Copyright © 2021 Sylvia Lowik All rights reserved

The characters and events portrayed in this book are fictitious.
Any similarity to real persons, living or dead, is coincidental and not intended by the author.
No part of this book may be reproduced, or stored in a retrieval system, or transmitted in any form or by any means, electronic, mechanical, photocopying, recording, or otherwise, without express written permission of the publisher.

Harbour Cities Midland

Dedication

Thank you to my husband, Nick, who supported me through it all.

Without all the encouragement of my Twitter friends, who know me as Nettie Sars, I would never have made it.

I owe a big thank you to my neurosurgeon Prof.J.J.Van Overbeeke, who saved my sight nearly 20 years ago.

Harbour Cities Midland

The Book of Light

It is unequivocal that human influence has warmed the atmosphere, ocean and land.

Widespread and rapid changes in the atmosphere, ocean, cryosphere and biosphere have occurred. The scale of recent changes across the climate system as a whole and the present state of many aspects of the climate system are unprecedented over many centuries to many thousands of years.

Human-induced climate change is already affecting many weather and climate extremes in every region across the globe.

There is evidence of observed changes in extremes such as heatwaves, heavy precipitation, droughts, and tropical cyclones, particularly their attribution to human influence.

ISPCC Sixth Assessment.

Eugenics is the practice or advocacy of improving the human species by selectively mating people with specific desirable hereditary traits. It aims to reduce human suffering by

Harbour Cities Midland

"breeding out" disease, disabilities and so-called undesirable characteristics from the human population.

First Law of the Church
of Light, Prior Galton the First

    Survival of the fittest or natural selection: The natural process by which organisms best adjusted to their environment are most successful in surviving and reproducing.

Father Spencer 1264 AE.

Chapter One

It was one of those days in April which could make you believe summer had already arrived. Gulls, squealing like a bunch of squabbling fishwives, were swooping around the cliff tops, diving into the glistening water in the hope of catching their breakfast.

The unexpected sound of excited voices drifting up from the isolated beach below made the boy drop flat on the narrow path high above and crawl to the edge of the cliff. He had to move the gorse bushes carefully, ignoring their prickly branches.

The sight of a girl, stark-naked, striding into the surf and gracefully diving into the water made his breath catch in his throat. He never saw a woman that beautiful and…, and what? The only word he could come up with was 'shiny'. She was all gold and copper, like a jewellery box he had once stolen from a church. The women in Diggers' Peninsula did not look like that. He felt himself flush despite the cool sea breeze drying the sweat on his back.

He couldn't see who the girl had been talking to without having to lean precariously over the edge. He didn't want to risk it. Being spotted by any of the inhabitants of the Island would mean a death sentence. His people were strictly forbidden to set foot on it by the ruling of the Church. He knew all too well how those bastards treated anyone disobeying their laws no matter where you came from in the Archipelago or who you were. And it would not only affect the offenders but their whole family, and sometimes even their entire village would feel the wrath of the Prior. It had been a shock this morning when his leader had informed them the ruler of Midland had ordered him to rob the most important family on the Island.

"Damien heard there would be a double wedding tomorrow. Two of their brats will be sacrificed on the altar of their fucking Tree. People have been arriving with gifts from all over the Archipelago for days. The loot will be enormous if we can get at it and leave without getting ourselves killed. If we can't, he intends to send a full raiding party, and we can whistle to our share."

No one had dared to raise objections. You did not disobey an order from the White Fort nor their boss.

It was why he now found himself on a narrow ledge below the steep walls of the Harrington stronghold, his eyes following the girl while she swam out to a large iron cross sticking out of the waves. There must be buildings from the time before down there. They were everywhere. His remarkable knowledge of the water charts was one reason Solo even allowed him on his crew. The other being his sister.

He wished he could watch forever, or at least until she would come out again, but he must go back and report how the girls had suddenly appeared on that deserted beach coming out of nowhere. There must be an entrance to the House down there. He could bet his life on it. Solo might even praise him, which would make a nice change from his usual contempt.

The lad shuffled back from the ledge and sprinted through the woods as fast as he could. The trees and shrubs still recovering from last winter had not yet grown impenetrable. And he would have to cross the Sevenoaks woods for many miles until he would reach the small cove where Solo was waiting for them with their boat.

The boy stopped for a moment to get his bearings. The fresh smell of early spring and the vivid green of brand-new leaves around him reminded him of the girl with her fresh young body. How would it be to bed someone like that? He felt aroused just thinking about it. She had looked like a mermaid when she walked to the sea, her skin glistening in the sun and her auburn hair coiled in thick ropes around her head. He took a deep breath.

Suddenly two massive arms encircled his body, lifting him off the ground.

"Daydreaming is for corpses, Boy. Anyone could have sneaked upon you, you little squirt. Wait till your big sister hears about it."

Wulf grabbed him in a bear hug and planted a sloppy kiss on his head. Being two heads taller and already given his name two years ago, you would never guess he was six months younger.

As yet unnamed and therefore going by the name Boy as was the tradition, the boy liked being part of the same scouting group but wished his sister and friend would have chosen one with another leader. Solo had mainly taken him on as a favour to his sister, Yaya, in the hope she would finally be his mate, but when she wasn't around, the jerk never let a chance go by to ridicule her 'weakling' brother.

Boy tried to wriggle free, wanting to get word about his discovery to Solo as soon as possible.

"Let go, you big oaf. This isn't funny. I nearly stuck you with my knife."Which hands were you going to do that with?" his friend asked.

Boy immediately threw his head back, smashing Wulf's face. The big guy let him go with a yelp and clutched his nose, the blood spurting out between his fingers.

"I would have used these hands," Boy replied, starting playfully to use the big man as his punching bag.

"Hey, you little punk. That hurt like hell. Why were you running back?"

"I have good news for Solo. While I was on the cliff behind the castle, I heard these girls below on the beach. They appeared out of nowhere. One of them went swimming butt-naked. It was amazing. The girls, I mean. There must be a way to get into the house down there. The beach is easy to get to, and you can't see it from the walls. We could save ourselves a lot of trouble."

Wulf scratched his head, wrinkling his forehead.

"I am not sure. Shouldn't we first finish our tour around the walls? I will go back with you and maybe have a bit of an eyeful as well. Or if we are lucky, a handful."

"No, be serious. Delivering an easy way in is my chance to make Solo finally let me choose a name."

Boy, seeing his friend's doubtful expression, started pulling him back to the waiting boat.

"Come on. What are you waiting for? Let's go."

Wulf rubbed the back of his neck and stood there immovable as a rock.

"Solo gave us strict instructions to scout the whole perimeter before reporting back. You will never earn a name if you keep trying to do your own thing. Shit, Boy, Solo already has it in for you. Let me spell it out again: we don't make the decisions. We follow orders, nothing more, nothing less. If you want to stay out of trouble, that is. You must know what happens to people who don't. The last ones are still digging latrines in West Drayton. Your sister won't be able to help you. You can tell him after we have finished."

"But what will Solo do to us, eh, if he finds out later, he can get in the house without being noticed, and we didn't tell him straightaway? One of us getting caught spying would ruin everything. You know what? Why don't you go on if you want, and I'll run back and tell him? Let Solo decide if it is worth checking out that beach. It won't take long. At least one of us will bring back the information he wanted, so what's the difference?"

"All right then," Wulf slumped his shoulders.

"But I'm coming with you. I'm not letting you go back and face him by yourself. I know what a jackass Solo can be about discipline. At least we'll be digging those shit holes together."

"Come on then, hurry. I promise you Solo will be fine once he hears what I have found out, I'm sure."

With these words, Boy raced off, not waiting for his friend to change his mind. Wulf sighed and tried to catch up with him, doing so just before they broke out of the woods and climbed down to the cove where Solo looked up at them, clearly surprised that they were back already.

Chapter Two

Astrid climbed up to the sunny courtyard lifting her hand to shield her eyes from the sun. Seeing it packed with people heralding yet more guests, she was glad they had escaped to the beach that morning. From now there would be no more opportunities to escape her duties.

Waking up this morning, she had only to take one look out of her window to make up her mind about sneaking down to the beach below the castle cliff. She had persuaded the more cautious Marion to join her. The latter probably only demurred in the hope to keep their visit as short as possible.

When she had started to shed her clothes to go in, her friend wide-eyed had shrieked: "You're not going in, are you? You'll freeze to death. It might already feel warm, but the water will still be ice cold. Besides, you'll never hear the end of it if your mother finds out."

"They're all far too busy to miss us. Besides, if I have to listen to one more of Father Sirio's lessons about doing our duty to the Tree of Life tomorrow, I'll jump from the highest tower I can find."

With these words, she had given her friend a playful push and run into the invitingly shimmering sea. At first, the cold made it nearly impossible to breathe, though as she started to swim with long, firm strokes towards the church steeple, it had felt a lot better.

The incredible feeling of washing away all the smoke, grime, and boredom of winter had made her spirits soar. It had been so kind of her brother to teach her to swim all those years ago. Life would have been far more unbearable would it not have been possible to escape the restrictions of becoming an Island woman by being able to swim away from it all. Alas, she always had to go back. This time it would be harder than ever. Her wedding was looming ever closer, and Nicholas was behaving like a stranger. Her mind shrank away from thinking about their last meeting.

Holding on to the church railing, floating on her back, she had felt the warm rays of the sun on her face. Strange to imagine that once there had been a whole community living right below the waves. She wished she was allowed to know more about those mysterious times.

Once out of the water, the wind had felt like an icy breath on her wet skin. Running as fast as she could for the shelter of the dunes and the comfort of her warm clothes, she felt reborn. Marion, lying with her arms over her eyes, seemed to have dozed off. Astrid had wrung a bit of water on the face of her unsuspecting friend, and the poor girl had jumped up with a shriek. Slapping her friend on her arm, Marion had started to hurry her back into her clothes and through the tunnel to the basement before somebody noticed their absence. Being found out would have them scrubbing pans until kingdom come. It would have been worth it, though.

The girls had to squeeze through a crowd of people to get to the main house. Stable boys were leading a group of magnificent horses away, and men in bulky clothing laughing and shouting for the servants seemed to be everywhere.

Trying to be heard above all the noise, Marion, her eyes shining, yelled: "Hey, I think your master Redwood has arrived."

"First of all, he is not my master yet, and it seems you are more excited to meet this guy than I am," said Astrid, her face clouding over, the happiness after her morning swim disappearing.

"Well, I am interested in the man my best friend will marry, even if she is not. You never even met him, did you? Your fiancée must be pretty old to have been friends with your father."

"Oh, stop. My father met Henry at my mother's court when Henry was only twelve. He is at least fifteen years younger. They told me the Tree charts only had two matches for me. If they had matched me with the other one, I would have become your stepmother."

"What? Who told you that?"

"I am not allowed to say, or he would be in a lot of trouble. "

"My brother has been talking again, has he? Astrid, he could get into a lot of trouble. You are taking advantage of his crush on you. That is not fair."

Astrid, her voice trembling a bit, tried to defend herself. "I only wanted to know if they could have matched me with Nick and were not telling me because Redwood is my father's friend and from a Great House, and they just threw your father in to make me happy with their choice."

Marion reached out to pat her, smiling apologetically

"chatting, Astrid turned her head back just in time to walk face-first into a man's smelly cloak. Ouch, watch where you're going."

"Young lady, I think it is you who should be watching where you are going. I think an apology is in order. Be quick about it if you don't want me to tell the master."

. The owner of the cloak reeked of stale horse sweat. He was dressed like a Northerner, far too hot, and was trying to take off his coat. Despite his stern words, his bright blue eyes sparkled with amusement. He must have thought Astrid, barefoot and with her hair still dripping from her swim, to be one of the house's maids. They had not bothered to dress this morning and just thrown their cloaks over their nightgowns.

" Sir, I'm so sorry," Astrid said, making a small curtsy, poking her friend in her ribs not to give anything away. "Please don't tell the master."

The stranger looked her up and down and started to smile. It changed his whole face, and the girls could not help smiling back.

"You got me there for a minute, cheeky lass. You are the spitting image of your grandmother. It is little Astrid, if I am not mistaken? Not so little anymore, I see. You probably won't remember me. You were about four years old when I saw you last. Let me introduce myself, Henry Redwood, at your service, your future husband." He made a reasonable effort of taking a courtly bow.

Astrid, probably for the first time in her life, was speechless. So, this was the man she would be marrying tomorrow and follow to the far North. She had seen a picture of him, but the likeness had not shown her that wonderful smile and his sense of humour. She stared at him, trying to take in as much as she could while he turned to Marion.

"And who is this other fine young woman?"

"Marion Selby, sir," stammered her friend, utterly overwhelmed by the attention of this very handsome man.

"Ah, you must be the daughter of Selby, Protector of the West and the famous Commander of our troops. I am looking forward to meeting him at the wedding tomorrow. Speaking of which, we should all better be on our way, as I don't think Ingrid would be pleased I met her daughter, my future bride, in such a state of undress. Even if you two are not, I'm still scared of her." He winked at them and sauntered toward the keep.

The girls looked at each other and immediately

started to giggle so hard, they collapsed in a heap.

" By the Lady," gasped Marion, "he is gorgeous. I would almost trade your brother for him. We are not even wearing shoes."

"Who cares what he looks like? He is not my Nick."

"Stop fighting what you can't change. At least your chosen one is handsome. Did you see how he was looking you up and down? Lady, his voice. My legs are still like jelly. What did you think of him? Isn't he lovely? I am sure it will be easy to fall in love with him and forget all about Nicholas. He doesn't look old at all. He sounded so nice."

Astrid sighed. The silly girl was practically swooning.

"Stop babbling. Since when does anybody consider your feelings when they choose a husband for you? It is just an arrangement serving the Tree and the Church. I will never love anyone like I do Nicholas, no matter how nice or handsome he is."

Astrid ran to the kitchen entrance with angry tears welling up as she did not want even her best friend to see how this unexpected meeting had deeply affected her. It had all become too real now. She hated it.

Looking around, she saw her wedding dress hanging on one of the hooks on the wall, all foamy cream lace and the softest of Sinise silk. She pulled her pillow over her head and screamed.

Did everybody and everything have to remind her of that awful wedding tomorrow?

"Hello, dear," said Trudy, coming in with a big pile of laundry. "Did you have a nice swim?"

Her former nurse and Nicholas' mum smiled as she said it, and Astrid decided not to deny it as her nurse knew her better than anyone except maybe Marion.

"It was so great, and I felt fine until I bumped into Henry Redwood," she wailed, flopping on her back, nearly disturbing a pile of clean and ironed dresses.

"Please be careful, dear. You'll make those clothes all crumpled and dirty again before I can pack them. What is wrong with Henry Redwood? You could do far worse. As far as I can remember, he is a charming and handsome man. You'll soon get to like him and hopefully even love him."

Astrid threw her arms in the air, moaning: "Our Lady, please help me. Why can't everybody stop talking about it all the time? It's driving me insane."

"Well, child, it's a bit too late to stick your head in the sand and hope it is not going to happen. I would enjoy my last day of freedom instead of moping in your room if I were you. Go and make yourself presentable and go and find your brother. Weren't you supposed to choose one of his pups?"

In all her dismay about the coming events, Astrid had forgotten all about her brother's present.

"You always know how to cheer me up, Trudy,"

she said as she went up to her and hugged her.

    She brushed her hair and threw on her riding clothes. Her mother would complain, but she needed the comfort of them.

    She heard Trudy calling after her, "Don't be late for lunch."

Chapter Three

Determined to make a getaway as soon as possible, Astrid joined her parents and their guests for lunch. To her embarrassment, her mother pointed to a chair between herself and Henry, beckoning her to sit there, frowning at her daughter's choice of apparel.

He smiled, winking at her and returned to his discussion with her parents about the situation with Damien in Midland. She thought she would die of boredom and looked longingly at the table where her friends were sitting having fun. At least Nicholas, seeing her look, waved and mouthed 'later'. She nodded to let him know she was game. Maybe they could spend some time together after lunch and talk about last time.

By the time lunch was finished, her parents had suggested she take Henry on a tour around Sevenoaks. Why on earth did she have to spend her last free afternoon with that man? She had her whole life to do that. She needed to talk with Nick. When she shook her head about to refuse, her mother pushed her chair back, practically dragging her from the room, fiercely whispering in her ear: "While still living under his roof, you'll never be too old for your father to give you a whipping. Stop acting like a silly child. Go and make sure our guest has a good time this afternoon, or else I will take a belt to you myself. I will tell Henry you will meet him at the horses."

Astrid was shocked into silence as her mother

never got this angry with her. She was usually the lenient parent, settling the many arguments between her wilful daughter and her even more stubborn husband before they escalated. Henry must be important to them.

She found him waiting at the stables, holding his horse's bridle.

"Sorry to take you away from your friends. I will try not to bore you again.

It has been quite a while since I had a look around the Harrington properties. It will be good to be out in the sun. A few weeks ago, we were still shovelling snow from our roads."

Astrid tried not to shiver. She had asked her father to tell her more about Scotia after she heard she would live there. The information had not done much to make the prospect more alluring. If any, it had made her even more desperate to avoid that fate.

Pretending not to notice the look of reluctance on her face, Henry continued: "It will be good to spend the afternoon away from all the preparations for our wedding and get to know each other a bit better, don't you think? Tomorrow there won't be much chance for that. There will be too many guests to entertain. Afterwards, we will probably only have a few days before we leave for Scotia."

Lady. If he was going to be talking about that wretched wedding, she might as well have stayed home and let her mother and friends go on about it.

Astrid abruptly changed the subject: "Let me show you Cityview first. You can see London City on a clear day like this. Even from that far, it is beautiful. I wish I could visit one day."

Henry nodded and told her it was his favourite city too.

They led their horses down the road to the harbour of Sevenoaks. A significant number of boats lay moored at the floating quays. Cranes were creaking as produce from all over the Archipelago was hoisted up to street-level big wooden platforms. From there, the waiting carts would take it to the warehouses of the Harrington company.

They made their way over a narrow stone bridge spanning the river Lint and continued on the Reigate road while Henry told her about the places he had been all over the Archipelago.

When he came to describing his own home, he tried to make it sound as wonderful as possible.

"We might not live close by the sea, but the Wasting Loch, or Lake as you would call it, is large enough to provide great sailing. I heard from your parents you love to be on the water and even have your own sailboat. People always talk about how cold and bare Scotia is, but it looks splendid in summer, with the heather blooming in the most amazing colours of yellow and purple. Neither do they mention how beautiful our mountains and rivers with their spectacular waterfalls can be. If you are willing to give it a chance, you will get to love it as much as I do, I am sure."

Astrid sensed how much he loved his home. She wondered if one day she could feel the same for that faraway, chilly place.

"You will fit right in, flower," her dad had said, pulling her plaits. Women in the North are allowed far more freedom than in the South."

The rest of the ride, they were mostly quiet. Both were enjoying the afternoon sun and nature going riot around them.

Back in the courtyard, Henry suggested he take both horses to the stables so she could get ready for dinner. Astrid accepted his offer. She wanted to look her best tonight. However, she wasn't sure if it would be for Nicholas or this fascinating man.

Chapter Four

"You're late, child."

Trust her father to reprimand her in front of everyone.

"Have you got nothing to say?"

Ingrid put her hand on her husband's arm and whispered something in his ear.

"Your mother says you're late because you had to help her. I still find that no excuse to make our guests wait. Henry, I do apologise."

Henry gave Astrid an encouraging smile.

" It doesn't matter, Gregory. We were a bit late to coming back from our ride. Your daughter has done her best to show me all the nice places around here. I had a lovely afternoon. You must admit it must take quite a bit of time to look so lovely"."

He gave her a wink, and everybody smiled at his chivalry. Henry spent most of the time discussing the situation in Midland with her parents.

As soon as it was politely possible, Astrid said goodnight using the excuse of needing her beauty sleep to retire early.

She found her little sister in her bed, vast asleep, curled up like a little kitten deep under the bedclothes. The little minx had crept into her room again. She looked so sweet in her pink cotton nightgown with her hair sticking out all around her chubby little face. Astrid crawled in beside her. She would miss their nighttime cuddles too.

Nicholas had disappeared before she could speak to him. She wondered again what had made him change his attitude towards her so suddenly.

She was still smarting from the way he had refused to let her give herself to him the night before. She had slipped into his bed and crawled under the covers stark naked. Instead of making passionate love to her, he had gently wrapped her up in his blanket and urged her to leave. He had told her again they could never be together like that, not now nor in the future. It had crushed her. The shame of being rejected made her incredibly sad but angry too.

Tired from her conflicting feelings, she fell into a restless sleep only to be woken by an incredible thirst. She carefully got up not to wake her sister and went to the sideboard to get some water.

Behind her, she heard her bedroom door open quietly and started to turn, smiling. Nicholas, he must have changed his mind.

Instead of her beloved, she saw a tall figure looming up in the darkness. For a split second, she hoped she was dreaming but was soon abused of the idea when a pair of calloused hands pulled her against a body encased in tough leather smelling of smoke and fish.

"One sound, and it will be your last, do you hear me? Do as I say, and no one will get hurt."

The only thing she could think of was to stop him from finding her sister. She had to stay quiet as much as she wanted to scream and fight. The brute shoved a piece of cloth in her mouth and tied another one tightly around her eyes. He threw her over his shoulder as if she weighed no more than a bag of feathers. His grip was so tight she could barely move. Her head, bouncing on his back, made her feel sick. He took her downstairs, where she felt the cold air outside chilling her bare legs. She noticed the distinct scent of smoke.

Another voice spoke, a woman's.

"Hurry, we managed to get most of the stuff. What are you doing? Who is she? Leave her. That's not what we came for. Dragging her along will only slow us down."

The man holding her just grunted and told the complaining voice to fuck off and get her ass to the basement.

Astrid's mind reeled, 'Oh no. I must have left the gate open in our hurry not to get caught this morning.'

Another gruff voice sounded close by, a man this time.

"We took care of the guards. It was easy. Half of them were asleep. We must go now before anybody else wakes up. I've created the diversion, as you told me, but it might not hold them back that long."

The acrid smell of smoke started to become ever more noticeable. Astrid heard everyone around them beginning to cough. The cloth covering most of her face at least prevented her from having to do the same. The man carrying her started to run. By the hollow sound of their footsteps and a musky smell, she knew they must have reached the basement. A cold, salty draft was coming from the door leading to the outside.

She bore some more uncomfortable jerking up and down before she was thrown unceremoniously down, getting drenched in the process.

"Get back in the boat, Boy, and you, guys, heave. They'll be a bit busy, but I still want to be out of sight of those towers before someone starts shooting at us."

She heard the men swearing and the creaking of oars. Her first instinct was to try and get away before it was too late. She wished she could jump overboard, but sense told her she wouldn't stand a chance against these people.

They took her gag out and uncovered her eyes once they were out of sight of the island.

Cold, wet, and shocked, Astrid wanted to give in to her despair and weep. She bit her lip and shook herself out of it. Her innate bloody-mindedness, which often had gotten her into trouble, came to her rescue. She would find a way out of this. No matter what it would take. There wasn't much she could do now but wait for an opportunity to flee.

"You can sum up survival in three words -- never

give up. That's the heart of it. Just keep trying," an ancient philosopher once said. She was a Harrington, and that should count for something.

Shivering, she sat up and stared back at her home, which was rapidly disappearing in the dark.

Chapter Five

Boy was looking at the girl Solo had stolen from the keep. It was her. She looked so different from the glorious vision he saw on the beach. Why had Solo done it? He never mentioned he wanted to take a hostage.

He threw a woollen blanket over her. Even though it smelled of sweat and grease, she would be grateful for its warmth. They had tied her hands and feet with some rope. They must have been worried she would jump out of the boat when she woke up and realised where they were taking her.

A movement under the blanket showed him she was trying to loosen the ropes by wriggling her hands and feet. He saw his sister go up to her.

If the girl hoped a woman would be a bit friendlier, she would soon find out how wrong she was. He heard her ask for some water.

Before he could get up to give her some, Yaya shoved him back down and snarled: "You can wait until we land. It's a good exercise for such a high and mighty brat as yourself to learn what it's like not to get everything the moment you want it. Islanders. Always thinking you're better than the rest of us."

She spat in the water, her towering presence

making the girl cringe

"You'll soon find out we do things very differently here."

Then his sister smiled, which somehow looked worse than her scowling.

"Right, Boy, here's where you come in" Solo changed places with him at the rudder and shoved Yaya aside to sit right next to his hostage at the back of the boat, calling out to him: "Make yourself useful. I want to be home and sit behind a large beer within the next half hour. Raiding is a thirsty business. Hold on to your horses, princess. We don't want you to go overboard before we had some use out of you."

Boy saw the girl trying to make herself as small as possible. She seemed terrified of Solo.

The boat picked up speed. They had reached the reefs. He had to make it tack left and right, sometimes catching the waves smack on the side. They entered the foaming surf at a terrifying speed, making the boat teeter high, hanging motionlessly in the air to then plunge like a dead weight. He loved the challenge of it but was too worried about the girl to enjoy it now. She looked like a ghost. Living on the Island, she must be used to being on the water but looked clearly about to be sick.

Before he could issue a warning to his boss, she vomited all over Solo's back.

"What the fucking hell, you little bitch." Solo

sprang up, right when the boat was making a sharp turn making him nearly fall overboard.

"Hold on, man, nothing you can do about it now. We're nearly there. Then you can jump overboard and wash," the boy who was skilfully piloting them to the shore tried very hard not to grin. His sister had no such inhibitions. She laughed out loud.

"Green suits you, Solo. You should wear that colour more often."

The others started to laugh too, which didn't do much for the big man's temper.

"Let me see if you'll all find it so funny when you're cleaning my boat from all that crap. Bunch of assholes."

In one swoop, he picked up the girl and jumped overboard. Just when he thought Solo was about to drown her, he hauled her up again and stuck his face into hers. Pure hatred shone from his eyes. He shook her so hard her head flailed from side to side.

"Let's see how well you can swim."

He threw her in the water, her hands and feet still tied. No matter how hard she thrashed, she started to sink below the surface.

Boy let go of the rudder and jumped overboard. He grabbed her and turned her on her back, holding her up above the water. She gulped for air and was still thrashing in her panic.

"Stay still until I'll get you to the beach and untie

you. At least you're clean now. Try and do what Solo says, or it will just get worse for you."

She followed his advice and let him guide her to the beach, where he sat her up on the dry sand, still warm from yesterday's sun. He pulled a knife from his belt to cut her bonds. She shut her eyes and involuntarily let out a cry. When she tried to get up, she fell back onto the sand as if her bones had turned to jelly.

"Here, let me help you."

"Stop pussyfooting around with that Gen whore, Boy."

Solo shoved him aside, dragged the girl up, and threw her like a sack of coal over his shoulder.

"Don't you get any ideas about this one, son. Damien has her down for a high ransom. If we lose her on the way to the Fort, it will be your guts he'll rip out, not mine. Go and help your mates drag the boat ashore and clean it. I'll look after the wench from here. And you, my darling," the swine gave her a whack on her behind, "If you barf on me once more or annoy me in any other way, I'll make you regret ever to have been born, ransom or no ransom."

With this warning, Solo turned around and strode away.

Ignoring his boss, Boy followed a little bit behind. He saw Solo dropping her like a sack of potatoes in front of his mother's tent. Looking down on her, his boss made a mocking bow, sweeping his arm around the settlement.

"Welcome to Hell's Kitchen, your first stop. Hey, Sara, take this inside and clean it up. It will need some suitable clothes and shoes before we leave for the White Fort. You, my treasure, don't give her any grief, or I'll come over and deal with you."

He abruptly turned his back on them and strode into the village, whistling a cheerful tune.

Chapter Six

The tired-looking woman who had appeared when the brute had called her took one look at Astrid and gently guided her inside, sitting her down on some soft woollen blankets. It smelt like a herb garden, eucalyptus and garlic fighting for dominance.

Seeing her shivering in her wet nightgown, the woman immediately stoked up the fire and urged her to take it off, handing her another blanket to wrap around herself.

The shock of her abduction and the horror of her near-drowning took their toll, and she started sobbing. The woman patiently waited until Astrid had calmed down a bit.

"Would you like something to eat? It will make you feel better and warm you up."

Though marked by a hard life, her face showed the strong features of a once beautiful woman. She sat down opposite Astrid and, in a soft voice, introduced herself.

"As you might have heard, my name is Sarah. What is yours, dear?"

She seemed nice. Maybe while the awful man was away, she could persuade this woman to help her get away.

She swallowed as her mouth was parched and managed to whisper: "Where am I? Can you help me, please? I don't want to be here."

Before the woman could say anything, an angry

voice interrupted their conversation.

"Mother, Solo told you not to talk to her and just tidy her up. Give her something to eat so she'll be fit enough to walk. She needs travel clothes and suitable shoes. You and JonahBoy are so soft. For fuck's sake. Can't you for once do what he asks. Solo will be here soon. He has gone to check on his brother. He'll want to get a move on as soon as he is done. Can you pack some food for Boy and me? He will be coming with us to see Damien."

It was the woman who had been so vile to her on the boat. She towered over them, scowling. Every part of her body was covered in black and red tattoos depicting horses, stars, and words in a strange language. Even on the woman's forehead, three symbols stood in a triangle. Her ears were adorned with multiple rings, and she was dressed in a tight brown leather bodice over woollen leggings, the latter embroidered with blue, wavy lines. With her tightly braided tresses dyed a vivid green, making her look even more barbaric, she stood out against the muted colours of her surroundings. On her back, she carried a sword that looked ancient but shone as if it were made yesterday. Heavy black boots studded and capped with metal completed her look.

Last night on the boat, Astrid had been too miserable to pay much attention to the woman's appearance. Unbelievable this woman, scowling at her mother, was in any way related to that kind boy. She hadn't caught his name.

Harbour Cities Midland

Everyone seemed to call him Boy.

"Stop barking at me, girl. I'm still your mother, no matter how high and mighty you think you are. I was just about to offer the girl something to eat before you so rudely interrupted me. I don't want your brother to go with you and that idiot friend of yours. Taking a girl from the Island is a major offence. The monks will be on your tail before you know it. Please keep Boy out of it."

Squatting down in front of Astrid, she gently took one of her hands.

"Don't mind her, dear. Her bark is worse than her bite. Have some of this hot potato soup. You must be hungry. It will make you strong for the walk."

"How long have I been asleep? Is this village called Hell's kitchen?" Astrid needed to know where she was and how long she had been missing from home.

Looking at her daughter with a stern frown, the woman, Sara, patted her hand: "That must have been one of Solo's stupid jokes. You are in West Drayton. You arrived here only an hour ago, and it's early in the morning now. Please do eat and drink something before Solo comes for you. I'll get you some of Boy's clothes. You are both about the same size."

The awful woman, satisfied when she saw Astrid accepting the soup, left but not before she had told her mother that it was her brother who had insisted on going with them.

"Mama has she..? The boy who had saved her

from drowning stopped in his tracks when he saw Astrid sitting upright and looking much better. His eyes widened at the sight of her. He looked to be close to her age, maybe a bit older.

"And this is my youngest, Boy, who hasn't got his proper name yet. Hopefully, that will change soon. Have some soup, Baby, or, knowing how patient Solo is, I know you will go hungry today. After you finish, take this young woman and these travel packs outside. I don't need to see Solo coming in here bullying that poor girl some more."

"Please, mama, don't call me that," the boy shot a glance at Astrid, his cheeks burning. His mother handed him another bowl and stroked his head. He pulled it back, looking very embarrassed to be treated like a little boy. He reminded Astrid of her sister, who always became mortified when people treated her like the baby of the family in front of strangers. The boy accepted the food thanking his mother, and started to wolf it down, managing to talk simultaneously.

"I convinced Yaya to take me with them. Solo will ask Damien to name me. I asked Wulf to come, but he couldn't. His mother forbade it."

"She is a wise woman. I wish you weren't going either. No good will come of it. I guess there's no talking you out of it? We can wait for a travelling priest to do the naming. It will be just as valid as having that awful man do it. Did you warn this girl about Solo?"

Turning to Astrid, frowning: "Be careful with that

man. He blames all his problems on the people of your island. Boy, if you get the chance during your trip north, tell her why. Now up, you two get. Young lady, you go and get changed and join my boy outside. And you, Boy, go."

Sara ushered her son out and pointed Astrid to a screened off partition to change. When Astrid was hesitating to leave the tent, Sarah gave her shoulder a gentle tap and whispered: "Keep your head down and try to stay near my lad. He's a good boy."

She never got to tell the kind woman her name.

It was only just getting daylight, and hard to get an idea of the size of the village. Trees and bushes half hid most of the dwellings. Smoke was already spiralling up in the air through openings in the top of the yurts. Dogs barked at the sight of their small group. In the distance, she could hear waves crashing onto the reefs.

A rough voice cut through the morning silence: "What are you two standing around for? Let's step on it. I want to be in Amersham before nightfall."

Without looking back, the man, who had stolen her from her home, set off, not looking back if they were following.

Boy gave her a shy smile and gently motioned her to start walking.

The woman Yaya popped up from one of the other tents and made up the rear.

Chapter Seven

It was hard for Astrid to keep up with the others. Solo set a gruelling pace. The food and rest she had in the small village had restored some of her strength but not enough to keep this up.

With the sun burning remorselessly on their heads by noon, she started to feel tired and very thirsty. Her feet, not used to the poorly fitting leather sandals they had given her, were killing her. She could feel the chafing making blisters on her feet.

"Can I have some water?" she whispered to the boy who had not left her side and been a comforting presence all morning. They had both been silent not to attract the unwelcome attention of Solo, who was striding ahead with Boy's sister beside him. Around her, Solo seemed a bit less inclined to taunt Astrid, too busy as he was to impress the proud woman.

Boy pulled a water bottle from his belt and handed it to her, putting a finger to his lips with a nod to Solo. Astrid took a deep draft and felt better.

"Thanks," she whispered, handing him back the bottle. He took a sip, too, before securing it to his belt.

After what seemed like an endless hike, Solo finally allowed them a short break on the bank of a narrow river. If Astrid hadn't felt so worried and scared, she would have been happy to stay at the clear burbling stream running over the pebbles and bordered by a riot of wildflowers forever.

Solo scurried off into the small thicket behind them to relieve himself. She heard him order the woman Yaya to keep an eye on the two love birds. Astrid sank onto the soft grass of the bank and took her sandals off to cool her feet in the water.

"Are you crazy. Don't they teach you Gens nothing?"

Yaya yanked her back from the water before she could douse the heat of her blisters in it.

"Your feet will get all soggy. You won't make the next mile without completely ripping open your feet. Show them to me."

Astrid stretched her right foot towards her. When Yaya saw the huge blisters, she roughly grabbed hold of the foot and put a tight bandage slathered with greasy ointment around it. It hurt like hell at first, but soon the burning sensation had entirely turned into a pleasant numbness. Astrid meekly gave the woman her other foot to treat, thanking her.

"Boy. Give her some bread and water, and you, my girl, you better keep up, or we'll be late getting to Amersham, and Solo won't be pleased."

"Thank you, sis. I forgot about the elk grease. Why the hurry to get to Amersham?"

Looking round to see if Solo was still out of

earshot, Yaya said under her breath: "Eric was not well when we got back. He's had one of his turns again. This time mum couldn't do much for him. Solo heard from one of the other women, who have relatives in Amersham, there'll be a monk in town only stopping there today. He's famous for his knowledge of the Healing Arts. Solo hopes the man can give him something for Eric. If he misses his appointment, we're in for a lot of trouble. He will blame us for not getting to Amersham on time. Especially her."

Solo returned, and Yaya went to sit with him.

"What was she talking about? Why does Solo hate me so? He doesn't even know me." Astrid said to Boy the moment his sister was gone.

Boy moved a bit closer to her.

"Believe it or not, Solo is a compatriot of yours, born on your island. His parents were fisherfolk. When his brother was born, they found him to be a defective and had to hide him from the monks. They..' He took a bite out of his bread, swallowed it and spoke loudly:" This is the River Gade. It was a tiny stream before the floods but now flows from the top to the bottom of Diggers."

Astrid looked over her shoulder and saw Solo approaching them.

"If you two have enough energy to jabber, we can start walking again. This time, I will keep the little bird company to make sure she doesn't fall behind. You can walk with your big sister."

With a grin on his face, Solo yanked Astrid up to the path. She had to run to keep up with him and felt grateful for the bandages the sullen woman had given her.

After more miles of monotonous tramping through woods and heathland, she finally saw some signs of a settlement. Fields with cabbage, onions and kale coloured the side of the road a variety of green. Further afield, people were preparing the soil for planting the summer crop. Some of them looked up but, seeing their small group, went straight back to work. People had to take advantage of the fertile time between the chilly and wet winter and the blistering summer heat. Soon fast-growing wheat and other grains would be shooting up, competing with the long stalks on the grapevines.

"Imagine having to break your back in the dirt each year every year. I'd rather drown myself." Solo was talking more to himself than to her. Since their stop, he had only spoken to hurry her along, never forgetting to tell her what a useless person she was.

"You're happy enough to eat their produce, though, especially when it's in liquid form," Yaya's spoke up from behind, encouraged teasing him a bit by his apparent good mood.

"Yeah, but I only have to pay for it, preferably with other people's money," Solo snickered.

They had reached the rough stone walls

surrounding the small town of Amersham. The gates were wide open. Two dishevelled looking guards were standing in the shade of some trees, chatting with each other. After a cursory glance at a sheaf of papers Solo waved in front of their faces, they waved them through.

He took them to a large field behind some stables, saying he saw no reason to waste good money on an inn with this nice weather.

"Here," Solo handed Yaya some money, "Go and get something nice for our evening meal. I'll be back soon after you after I've done with my business."

The woman didn't look pleased to be treated like a servant. She went off to the food stalls after asking the boy to set up camp and keep his eye on the girl.

Astrid was more than happy to sit down finally. She felt exhausted. Any thoughts she might have entertained of escaping during their stay in the little town disappeared as soon as she had a good look at its inhabitants. Most of them looked just as dangerous and untrustworthy as Solo and his mates.

On top of that, the boy had warned her that Solo would hold him responsible and probably kill him if she ran away. Despite the fact that he had taken part in her abduction, Astrid felt he was not as horrible as the others and genuinely tried to make things easier for her.

As if guessing her thoughts, the boy turned to her and said, "The gates will close at sundown. If you got out, Solo would get the whole town to hunt you down. You wouldn't get far with your feet the way they are. They would sell you to the next person coming through, making sure no one would ever find you. The rule in this land is 'losers weepers, finders keepers'. Please promise me to stay with us until we get to Damien. He is terrifying, but the prospect of getting a high ransom for you will make him keep you safe. In case you were wondering, Damien himself will never touch you. He is not into women. He prefers to spend his time with men."

"What do you mean 'not into women'?"

Boy looked a bit surprised, a flush creeping around his cheeks.

"Is he like a monk, maybe? They don't take wives and live with other monks."

Laughing, he said, "He sure isn't a monk. I forgot how isolated from the real world your Island is. Damien will never touch you. He will trade you back to your family for a hefty ransom. To do that, he has to keep you in one piece. Until we get there, Solo will have to behave himself.

Astrid's mind was whirling with all these strange ideas. The ransom thing puzzled her the most. Boy was talking as if it was an everyday occurrence here.

The sister came back with the food she purchased, the smell making Astrid's mouth water

The boy looked up from where he was lying near the fire.

"Let's give her some now before Solo comes back. It will be much harder for her to keep up tomorrow with her muscles all sore from today. She'll need her strength. Solo wants to get to the fort as soon as possible."

"Don't get too attached to that little wench, brother. She's just a large sum of money to us and nothing more. On top of that, Solo will not keep his paws off her if he has even the slightest notion you're sweet on her. Just to show you who's boss. Your job is to keep her moving and get her to Damien on time. She'll be worth nothing to Damien if Solo doesn't leave her intact. She will be in even more shit than she is now if he gets at her."

"Alright, alright, I get it. You don't have to keep on about it."

While his sister wasn't looking, he slipped some of the food she had brought to Astrid, whispering to her to eat it fast before Solo came back.

As if he had conjured the guy up by just talking about him, there he was, looking even more grumpy than when he left

"Hope you left me something to eat. I'm starving."

He dropped himself down beside Yaya, who hastened to offer him some pies and sausages, adding a small jug of ale.

"How did it go with the monk? Could he give you something for Eric?"

"No," Solo growled, hiding his despair behind his usual gruffness.

"When I told the monk what medicines Eric was taking at the moment, he said there was nothing more anybody could do for Eric here in Midland. He told me to keep him calm and not let him do heavy work. That might keep him alive a while longer. The guy suggested that he could give me something to end Eric's suffering when things got too bad. I punched him for even mentioning it. Stupid quack."

"Shit, why did you do that? Maybe we should take the girl and set up camp outside Amersham. He will have the Churchwardens after you before long."

Solo sneered at Yaya.

"Fuck that. I am not running from some stupid monks. We'll leave the moment the gates open again tomorrow. Will you be joining me for a bit of a cuddle tonight, or what?"

At Yaya's haughty refusal, the uncouth pig burped loudly, wrapped himself in his blanket and was soon snoring hard enough to frighten the horses.

Yaya looked furious, shaking out her blanket with abrupt movements and throwing herself on it.

"Crap. He's such a stupid fuck. Now Damien will keep a big chunk of the money to pay compensation to the monks. If we even get to the fort without being caught by those wardens. You take first watch, brother. Wake me when you get too tired."

Astrid shuffled back to sit with her back to the stable wall, still warm from the sun as far as she could away from the others. It made her feel a little bit safer.

She saw the boy settling before the dying fire wrapped in his blanket. And tried to stay awake fearful of what might happen if she closed her eyes, but the long walk and all that had gone before made it impossible.

Chapter Eight

The morning after the raid on Harrington House was beautiful, which felt like an insult to the people who had lost friends and family in last night's events.

The night before, Nicholas had gotten word to join the men going out to get Astrid back and stood ready to join the troops in the harbour

"Please look after yourself, son." Trudy could not stop herself from touching her son, tugging his clothes into place and telling him things he should or shouldn't do to stay alive. He shook off her hands. He knew she meant well but still felt angry about her deception all those years.

A few days ago, his mother had called him to her room and sat him down. She had tried to impress on him that he had to let Astrid go for his own good and hers. When he resolutely had refused to pay her any heed, she finally told him the truth.

"Nick, dear, your father did not die at sea. George Harrington is your birth father, which makes Astrid your half-sister. If the monks get the slightest whiff of a romantic relationship between the two of you, you will find yourself packed off to the furthest corner of Midland. They might even lock you away on the Continent, and we would never see each other again."

He had felt the blood draining from his face. His body hurt as if she had given him a physical blow. He had looked at her and asked: "Why? Why did you let us be together for so long? You saw what we mean to each other? I love her, and she loves me."

"Her… your father and I thought you would both grow out of it. We were wrong. I am sorry. I should have told you sooner. We were worried you would not be able to keep our secret from her. No one but us knows, and it has to stay that way. Too many people will get hurt if this comes out."

He had fled the house and wandered for hours before he went back, determined never to tell his friend, no his love, this conversation had ever happened.

He turned to leave her without saying goodbye, but once at the gate, he ran back, put his arms around his mother and said: "See you soon. Mum, I do love you."

After one more embrace, he had joined the last stragglers filing out of the gate to the harbour. He found the sight that met him there extremely exciting despite the dismal reason for all the activity.

The ordinarily quiet quays were swarming with soldiers. Pennants were waving in the wind from every ship, giving them almost a festive air. Astrid's grandfather had sent three trireme warships. Their crew was in the process of distributing the men waiting on the quay. It would be a tight squeeze to get them all on.

In the middle of all the folk milling around, one person dominated the scene. The Commander stood on a large crate and shouted orders to the men, his own and everyone else's.

"Experienced soldiers first. I know you all want to help, but we have limited space. Every ship has a steward who will check your papers. No pushing, or we'll send you away immediately."

Further away, Nicholas saw Astrid's future husband on the flagship deck showing the Harrington soldiers where to stow their belongings. On the other two, the Commander's lieutenant's men were doing the same. Henry must have been looking out for him and waved for him to come over and join him on the deck.

"Why don't you put your things in the Captain's quarter. We'll have a meeting there once we're out of the harbour. Captain Finn will be assisting the ship's captain. We hope to leave within the next hour. According to Finn, there's a storm brewing. If it were not for Astrid, we would have waited it out, but we don't want the trail to get too cold, so we'll have to risk it."

Looking at the older man, Nicholas could not help grudgingly admiring him. Yesterday, Henry was within sight of getting married to a beautiful girl, daughter of one of the most outstanding Companies in the Archipelago. Today, two of his best friends were dead, and his bride-to-be was taken by

Midlander scum. Nicholas couldn't for the life of him, imagine how Henry managed to look so calm and in control of the situation. He seemed determined to find Astrid and punish her abductors.

No wonder Astrid likes him, he thought. I still find it hard to see her as my sister. Would it have made any difference if we had never found out and ran away? Would we have been happy? But then what if she had found out later? She would have been disgusted and hate me.

Thanking Henry, he went to find the cabin, vowing he would disappear after making sure Astrid was alright. She would be much better off with this guy and would never have to know what his mother had told him. He wanted to keep her father's reputation intact.

Chapter Nine

He was the first to arrive at the large cabin and felt a bit awkward going into someone's private quarters, especially the captain's. He walked up and down for a while but then let himself in after knocking a few times. Henry had sent him, so it should be okay.

He had just sat down before the large window at the back of the cabin when the door opened with a bang. "No one here yet?" Lowering his large frame under the door jamb, the Commander entered.

Nicholas jumped up, looking a bit guilty at being caught doing nothing while everyone seemed to be so busy. He felt he had to explain himself to this awe-inspiring man. "Henry told me to bring my travel things here, sir. Is there something else I can do?"

"Well, as a matter of fact, you could go down to the galley and get us some ale and maybe a bite to eat. Word has come in from fishermen working west of the city. They saw a small vessel going in the direction of Diggers' Peninsula. From what they could see from a distance, there was only a small party on board. I hope Finn will be as good as his word and get us through those reefs. We will take fifteen men to go on land. The ships will anchor out of view on the other side of the rocks. If all goes to hell and we don't come back within a day, they have orders to go South to the port of Penn Station and march North."

The Commander sat down with a sigh and started to peruse the maps scattered on the table.

Nicholas hurried to the galley and came back with the requested refreshments. When he returned to the cabin, the meeting had already started. The Kentish ship's captain Atanur sat next to the Commander with Henry on his other side. Captain Finn was standing over the table, pointing out the proposed route on a map. To Nicholas' surprise, William was there as well. His friend looked up and gave him a wink mouthing the word 'later' to him.

"The surf will be extremely turbulent before the coast of Diggers. We will take one of the larger lifeboats. As far as I know, there are only two small villages in that part of the peninsula. They should already have moved to their summer location near the beach. As for Astrid, she might already be on her way to the White Fort if they mean to ransom her. Damien insists they bring every hostage to him first. If you thought his two older brothers were bad, he is even worse. After his eldest brother died from a sword wound, the word goes that the mongrel poisoned his other brother to grab control over Midland. He is a piece of work. I can't think for the life of me why the Prior has not executed him already. Word is that they have an understanding."

"Well, bad things happen to bad people. Only a

shame there's one more of that viper's nest still alive. At least there isn't much chance he will surprise us with more of that rotten seed," Henry remarked

They all chuckled at that and started laughing even more uproariously when they saw the surprised look on Nicholas's face.

"Don't worry about it, young man. Someone will explain it to you one day. Better you don't know about such sins."

Feeling a bit embarrassed, Nicholas mumbled an apology and went outside to see if he could see the coast of Midland yet. He turned when he heard someone coughing behind him. It was William.

Nicholas embraced his friend, exclaiming, "I never thought to find you here. You never said anything during the meeting yesterday at the house. Your father seemed dead set against you coming."

"I simply slipped on board during the embarking. When my father found out, we were well on our way, and it was too late to do anything about it."

William sounded quite proud of his deed.

"He has told me I to stay well away from any fighting. I'm here solely in the capacity of a representative from the Church. Guess he thought it would be easier to manipulate me than Father Sirio. I just want to help find Astrid. She's my best friend too," his voice wavered.

Before Nicholas could comfort William, a shrill whistle from the lookout had the others outside at once. It was a long line of rocky shore with some sandy beaches carved out of the bedrock. They were still too far away to see any signs of habitation. Nicholas could see the white heads of the surf between them and dry land. It didn't look as dangerous as they all had been making out.

"It doesn't seem too hard to sail through, does it?" Captain Finn was smiling, making his eyes practically disappear in his grizzled face. William seemed to have disappeared.

"Below those smooth looking waves, there are a lot of old buildings from the time before, waiting to rip a hole in your ship for the surf to smash it to pieces. If you do make it to the shore, the villagers will kill you or take you prisoner. I don't know which is worst. But don't worry, son, I'll get us ashore in one piece. We've agreed to land a few miles south of a village called West Drayton. We think it the likeliest place for them to have gone ashore as the passage through the reefs is easier there. We have to make sure they don't spot us. If they get even a whiff of us coming for them, they'll disappear in no time. Would you prefer to sit this part out on the ship? We have enough experienced men without having to risk the life of a young lad like you, who still has a lot of living to do."

Nicholas was very tempted to accept the offer and stay with William. He would probably be more of a hindrance than a help. If he stayed on board, though, everyone would think him a coward.

"No, thanks, sir, I want to help get her back. We lost eighteen of our people, and by now, there may be more. We can't let those people get away with it."

Captain Finn fiddled with his moustache and bit his lips.

"I'm a bit worried, as you're not eighteen yet. They can't have told you about the culling."

"Culling? What do you mean? I mean, I know what culling is as we do it with the deer when their number becomes too many. Are we going to hunt after the raid? I don't understand."

Finn was looking ever more uncomfortable.

"Maybe the Commander should explain it to you. I have spoken out of order. It might not come to that. Forget what I said."

Finn abruptly walked away, finding something to busy himself with on the other side of the deck, leaving Nicholas even more rattled than he already was. He decided he would find out soon enough what Finn had meant. Bothering the Commander at a time like this with his ignorance was out of the question. Soon the whole venture would begin, and he would undoubtedly get an answer to all his questions.

Chapter Ten

Captain Finn, fourteen of the Commander's finest, Nicholas, Henry, and the chief himself lowered themselves down in the sloop, bucking up and down the waves like a wild horse.

The crossing through the surf was wild. Nicholas had to close his eyes now and then, fearing for his life. Captain Finn, his plaits whipping in the wind, was at the helm shouting his directions to the rowers, seven on each side of the sloop, who were pulling for all their life's worth, their faces taut with the strength it required to keep their boat on a steady course. After many hair-raising moments, they reached a narrow pebbly beach rimmed by ancient oak trees and large holly bushes. Here and there, a lone pine stood sentinel. They left two men to guard the boat. The rest formed two lines and set off at a fast pace. No sound could be heard but creaking their leathers. The commander had impressed on them the need for stealth. Not one of them wanted to be responsible for giving their location away to the locals.

Spotting spirals of smoke in the distance, the commander held up his hand. Everyone came to a halt.

"You two, go and scout ahead. I need numbers and locations. There should be mainly women, children, and old ones in the village. At this time of day, most of the men will have gone out to sea to fish. I'll stay here with the lad and half of you while Henry will take the others round to the other side of the settlement. If someone sees you, kill them. We can't have anyone sending out a warning to their men."

The two scouts hurried away, and Henry took his group to the other side.

The Commander addressed Nicholas and his men: "We'll go a bit closer. I've arranged a signal with Henry when to start the ambush of the village from his side. We need the scouts to report back first. The only thing we have to do now will be the hardest. Wait."

Nicholas was a bit shaken by the straight order to kill anyone they met. He knew the Commander hated the Midlanders, but surely women and children should be exempt? They could never hold them responsible for what their men did. He had heard a lot of the women were victims of kidnapping themselves. The words of Captain Finn sounded in his mind. "They have never told you about the culling."

A rustling of leaves and the fast footfall of one of the scouts returning made them all tense up. The soldier was entirely out of breath and could barely get his words out: "You were right, Sir. There are not many boats on the beach. The village consists of a large meeting house and five yurts. There are only two paths out. One leads to the sea and the other inland."

"Good, we'll put three of you on the beach to catch any runaways. The others can come with me to the village.

Do you all know what you have to do? We need one of them to tell us where they have taken Astrid. The rest is a waste of space," seeing Nicholas going pale, "Nicholas, why don't you join the three on the beach? You can keep an eye on the sea in case their men return early."

He took a bird whistle out of his pocket and blew it once.

"That will let Henry know to go to attack the village from his side."

They all started to run in the direction of the village. Nicholas felt very confused. It was not at all as he had imagined a raid to be. He had seen himself heroically waving a sword, vanquishing Astrid's abductors and punishing the men responsible for the fire and subsequent deaths. He did not come prepared for the slaughter of innocents. His mouth was dry, and he felt bile rising in his throat. He wished he had stayed on board.

Once on the beach, he heard women and children screaming and crying. Then and that was worse, the sounds stopped one by one. He hoped sincerely that some of the women and children had a chance to get out unharmed.

The bushes at the edge of the beach moved apart as an older woman clutching two small children rushed onto the beach, looking frantically around for a way to escape. Before Nicholas' shocked eyes, one of the Commander's men stormed at her, his sword raised high and hacked both children down within seconds. The woman, her eyes blazing, gave a piercing scream and threw herself at him, scratching his face and kicking him. He just laughed cruelly and gave her a big shove pushing her to his colleagues.

"Shall we first have some fun with this hellcat?"

To Nicholas' relief, the oldest amongst them shook his head and said: "The Commander will have our heads. You know he disapproves of that sort of thing."

The first one shrugged his shoulders and brutally put his sword through the poor woman, then cleaning it on her apron.

Nicholas felt as if his head was exploding. He was in some sort of nightmare and would soon wake up. Surely? Looking inland, he saw thick black smoke coming from the village. One by one, the rest of their party gathered on the beach. All of them spattered with blood and stinking of smoke.

When the commander saw the three pitiable bodies, he ordered Henry and two others to take them to the village and add them to the pyre. He turned to Nicholas, seemingly unaware of the boy's utter horror.

"Some of the women gave us a lot of resistance, which I hadn't expected. It gave a few of their people the chance to escape. I would've liked not to leave any witnesses, but we have to get back to the ships as soon as possible and have no time to hunt them down. Henry was able to get the information about Astrid's whereabouts from one of the villagers. A few of their people took her north. They'll be taking her to the White Fort, just as I feared. Before she could tell us what route they took, she managed to get a knife and cut her throat. By the Tree, these people are real savages."

Henry appeared through the opening in the trees, looking quite sick. He didn't look Nicholas in the eye.

Captain Finn pulled Nicholas aside.

"Don't take it too much to heart, boy. Except for the woman we interrogated, it was all swiftly done. Culling is a necessary evil. Luckily, we don't have to do it very often. Do you think they were sorry when they killed our people yesterday?"

Before he could form a coherent answer, Nicholas ran into the sea and emptied his stomach. He heaved until only yellow bile came out. Tears were streaming down his face. Why was everyone so callous about this? He felt so dirty as if he would never be clean again. Behind his back, he heard the Commander bellowing out his orders.

"Right. Listen up. We will return to our ships and send one back to Sevenoaks to tell the people waiting at home they have taken Astrid north. We will sail to Luton to ask the Prior's help with dealing with the White Fort."

Chapter Eleven

Compared with what had gone before, the trip back through the reefs hardly registered on Nicholas.

The Commander beckoned him, Henry and Captain Finn to join him in his cabin. William was already seated at the table.

"My apologies for not letting you all freshen up first, but time is of the essence. We're sailing to Luton to ask the Prior to intermediate for us. William, we will stop at the harbour near the White Fort to drop you off. You have to contact the local priest so he can help keep an eye on Damien before he does something stupid. Being a man from the Church, you should have immunity."

"How will I make him listen to me? "William was holding his hands up as if to ward off this plan.

His father was having none of it.

"You are all we have got in the way of clergy. We need to make sure Astrid stays unharmed until we can contact the Prior. Damien might think twice about harming her with a member of the Church looking over his shoulder and reporting back to Luton. Use your imagination. Those monks must have taught you something, didn't they? You always were good friends with Astrid. Don't you want to help her? I know you don't have the stomach for war, but I hope I did not raise a coward?"

William, his lips a straight line in his face, bowed his head and nodded, everyone's eyes on him.

"Sir, why don't I go with him." Nicholas wanted to do something positive after the spectacle he had made of himself on the beach. He felt sorry for William, who they used to tease for being such a tender-hearted soul.

"Warrior monks often accompany their brothers on peacekeeping missions. It will make William look more like a genuine messenger from the Faith."

The Commander looked from one to the other.

"That might be an idea. What do you think?" He looked at the others.

"He will need someone to give him the Warrior monk tattoo, sir. I don't know what his mother will think of that. He has not taken the oath yet."

Henry sounded sceptical about their plan.

Nicholas and William exchanged a quick look. Henry continued, "Do we even have anybody on board? Who knows how to do it? Tattoos like that are not easy, and they'll hurt like hell. I hope you know what you are setting him up for?"

He was looking at the two boys, his arms crossed in front of his chest.

Nicholas stiffened. He wanted to show this man he

was not a child.

"If there's anybody on board who can do it, I'll go with William. I'm not afraid of a bit of pain."

"I'll do it."

Captain Finn stepped forward. He stroked his sleeve up, and to everyone's surprise, there was a detailed picture of a warrior surrounded by lots of small weapon symbols. Even the Commander was surprised.

"Here I had you for a pirate in your former life. Right, go back outside and tell the purser what you need. And for fuck's sake, give the boy some whiskey. He already looks green about the gills."

To Nicholas' relief, William followed Finn and himself down below. He would need his friend there.

He heard the anchor rattling up. The Commander seemed to be in a hurry. They had only a few hours of daylight left to get before the coast of White Fort town. With the dangers lurking underneath them, the seas were too treacherous to hazard a crossing after nightfall. The next day they would drop William and him off and make sail for Luton.

It had been a harrowing day with more to come tomorrow.

Chapter Twelve

Father Sirio, priest and scientist of the Church of Light on the Island, sighed and set to work, only to be interrupted by a knock on the door. He stood up to open it and found a man, one of the captains of the rescue mission, breathing hard on his doorstep. He ushered him in and closed the door behind him.

"Before you start telling me your news, let me send for some refreshments. You look like you need it."

He pulled a bell and told the servant that the officer would like some refreshments to please serve them in the dining room.

"I will join you in a minute. Make yourself comfortable. You must be hungry."

The man accepted gratefully and followed the servant downstairs.

Sirio closed his eyes for a moment and took a deep breath. It was time to hear what had happened on Diggers' Peninsula.

"I see they've been looking after you. Is there anything else I can get you? I've got some lovely rum here."

He pointed at a table loaded with decanters.

The captain, still eating, shook his head.

"Thanks for the offer, but I better keep my wits together. I need to sail to Kent today to bring the news to the court ."

He hastily swallowed his last mouthful and started to tell the priest what had happened in West Drayton.

Father Sirio tried not to let his feelings show upon hearing about the unsanctioned slaughter of a whole village. It was not what he had expected. It should merely have been a rescuing operation. This time the Commander had gone above his authority one time too often. There would be a high price to pay. No wonder he had not been able to contact Luton. They must be preparing an answer to this breach of their authority before they would speak to him.

"I hope the Commander knows culling without dispensation from the Prior is illegal? I know he was not himself, losing one of his oldest friends, but I expected more restraint from such an experienced leader. We are supposed to be the civilised ones in the Archipelago. Now I'll have to speak with Prendini to explain. There were tribes higher on the list than that one in. What was it called again?"

"West Drayton, your excellency," the captain was a bit taken aback by the priest's reaction.

"Ah yes, West Drayton. Thank the Lady that there weren't too many people in the village at that time of day. They were never candidates for culling. We may have ruined one of our experiments."

In his dismay, Father Sirio was thinking out loud, forgetting this was Monastery business only. He shook himself and bit his lip.

"So, the Commander has set sail for the harbour of the White Fort? They won't let him moor, and the plan of sending young William as a representative of the Monastery supported by Nicholas is risky. Let's hope Luton can intercept them before they come to any harm."

The captain, his eyebrows practically disappearing under his wig, stared at him. The poor man had already heard too much. He would hopefully be too tired to remember too much of it. He needed to send him on his way.

"My dear Captain. You must be exhausted. Why don't you go and let one of the guards show you a room in the Barracks via the baths?"

The man was more than happy to leave Father Sirio's quarters, having heard enough to be afraid of the ruination of his soul. Bowing deeply, he hurried out of the room.

Well, he had to speak with the Prior. He might have to go through London as Luton seemed to be blocking him. They would be less likely to ignore a call from someone else.

Sirio locked his rooms and went down to the nave of the church. He disappeared behind the large picture of the Lady in one of the side chapels.

He put his hand on a sculpture in the wall, and a door silently slid open to reveal broad marble steps leading to the catacombs below the building. Lights sprang on when he walked the corridors, extinguishing behind him as he went along.

Not paying any attention to these features, which would have appeared a miracle to the lay people in The Archipelago, he hurried on. He came to what seemed like a dead-end but opened at another touch of his hand.

He entered a bright room with a large screen taking up most of the back wall and sat down opposite it, his hands rapidly playing over a desk lit by buttons of every size and colour.

A face sprang up on the screen, and a voice said: "Sirio. I didn't expect to hear from you so soon? Has anything happened?"

Oh, good. One of his old classmates was on duty tonight and would surely help him.

"We had a bit of a disaster on our end, and I need your help, no questions asked. This call has to stay between us for the moment until Luton brings out the official news about it. I need you to patch me through to Luton. They are being very evasive, but I have to ask them what they want me to do on this end to salvage what I can. Can you do it?"

There was a long silence on the other end, and the screen went blank for a bit.

When it lit up again, his friend spoke up again: "I had to move to one of the other cells. Of course, I will help you, my friend. It is the least I can do for you after last time. I will rustle up a contact code and send it to you. Take care and let me know how it went. Good luck."

Sirio let go of the breath he had been holding and copied the number that appeared in the corner of the screen.

"Thanks. You saved my flock and me a lot of trouble. If I can ever do anything for you, let me know. I have to hurry. Bless you."

A few moments later, a young face appeared on the screen and stared wide-eyed at him.

Before he could do anything, Sirio started to talk as fast as he could.

"By everything holy, don't disconnect me. I have important news for Macron. Just tell him it is about the situation on the Island."

He had contacted the Priory the night before and reported the attack on Harrington House and its disastrous result to headquarters. They had told him they would contact him with further orders. But he needed to know if they had already heard about the destruction of the village. It would take a lot to deflect the wrath of the Prior. Or better, it would take the company a fortune to make it all go away. At the same time, he wanted to get an update on the Astrid situation.

"Macron told us he would call you later and until then not to let you through. I...."

" That might be, but when he hears my news too late, there will be trouble. Put me through, or I will report you to the Prior himself."

Sirio usually was very courteous, and the young novice on the other end must have heard the emergency in his voice because a minute later, the irritated voice of the Secretary of the Church of Light in Luton sounded over the speakers. Macron showed his displeasure by not appearing on the screen.

"What did you not understand about not contacting us before we called you? You might have been a High Priest for a long time, but that doesn't excuse you from following an executive order. We are discussing our answer to the invasion as we speak. We are about to contact that scoundrel Damien to see what he has to say for himself. You are just holding up procedures, and you will have to come up with a very good reason to disturb the high office's business. What is so important that would excuse your behaviour and not let us fine you for it?"

Sirio clenched his teeth. The little upstart just loved to make everyone feel inferior. They were from the same year, but the man's ambition had been enormous, and he had wormed his way into the second-highest post with a keen eye on taking the Prior's place at the next election.

"You might want to hear my news before you do that, as it will affect your negotiations. Our Commander has gone outside his book and culled most of the population from a Midland village. He was angry about the attack and losing his friends and Astrid. As far as I know, most of the men were at sea at the time, but their women and offspring are gone."

Sirio heard Macron swear on the other end and

mumble something to someone or others in his room.

"That old idiot should have been thrown off the Island ages ago. We will contact Damien and will let you know what we decide. Don't do anything else yet. You people have done enough harm as it is for now. We are so close, and this could set us back at least two generations. Be sure we will review your post at our next Church Council. There have been too many mistakes. And about the son of Harrington. Send him to London. We will assess the case. If he can't be restored, he will join the other on the Ship. I see you don't like it, but don't interfere. Did you forget the first rule of Science? Don't get attached to your specimens. Now let us do our work."

The screen went blank without any of the usual greetings, and silence returned in the subterranean room.

Sirio shook his head and went back upstairs. He didn't worry too much about Macron's display of power. The families from the Island always supported him, and in the past, his contributions to the Plan were far too valuable to them to substitute a prominent scientist at such a late date.

He would have to see what they came up with and do his best to reduce the damage as much as possible. He'd better get organising the funds to pay the undoubtedly high fine the company would get. He knew how important Astrid was for the Priory's project and trusted them to get her back as soon as possible.

Chapter Thirteen

Astrid was woken by the sound of a low voice growling: "Let her sleep. I'll keep watch until tomorrow. I have a lot of thinking to do."

Her heart hammered when she saw a dark shadow slithering towards her.

"Lie still and don't make a sound, or I will kill you, everybody be damned".

Before she could react, a large, calloused hand clamped over her mouth and nose like a vice, and she froze with terror. She could barely breathe. The weight of a heavy body smelling of sweat bearing down on her made it impossible to move.

"It's time to get to know each other a bit better, I think. I've seen the lad making eyes at you all day. I can't blame him. After I've finished with you, I might let him have the leftovers. Damien wanted you undamaged but didn't mention which part of you."

He whispered those last words, licking her face and groping her wherever he could.

Astrid trembled like a leaf, having this brute crawling all over her, pinching her. His teeth were gleaming close to her face.

"Now, I'll take my hand from your face. Nod if you won't scream. If you lie, I'll put this knife into that lovely body of yours. Then I'll deal with the others."

She felt something sharp sticking through her shirt into her side. Solo's breath smelled of beer and garlic mixed with the oily smell of fish. She felt bile rise in her throat. Petrified, she nodded. His hand let go of her face. Gulping air into her starved lungs, she looked frantically around for help when she felt his rough hands shoving up her shirt and tearing at her trousers. This just wasn't happening. Should she scream? Who would come? Would he kill her? She decided to try to make him see sense.

"Please don't do this," she whispered. "Let me go. My parents will pay anything. Your boss won't pay you anything if you molest me. Your woman wouldn't be happy either if she finds out."

"Well, I won't tell anyone if you don't," Solo smirked.

Astrid lifted her head, seeing the two small, unmoving mounds by the fire, hoping they could do something to make this nightmare stop.

Seeing her look, Solo whispered: "Waking them will do you no good. The boy is no threat to me, and his sister won't want him to get into trouble. You will only make me have to kill him or both."

She started to struggle again to get out from under him. He hardly seemed to notice. His weight was enough to stop her from moving away. By now, he had managed to undo his own trousers as well. She felt his hands mauling her breasts as he was trying to mount her. She stiffened. She'd rather be dead than let this beast defile her. Her life would be over. She opened her mouth to scream, not caring about the consequences. But before she had a chance to utter a sound, his eyes narrowed. He let go of her with one of his hands and reared up. The last thing she saw was a giant fist coming at her. Everything went dark.

Chapter Fourteen

Yaya woke by the muffled sounds of a struggle. Groggy with sleep, she sat up, gripping her knife, thinking some men from the village might be trying to earn some easy money by stealing their prisoner. Peering in the direction the sounds were coming from, she saw what Solo was up to and decided not to interfere.

What did she care about that Island wench, who'd only make her brother get into trouble? Boy seemed besotted with the girl. She knew him well enough to have seen the signs. It would only mean a mess if she woke him, trying to stop that idiot's bit of fun. Boy would want to save her, the little idiot, and get himself killed in the process.

Despite feeling a bit guilty to let a man abuse another woman like that, she turned her back to the scene, plugged her fingers in her ears and waited for it all to end while praying Boy wouldn't wake up or all hell would break loose. She told herself she would have to choose and knew who it was going to be. They would probably all end up dead. Solo, when thwarted, could be a force of nature.

Yaya never got back to sleep that night. She heard Solo come back to the fire and start snoring. From the girl, she didn't hear any sound. Yaya hoped her stupid partner hadn't killed her. That would genuinely mess everything up. She got up to take on the last watch.

Her brother woke up just before daylight rubbing his eyes. He looked around to see Solo still sleeping and the girl sitting upright staring at them.

"I'll see if she needs something."

She saw Boy bend over the girl and talk to her. She recognised his expression of anger and hurried over to them. The girl's clothes were torn, and she was shivering uncontrollably. The right side of her face sported a big bruise, and her eye was entirely closed by a dark purple swelling. She was white as a sheet and didn't look them in the eye. Boy tried to talk to her, but she just looked at him as if she didn't know who he was.

Yaya took the girl's arm and started to walk her in the direction of their fire, snapping at her brother, "Mind your own business, Boy. She got up in the night and walked right into the stable door. Didn't you? Her body is hurting from all the walking we did yesterday. Just keep away from Solo and don't ask any questions. That will just make it harder for her and both of us. Give her something to get herself tidied up."

Boy handed Astrid a wet cloth to wash her face and rummaged in his bag for his spare clothes. She silently accepted them and stumbled, barely able to keep upright to the back of the stable where there was a water pump.

Yaya felt her blood run hot and cold. Her brother looked over his shoulder to where Solo was lying, his eyes burning. He rose to go, ready to have it out with him. Before she could do anything to stop him, the girl was back.

"Please, don't."

"What happened? Has Solo..?"

But the girl walked right past him and went back to the pump again. When she returned, she sat down beside their bags, hiding her face by letting her hair hang in front of it. Her brother looked as if the girl had slapped him in his face and went to get their things packed, stumbling as if he was in pain too.

Yaya, glad she had not said anything, offered the girl some food and, when she shook her head, urged her to at least drink something.

Astrid just looked up at her in dumb silence, pulling her coat tightly around her.

"Are you in pain?"

She nodded. Yaya rummaged into her pack and dug out a vial of medicine.

"Take this. It will ease your pains and stop any bleeding. When we get to the fort, we'll have a medic look at that eye. Can you see anything with it?"

The girl, shaking her head and still not looking up, accepted the medicine. She emptied the little bottle down her throat in one go, seeming not to care about its disgusting taste.

"Let's get you up. We have a long walk ahead. Tell me when the pain comes back. I will give you some more."

Yaya pulled her up and then abruptly turned and

hoisted her pack on her back. On her way past Solo, she gave him a hard kick and shouted for him to get up.

When Astrid tried to put her pack on, she moaned. With a thunderous look on his face, Boy hurriedly took the bag from her and motioned her to walk with him, but Solo, looking hung over but pleased with himself, wanted to have her by his side again.

He was whistling and hustling her along, giving her a leering wink now and then. Astrid looked straight ahead, ignoring Solo completely.

Chapter Fifteen

Boy asked his sister to move up and talk to Solo. To Astrid's surprise, she did so immediately and waved her back to walk with her brother.

He tried to start a conversation with her. She felt like she couldn't talk without bursting into tears and bit her lip, turning her head away from him.

He fell quiet, and they both trudged on.

"The tracks." His sister's excited yell broke through their silence, "Let's see if we can jump a train or else, we will never make the Fort today. The girl isn't going to last much longer, the way we're going."

The moment they halted, Astrid crumbled to the ground, her face alarmingly white, streaked black with the dust of the road. They'd been going at a pace that was hard to keep up with. Especially for a girl who had just been through hell and back. Hadn't he tortured her enough?

Giving a big sigh, pretending to do Yaya a big favour though he must be tired too, Solo said: "There is a convenient place to get on at the next water tower. I can't see her jump, though, in her state. It will be less risky to keep on walking. I can always carry her."

Astrid visibly shuddered just at the thought of Solo laying his hands on her for whatever reason, which made the brute roar with laughter.

Boy called Yaya over, "You and I can pull her aboard.

We've done it before with mum."

Solo bristled.

"Who made you in charge? We'll only wait for a train as long as she needs to recover. I will give it half an hour. If it hasn't come by then, we'll continue walking. I want to be in the Fort before nightfall."

Astrid gratefully accepted Boy's arm, letting him pull her up and half carry her the next hundred meters or so to a tall wooden contraption with a round vat on top. She had read about the big train running from Penn station in the south all the way north to the White Fort. It was an ancient machine. In any other circumstances, she would have been excited to try it out. It was what she always had dreamed of, discovering the world outside the Island experiencing all its wonders. Now it seemed just another obstacle to overcome and to listen to them, not without danger. At least she could have a rest waiting for it. Her whole body hurt from the exhausting track in the hot sun and the abuse from last night. The sight in her right eye was still blurry. It all faded into nothing compared to what he did to her afterwards. Her skin crawled just imagining it.

Glaring at her, Solo warned again: "We'll wait until the sun is halfway down the sky. If the train hasn't shown up by then, we'll walk. I'm not.."

He didn't get to finish his sentence. Loud voices came up from behind the bushes on the other side of the tracks. Quick as a flash, Solo drew his weapon. Yaya and Boy had theirs ready and stood beside him.

"That's a nice way to great your friends, Solo." a high voice piped up. A boyish face grinning with mischief appeared through the leaves.

Solo dropped his weapon and, with a rare smile, making him look nearly human, said: "I'll be damned, Peter the Piper. Waiting for transport too, I guess?"

A second tall, thin figure appeared behind the first.

"And Jo, of course. You guys are joined at the hip. Long time, no see. Last time I came up, you were on tour in the West. How did that go? I've often thought of exploring that way."

To Astrid's surprise, Solo embraced both men. Boy and his sister did the same, looking very pleased with this distraction.

The first man, who approached them, was the smallest person Astrid had ever seen. He was shorter than her little sister. He barely came up to her chest. His clothes were in various colours of green, making it look like one of the shrubs had gotten feet.

The one who followed behind him was a beanpole of a man wearing a white robe similar to an Untouchable. His hair, tucked into a topknot, was decorated with brilliant feathers. From his right ear, an intricate jewel dangled, sparkling in the afternoon sun. It was hard to see his features with all the paint covering them. His face looked like a mask. But the eyes looking out of it were kind.

The tiny man swept his large hat in a mock gesture and bowed to her. "Peter the Piper at your service, young lady. Boy, me lad, introduce me? Did you get married to this delicious creature without telling me? I am devastated you didn't invite me to the wedding. And to an Islander, am I right? How do you like our beautiful country so far, my dear?"

He was observing her with sharp dark brown eyes. She could see he was aware she was not here of her own free will. The bruises on her face and arms would tell their story.

Before Boy could answer, Solo stepped between Astrid and the newly arrived men, puffing himself up.

"She's a present for Damien. So hands-off. You may have a nice voice, and that friend of yours plays the violin like a demon, but any nonsense, and you'll be looking for other jobs. Hard to play or sing with no head."

"Keep your shirt on, young man. When have we ever pulled one over you? I am just making conversation. Hey. Do I hear something?"

They all heard it. The sound of a hundred horses galloping towards them, dragging metal chains behind, was hard to miss. The ground started to tremble. Soon the screeching rumble was accompanied by a high piercing whistle and the hissing of a thousand snakes.

Astrid, for one moment, forgot her misery, the sight filling the horizon taking her breath away. The pictures in

her schoolbooks had not done it justice. Seeing it hurtling towards them, towering over the trees belching out great clouds of steam, made her realise she had never really understood how huge the Midland train was. When it was still quite a distance away, it started to slow down. Everyone except her began running towards the tracks."Come on, you stupid girl. Come over here." Solo, his old furious self,
was beckoning her. Astrid, not wanting him to touch her again, froze.

"Come here, little one. I'll get you on that train in a jiffy." The taller of the two strange-looking men had come back for her. He guided her gently but determinedly to the metal tracks, all the while making calming noises as if she were a nervous animal.

Solo looked as if to interfere, but the train's closeness and the short window of time they had to get on it made his decision for him. He left Jo to deal with her. The man swept her up with one arm while with the other, he gripped one of the ribs of the carriage, swishing past them and swung them both into a dark space.

Chapter Sixteen

They landed in a tangle of limbs. "Well done, my girl. You can let go now. We don't want to give Solo a reason to start making trouble. Not that he usually needs one."

Her saviour gently undid the white-knuckled grip she still had on his lower arm. Only then did she dare to open her eyes to find that everyone had made it safely onto the train. Despite her body's soreness and the profound grief about all that happened the day before, she couldn't help feeling quite exhilarated at the enormous speed they were going. The wind was blasting through the wagon's open doors, making her hair whip around her head and drying the sticky sweat from the long, hot walk on her body. No wonder people paid lots of money to travel on one of these marvels. It must be even nicer to do it sitting on comfortable couches. Her parents had told them about their journeys with the Rail Nation. They had not exaggerated.

" Ah, the best way to get home, dear, I say." The man called Peter leaned back against his companion. To her surprise, the latter kissed his partner lovingly on the top of his balding head, winking at her.

Solo spat on the floor. "Get a room, you two. I'll have to see enough of that when we get to Damien's. Don't want to corrupt my little bird here." They ignored him.

"We'll be at White Fort Station soon," the boy had managed to worm his way between her and Jo. "You'll get a chance to rest and eat some proper food. Damien always makes sure his foreign prisoners are kept in good condition to get the best price. He knows your father will pay well."

Astrid swallowed, thinking how her father would react if he found out what that animal Solo had done to her. "How long will it take for a message to get to my parents?"

"Damien won't deal directly with them. The monks will take care of the exchange. He will ask Luton as they are close to the Fort. They often mediate in his cases."

She stared at Boy, not wanting to believe what she was hearing. "Often? What are you talking about? I've never heard of this. Surely the monks should make sure this will never happen in the first place? It is against their law to enter our lands without our permission. To do so, the monks will put you to death with everyone who knew about it and didn't try to stop it." Her voice became shrill.

He winced but still tried to explain, "The monks allow us to ransom hostages from the Gen folk when they enter our country. As long as we never set foot on their lands."

"Then you must know what the Monastery will do when they find out you and your friends did go onto our island and into our house to rob us and steal me away?" Astrid's cheeks were flushed, and her eye had some of that spark back he thought lost forever.

Boy sighed. "I know. It's all a big mess. We were supposed to watch your house to get information on the security.

We were never supposed to go in ourselves. Our chief Damien was planning to send his own men. Solo needs money to take his brother Eric to be treated. It costs tons of money to pay continental medics to do so. It pushed him to go in himself instead of waiting for Damien's men. They got lucky finding an easy entrance to your house. They saw people using it."

Boy's cheeks turned scarlet, and he looked away. Astrid felt the blood drain from her face. It had been her that morning on the beach.

They both looked at Solo, who seemed quite relaxed for someone who had just broken one of the strictest rules in Midland: Never disobey Damien or the Prior. Solo was talking animatedly with the pair who had joined them.

Astrid wondered, pointing at the pair, "Are those two such men who love other men? You mentioned it yesterday when we talked about Damien. Are there many people like that here?"

"No, not many but some. Why do you ask? My mother told me that it was never commented on in the olden days before the Monastery came into our lives and told us to multiply. There is nothing wrong with it. Peter and Jo are two of the nicest people I know. They met at a festival while touring Albion and have been together ever since. You must hear them play. There'll be a party tonight to celebrate our raid, and Damien hired them to sing. They're the best. I can't wait to hear them again."

Boy stopped talking when the train slowed down—this time coming to a complete stop.

Peter called out to them: "We're here. Let's get off before the train guards do their rounds. The Fort pays them well to leave this cart always last, but you never know if some bureaucrat from the company is checking up on them and changes the routine."

Jo carefully lifted Astrid off the car. She smiled her thanks at him. He softly squeezed her arm and signalled to Boy.

"Young man. Look after this young lady for us. And, before I forget, happy naming day tomorrow."

Astrid's head shot up.

"Didn't he tell you? This fine lad is finally getting a proper name tomorrow as he's done well during his last raid. They would never have been so lucky without his help."

Astrid gave Boy a furious look. Jo, seeing that angry stare, turned around and practically sprinted back to his partner.

"Well, I hope you will have a nice NAMING day," Astrid spat the words at Boy, finally finding a target for all the fury that had been building inside her.

"Glad to have been of service to get you what you want."

With these words, she pulled herself up as tall and forbidding as was possible with her sore body and filthy clothes before striding off to where the others were getting on a cart driven by a slightly dim-witted looking person.

Jo was miming 'sorry" over Peter's head, but the damage was done. She felt miserable. In one go, she had lost her trust and the hope of ever getting home with his help. He climbed behind them on the back of the trap, shoulders hunched, looking as miserable as she felt.

The driver took them over a pebbly road to high walls surrounding the White Fort, which lay in a vast lake from which it took its name, looking impregnable.

Everything around Astrid felt colder and darker even though the sun was still shining merrily, the heat radiating off the cobbled road, making her sweat.

Chapter Seventeen

The security at the White Fort's gates was far more strict than it had been in Amersham. Guards bristling with weapons checked their papers at two portals before they even reached the courtyard. They passed a beautiful pond covered in water lilies fed by a tiny waterfall.

Astrid noticed a lot of people hanging around the square. Some were pointing at them. There were only a few women amongst them. She didn't get much time to take in her surroundings as Solo marched them to the entrance of what looked to be the main building. It was a surprisingly beautiful villa, its wings spreading wide to both sides and fronted by a covered walkway. It was five floors high and looked very opulent. She hadn't expected to find such fine craftsmanship in this forsaken land. It could easily compare itself with the finest villas on the Island.

She felt Yaya and Boy following close behind her.

Peter and Jo had somehow made themselves scarce the moment they arrived.

Solo had to identify himself again before they allowed him in, which annoyed him no end.

"Don't you numbskulls know by now who I am? I've come here so many times. Is your brain so small you can't remember anyone's face if you didn't see it a minute ago?

Idiots. I bet Damien won't be happy when he hears you were wasting my and his time. Let us through immediately."

The warden used to abuse while doing his job, shook his head and held out his hand for their papers. He was clearly not worried about Solo's threats.

"Just doing what they pay me to do, mate. Damien will be more unhappy if we let people in without checking their papers properly. I know you two."

He pointed his chin at Yaya and Solo. "But these two I've never seen before. I see you have a pass for one of the others. I don't see this girl on any of your documents. I'm afraid I can't let her in. She has to go to the back outside until you got her a pass. The boss doesn't like it when someone brings strangers into his living room, not after what happened to his brother. That was a woman as well."

Solo's face became nearly purple. Patience had never been his strong point. He balled his fists and would have struck the man were it not for Yaya's hand on his arm. She squeezed it hard and told him to calm the fuck down. It had the desired effect.

He took a deep breath and growled at the man: "I have strict orders to bring this woman to Damien as soon as we arrive, so stop pissing us about and let us in."

Not able to control himself anymore, he shoved the guard aside and entered the building without even looking back if the rest of them were following.

When he saw them hesitating, he shouted: "Come on, don't stand there like a bunch of morons. That asshole better not stop you if he knows what's good for him."

Yaya grabbed Boy and Astrid by their sleeves and went after Solo, trying to catch up. He had disappeared into the dark shadows of an enormous entrance hall.

Trying to get her eye used to the gloom inside, Astrid stopped for a moment, awestruck by the vastness of the place. A sweeping circular staircase wound its way up through all five floors. There were beautifully woven carpets and wall hangings everywhere. The woodwork of the stairs shone by the polishing of many hands. Around them reigned an eerie silence. It was lovely, cool inside.

Unimpressed by all the splendour, Solo knocked loudly on a door at his right and barged in after pushing it open. Bright light coming through a multifaceted, colourful window streamed into the hallway and made it hard to see the person sitting under it. Astrid and the others hesitated in the doorway when they heard a cold voice coming from within the room.

"Still the ill-mannered peasant, I see. What have I told you about waiting until I tell you to enter? If you weren't bringing me such a nice package, I would have you whipped for disrespecting me. You did bring it, I hope?"

Without answering, Solo looked over his shoulder, beckoning Yaya to bring Astrid forward. He pulled her in front of him and gave her a push towards the grossly fat figure sitting behind an ornate desk. The man looked up with slitted eyes, not looking overly impressed.

"Doesn't look like much of a bargain. You're sure it's one of the Harrington devil's brood?"

Solo stuck his chest out: "She's the eldest daughter, and I reckon she'll make us a nice sum. We managed to grab a lot of nice stuff from the house as well. That will be following later with my men. I thought you wanted no delay getting your hands on this one. Before you complain we went too far, this lad found us a secure entry to the house. It would have been a shame to wait for your men and pass on this opportunity. We even had time to leave a nice token of our appreciation. More than twenty of them."

Solo grinned, having pulled Boy by his neck to stand with Astrid while giving him a little affectionate shake.

Astrid wondered what Solo meant by what he said. Feeling the boy standing close as if to protect her, she got the courage to look up. Only to see the mountain of a man had gotten up from behind his desk and was limping towards them. She had never seen anyone so obese in her whole life. Standing close, she could see Damien, for this must be him, had a large, bald head with multiple rolls of fat in his neck, making it nigh impossible to know where his head ended and his torso began. He had wrapped himself in voluminous dark grey robes edged by beautiful embroidery. The lovely clothes did nothing to make him look less frightening. His wide-set eyes were so pale they looked white. His ears looked like someone had put them on the wrong side of his head.

When he put out one of his pudgy hands to tilt her face up, she jumped back, feeling disgusted by the look of his fingers, which had blunt bulbous ends. The thought of those touching her made her nearly lose the little breakfast she had that morning.

"Now, now, child. I'm not going to hurt you. yet. But I will if you don't step back over here and let me have a good look at you. Your father will be paying me a substantial sum of money, so I need to check if my merchandise is undamaged and worth his trouble."

Trembling, she let him lift her face to the light.

"What the fuck.. How did this happen?" baring his teeth, Damien glared at the other three.

Solo, who felt his ears burning, decided to bluff his way out of the situation. Giving Yaya and Boy a warning look, he said: "It was a rough boat ride. She fell and hurt her face. Nothing that won't disappear in a few days. These pathetic islanders bruise easily. She will still be worth the same to her father."

"To her father maybe, but not to those shitty monks. You know when they see this, they'll have one of their medics check her thoroughly before they will agree to intermediate? She will be worth nothing."

Solo started to sweat profusely now.

"What. She should be fine by the time they make it over here. For the rest, she's in one piece, I promise."

"Well, I can't take your word for it. As far as I know, you're not exactly famous for your medical knowledge nor your gentle way with women. I'll let my doctor man have a good look at her and ask her some questions."

His pale face now showing red spots on his cheeks, Damien sat back behind his desk and pulled a tasselled cord. A door, hidden in the wall behind him, opened to let in four young men dressed similarly to their chief. They all had the same pallor as their boss too. With their eyes rimmed with kohl and their mouths painted scarlet red, they looked like scary dolls. They formed a tight cordon around her.

"Take her to Mallory, my lovelies. When he's examined her, let him come to me with a full report. But before that, bring her to the women's basement for a wash. She smells. Don't want Mallory to complain again."

Turning to Solo and his companions: "I'll deal with you lot later when I've heard back from my doctor. For now, you're free to go to the kitchens and get something to eat, but on no account, try to leave the compound. I'll be watching you."

There was nothing else for Solo and the other two to do but meekly leave the study, relinquishing Astrid to her new escorts.

Boy looked very worried when he saw her

disappear into the bowels of the house and tried to catch her eye. When she looked back, he mouthed:" I will find you." They whisked her away before she could acknowledge his message.

Chapter Eighteen

Boy wished he had put a stop to all this when there still had been time. He should never have mentioned that bloody gate. He knew Solo had done more than just hurt Astrid's face and had no doubt Damien would find out. They would be in deep shit. The man wouldn't give a damn that it had been Solo's doing and would find them all guilty by association. He worried about his sister too. They didn't see eye to eye about many things, but she was still family, and he didn't want anything bad to happen to her.

Solo didn't look to be too bothered or was pretending not to be. He growled: "Let's get something to eat. That doctor won't find anything but some bruises. I hope the little bitch keeps her mouth shut. I told her what would happen if she didn't. She can kiss her ransom goodbye and will never see her home again. When the monks hear she is damaged goods, they will tell her parents she died and let Damien do with her what he likes. They don't want someone who has been fucked by a Midlander to come back into their Tree. I should know that much."

"So, he did do it." Boy felt a rage built up in himself and balled his fists. But before he could say anything, his sister spoke.

"Why do you always have to ruin everything, Solo? Even for yourself. What will happen to Eric when Damien decides she's worth nothing anymore and sells her on to some farmer and hangs us from the walls of the fort? You can have any woman you want, but no, you couldn't keep your hands off that skinny islander."

Yaya was shaking with rage. She had been stewing on what she'd seen him do in Amersham during the whole trip up here and was now kicking herself for not interfering at the time. She could have stopped Solo. Why hadn't she? Because she had been afraid Boy would try to defend the girl's honour and pay with his life for it? Or because she did not want to see what Solo was? A total piece of shit.

Boy opened his mouth to say something. His sister told him to shut up and keep out of it. "You, brother, will be lucky if we can convince Damien you had nothing to do with this whole stupid disaster. Let us hope that he will leave you out of it."

"But what about Astrid? Where have they taken her? Will Damien sell her to the highest bidder if the monks don't want her?"

Boy felt desperate looking at his sister for help. He felt like he had shrunk to the little brother he always was to her.

"It's all up to that doctor, Mallory, and the girl herself. I hope she will only tell him Solo gave her a beating and leave it at that. We might get away with just a hefty fine for damaging Damien's property. If she talks. Well, you've just heard what will happen then. We will have to wait and see."

They had arrived at the kitchen, where one of the cooks, shoving them a plate of food in their hands, showed them the way to the mess hall. None of them felt much like eating, even though it had been a long time since they last had something. Not looking at the other occupants of the hall, they huddled down at a small table and quickly rinsed down the food with some sour beer and got up. Solo left to join some people he knew from other visits while Yaya strode away, turning her back on both of them.

Boy went for a walk on the fort's grounds. He wanted to find out where they had taken Astrid. People were giving him pitying stares when they saw him. News spread fast in the fort. He ducked his head down and started his search.

Chapter Nineteen

Elsewhere in the fort, a much cleaner Astrid was looking up at Mallory, the local doctor. He had taken one whiff of her and agreed with Damien that she needed a bath before examining her.

"And give her something decent to wear."
The servants in the bathhouse had given her a soft grey robe similar to those her guards were wearing. Mallory ordered them to stay outside the sick room. They grudgingly agreed.

What she saw was a powerful-looking man with a short grey beard and a halo of wispy steel grey hair around his head. His face was wrinkled and brown like a walnut. He didn't look like he belonged in a horrible place like this with his soft voice and kind manner. His intelligent eyes studied her.

"Now, my dear, Astrid, isn't it? My name is John Mallory, but everyone calls me Mallory. Let me first have a look at that eye of yours. It looks quite painful. Have you been able to open it at all since you hurt it?"

She shook her head silently, looking at her feet.

"I'm going to try and carefully open it. I want to see if there's any damage to the eye itself. Try not to pull away if you can. I'll do my best not to hurt you."

Very gently, he lifted her right eyelid and winced at what he saw.

"Did it hurt when I did that?"

Astrid shook her head, trying not to cry. That part of her sight had been in darkness since that harrowing night. All this time, she had hoped she couldn't see much with it because of the bruising, making it nigh impossible to open it. The compassionate look in the doctor's eyes told her what she hadn't wanted to admit to herself. She might have lost the sight in her right eye.

"When that bruise has gone, you might be able to see a bit better with it, but I'm afraid it looks like you will have lost at least some of your sight. Sorry, I can't be more optimistic. It is no use giving you false hope. Looking at the other bruises, I can assure you there won't be lasting scars on your lovely face. I will have to report this to Damien, I'm afraid. That young man, Solo, will be in quite a bit of trouble. Fortunately, the monks don't count physical disabilities acquired later in life as a reason to deny ransom. In a way, if this is all the damage he did, you should count yourself lucky. Knowing Solo, it could have been far worse."

He smiled friendly at her, trying to put her more at her ease.

"I now need you to undress, so I can see if there is no other damage. If that makes you too uncomfortable, you could just tell me. Did you hurt something else when you 'fell' over?"

His kindness was too much for her, and Astrid

suddenly found herself sobbing. Her shoulders were shaking. She desperately wanted to tell him about what Solo had done to her that night, but she kept hearing his warning in her head. What if Solo was right about the monks not taking her back? By keeping quiet about it, she would at least have a chance of getting home. Father Sirio had always been kind to them, but she knew the other monks were extremely strict, and he had been a bit of an exception. A fallen woman had no place in the Gen community. What would Nicholas say if he knew?

Mallory now started to look worried.

"Are you in pain anywhere else? I'm so sorry I couldn't give you better news about the eye. I will give you some ointment with Arnica for the bruising and a bottle of boiled water with blueberry juice to rinse your eye three times a day. It might give some improvement. Are you sure you don't want to tell me more? It will stay between you and me, I promise. I can't treat you if you don't give me all the information I need."

Seeing her extreme distress, the doctor fearing the worst, told her: "You know the monks will have a physician nun make sure you are alright? She will do a thorough examination. Whatever you're not telling me will come out. If you tell me now, I can help you deal with it. It will be our secret. Damien will be furious enough about the eye without me telling him he lost his ransom."

Astrid desperately wanted to tell him the truth.

This kind-hearted man might be able to help her. Telling the others had been out of the question. Confiding in Yaya, the woman would just have told her to get a grip and be happy she didn't have to go back to the island. The only other person she could have said anything to was that boy. She had seen him looking at her when he thought she was not paying attention. Somehow, he still seemed to like her. She'd been furious at him when they last spoke, but if anyone in this forsaken place could and would be willing to help her, it would be him. But what would this nice man think when she told him about what had happened that night? Would he still want to help her? Wouldn't he be disgusted by it all?

Astrid took a deep shivering breath, wiping her face with her sleeve: "No, for the rest, I'm fine, I'm just exhausted. It's all been so horrible. Could you maybe do one thing for me?"

Mallory promised to go and find the boy and give him a message to go and see his patient.

"You can stay here in the sick room. The guards are still stationed outside, but I will tell them to let the lad see you. They will do as I ask. There might be a time they need me themselves. I'll leave you now to tell Damien the bad news about your vision. Hopefully, he won't shoot the messenger, and with Damien, I mean that literally. The last medic didn't last very long when he failed to cure Damien's favourite pet boy. Let's be grateful my news isn't any worse, and we can let him tell the monks to come and pick you up. Why don't you go and lie down for a bit and try to have some rest ?"

Mallory walked out of the room and shut the door softly behind him. Astrid could hear him talking to the guards. With a sigh, she lay down on the bed, exhausted but felt too worried about her future to sleep.

Chapter Twenty

Astrid woke up with a start when he leaned over her. She cowered down under the blankets, thinking it was one of the guards coming to take her back to Damien.

"And? How did it go? Why didn't you call out to me when he did it?"

The boy sounded quite indignant.

"I would have protected you. I am not frightened of Solo. Yaya would have helped me. What did the doctor say?"

Astrid sat up and held up her hands as if to ward off all his questions.

"I told the doctor nothing about that. I don't want to ever talk about it again with anybody. He was very nice to me. He's going to speak to Damien and will tell him about my eye and nothing else, and that will be bad enough."

"What do you mean about your eye?"

She told him what Mallory had told her about the loss of her sight. Boy sat down beside her on the bed, shaking his head and putting his hands over his face.

"Oh shit. I'm so, so sorry. Does it still hurt? What will this mean for your release to the monks? I heard from the soldiers a message had been sent to Luton Island. The Prior will send a delegation. It won't take long for them to get the message and put the team of negotiators together. That will give us some time."

Ignoring his barrage of questions, she asked, "Some time for what?"

" I have been talking to some people. You'll have to leave before the monks arrive, or we'll be screwed. I haven't been able to think of anything else after I saw what he did to you. I could kill him. Do you know where they will hold you until then?"

"Mallory told me I could stay here until they arrive, but those four men will be in front of my door all the time, though. Are you going to help me get out of here? Help me escape?"

Astrid looked at him with so much hope in her eyes he would have fought Damien himself to save her.

"I will try. It will be dangerous. If Damien catches us trying to get away, he will have us both killed, ransom or no ransom. He likes to set examples."

"I don't care. The monks will find out I'm not a virgin anymore and leave me here if I stay. I'd rather die trying to escape. If I can get out of here and back home, I'm sure my family won't ask too many questions. They will be too happy to see me alive. Do you know a way out?"

"This is my first visit. I need to go and get more information about this place."

Boy hung his head, having to admit his ignorance. Astrid felt her chances to get away diminish again. She was thinking furiously. "There must be a map of this place. Do you think we can trust this doctor enough to ask him if he can get us one? He was very friendly to me. Maybe he can help us without getting into trouble. He should be back soon. Let's ask him. If the doctor doesn't want to get involved, he might show us a way out of here."

At that precise moment, the subject of their conversation opened the door and gave them both a big smile, seeing their guilty faces.

"Don't look so worried, children. Damien was livid when he heard you might have permanent damage, Astrid, but I managed to calm him down a bit by assuring him it wouldn't show after I dealt with it. Boy, go and tell Solo and your sister to stay well out of his sight. This evening there'll be a big party, and the minstrels who travelled with you will be playing. I heard you met them on the road. Their music usually puts Damien in a better mood. Believe it or not, the man is very fond of music. Now, young man, it's time for you to leave."

Astrid, her lips trembling at the thought of being locked up somewhere, asked, "Can I stay here with you? Maybe you can say you need to treat me and need to do it here. Damien would want me to look as normal as possible, don't you think?"

Mallory rubbed his head, frowning.

"I will send one of the guards to Damien to check if he allows it. He is in a foul mood, and I don't want to aggravate it by deciding to keep you with me without his knowledge. Using your condition might do the trick. He is still keen to persuade the monks to pay the full ransom."

The doctor went outside to ask one of her guards to take his message to Damien. They heard one of them leave. Mallory came back in, looking as if he'd made a decision.

"Until we get word back, Astrid, you stay here, but you, boy, will have to leave. I will let you know what Damien decides. Where will I find you?"

"I'll go to the stables. It's the one place where I'll be least likely to run into Yaya or Solo. They went off together to be alone for a bit. I'll be in the hayloft having a kip if you need me."

Chapter Twenty-one

After waiting for an anxious half-hour, the message came back that it would be alright for Astrid to stay in the sickroom as long as the doctor understood she would be his full responsibility until the monks came for her."

The doctor looked at the guard: "I will not ask you what he really said, as I don't want to frighten the girl. Did he say anything else besides threatening me with all sorts of ways to die a miserable death if something went wrong?"

Having no problem terrifying Astrid, the boy answered: "He wants you to know that you'd better make her look acceptable before the end of the day, or he'll have your head. There's a big party planned tonight, and he wants to show her off to the guests. He said they might give him a better price than the monks."

At these words, Astrid's blood ran cold, her face going paler than a ghost. Her hope of getting out of here seemed to diminish by the minute.

Mallory took her ice-cold hands and warmed them between his.

"Even Damien wouldn't dare to antagonise the Prior. Don't worry, dear. He'll wait for their offer before he does anything else."

With these words, Mallory gave the messenger a

firm push towards the door, asking him to make himself useful and fetch Mattie, then shutting it firmly behind him. He made Astrid some chamomile tea to settle her nerves. Her teeth chattered against the cup.

"Don't look so worried, flower. It's been a long time coming, but I think the moment has come for me to leave this snakepit. I know how to get out of the castle unseen, but I will need some help from two of my friends. You met them, I believe? Peter and Jo, the minstrels. Crossing Damien equals signing your death warrant, but I'm sure they'll help. I'll make sure their part in our escape will not be noticeable. The last person who got into Damien's bad books took five days to die. That man happened to have been a good friend of theirs. I know people in Midland who will help us stay out of sight for as long as it takes us to get you out."

Astrid's shoulders slumped with relief.

"Are you willing to do that for me? It must be perilous. You've just met me. I thought all Midlanders hated us?"

She felt hopeful and frightened at the same time. Maybe it would be better to stay put and take her chances with the monks? She still could not believe they would leave her with these animals because of some old church rules. Her father wouldn't allow it. It wasn't her fault she'd been abused by that monster. But then, she had not known about this ransom thing either. Nor that the monks were colluding with these criminals.

Mallory sat down, crossing his arms in front of him.

"I've been here far too long. I did things that made it necessary for me to be out of the Prior's sight for a time, and then something else kept me here. I was born on the Mainland, but my family moved to Midland when I was still a child. When I became a young man, they sent me to Luton, to the Academy to become a monk."

Astrid pulled back from him with a start. "What? Continentals can never mix with people from Albion. Our priest told us they would get sick just by breathing the same air we do. How can you live here without getting ill?"

Mallory closed his eyes and sighed.

"That's a very long story, too long. When we have more time, if we get more time, I will one day tell you the truth about Albion and the Mainland."

Astrid felt immensely grateful Mallory was willing to help them escape. The boy would be glad he did not have to arrange their flight all by himself. It would improve their chances to no end.

Chapter Twenty-two

A soft knock on the door interrupted their conversation.

"Come in," Mallory called. "And where have you been all this time, my little pup? Wasting all my money again on those card games, I bet?"

"I didn't waste it. I won." the little girl, who had slipped in the room, piped up proudly.

One could have easily mistaken her for a boy, dressed as she was in yellow trousers with a red shirt far too big for her, were it not for her delicate features and mop of long messy golden curls. The gold was in stunning contrast to her dark brown face. Her black eyes had such a sparkling, mischievous look they made Astrid feel like smiling.

Mallory shook his head, trying, not very successfully, to keep a stern look on his face.

"I will believe you this time. I could have done with your help with this young lady this afternoon. Astrid, meet Mattie, full name Mathilda, but don't call her that or she might stick you with one of those wretched pins she carries about her, the little she-devil. Mattie, this is Astrid Harrington. She is our guest. Now you're here, I would like you to go and fetch a boy who's hiding in the stables. Look out for a young man with light, curly hair and tattoos of the Diggers clan. You remember from your lessons what they look like?"

"A wave with a skull above it on his right arm," the girl said, beaming with pride to show off her knowledge. Astrid could not remember seeing any tattoos on the boy, but then she hadn't particularly been looking for any.

Mattie stared at Mallory's guest with great curiosity, not yet ready to leave this wondrous new person. "How did you get that black eye? Did you kill the person who did that to you? I would've done."

"That's enough, Mathilda. What did I tell you about killing people? Go and find the boy. Tell him Mallory sends you. Bring him here through the bedroom passage. I don't want our friends outside to find out he is here."

Excited to sneak around the guards, Mattie shot away like an arrow, leaving Mallory to shake his head indulgently.

"Guess she still has a lot to learn. She was gifted to me by Damien after I managed to cure him of a horrible backache. His men had found her wandering around after they ransacked a farm west from the Towers. At a guess, I'd say she was about four then. She doesn't remember much from her previous life, which is a blessing. The lady knows what happened to her before they found her. But she could tell me her name, Mathilda. She's a lively little thing with a good heart but has learned a few bad habits from the men around here. I've taken it upon myself to look after her and give her some kind of education."

"Won't you be putting her in danger by helping me? She might be better off staying here, where she feels at home? Surely they would never blame her for your actions?"

Mallory shook his head.

"Mattie is twelve now, and believe it or not, under that dirty face hides a beautiful girl. I think I know where she comes from and always wanted to return her to her folks. If I leave her here, she will be distraught. She has become very attached to me and me to her. The men treat her like one of their own now, but it will be a whole other story when she becomes a woman. Don't worry too much about her safety. She can probably look after herself better than we can. She had enough experience in the fort. The kids here are sometimes worse than the grown-ups. It is the law of the jungle out there. Eat or be eaten. Most of them have had to learn the hard way not to mess with Mattie. Damien doesn't care what those kids get up to, as long as they don't bother him. The boys can either join his entourage later or become one of his soldiers. As for the girls.. in his eyes, they are only suitable for having children and serving the men. For her sake, it will be better to come with us."

Behind them, Boy entered the room tugged along by Mattie, who looked as proud as a dog bringing her master a juicy bone. Mallory smiled at her and patted her head.

"Ah, thank you, Mattie, well done. Boy, I hope you managed to stay out of Solo and your sister's way? I have decided to leave this place too and will bring Mattie with me. Better if they don't find out what we're planning. Or do you trust your sister enough to help us? I need to know before I involve other people and put them in danger for nothing."

The boy vehemently shook his head. "We can't tell her. Yaya's my sister, and I love her, but since she's been part of Solo's crew and his lover, she has changed. Were you saying something about involving other people? Are you sure you can trust them? They don't know Astrid and me. The fewer people who know, the fewer can betray us. There's a large sum of money and status involved."

"Don't worry. You must know them as you all arrived together, and I would trust them with my life."

"Peter and Jo? They are minstrels, not fighters. What can they do to help us get away?"

"I've known both of them since they were small boys when they were studying the musical arts in the Monastery school in Luton."

"You were a monk?"

"Yes, I was, a long time ago. We have some planning to do if we are to escape out of this place with our lives," the doctor turned to his protege, "Mattie, can you get us some bags and fill them with food. Try to get some water pouches as well. Don't forget to add a blanket for each of us. Never thought your thieving little ways would come in handy one day."

The girl gave them a naughty grin and ran off to do as he asked.

"Boy, why don't you go and find your sister and Solo and spend some time with them or else it might look suspicious. Join them at the party tonight. It is your naming day, after all. It will look strange if you're not present from the start. The festivities will begin at sundown. At the end of the evening, I will ask my friends to sing Damien's favourite ballad to distract him. It's a very long one. Most of the guests will be either drunk or stoned out of their minds by then. The only ones who won't be drinking or using drugs will be the man himself and his boys. With such a large gathering, they'll be extra alert to keep their master safe. Their attention will more likely be on the people entering the room than leaving it. I'll be attending the start of the party with Mattie. She will go to the stables first. I've always insisted she disappears when things get too rowdy so it won't look suspicious. I will follow when Damien orders me to bring Astrid down, as I'm sure he will. He wants to parade her in front of everyone to show everyone how clever he was, stealing the daughter of the mightiest man on the Island. Boy, you can go to the stables a few counts after I've left. Just tell your sister you need to take a leak or something."

Boy nodded his agreement but stuck up his hand as if to ask permission to say something. He looked a bit embarrassed.

"I would like to be called Jonah from now on. I

might not make it to the naming, and this is what I chose."

" Great. It will be a lot easier to call you by a proper name. "

Mallory clapped the boy on his back and continued:" We will all meet up in the stables. I don't expect many people there during the festivities. Mattie will deal with them. No killing this time, Mattie, I've got a plan. Astrid, you have to stay in my quarters until I come and get you. Make sure you rest some more. We have a challenging journey in front of us. Peter and Jo's performance gives us the time we need to vanish before Damien gets wind of our escape and sets his hounds after us."

Mallory looked around at her and the others as if to seek their agreement. None of them could see any other option to get them all out of this hellhole.

Mallory pointed to the back entrance. "Off you go, children. May the Lady watch over you."

He told Astrid to get some more rest while he found her some warm clothes and a cape to put on later that evening.

Chapter Twenty-three

After everyone disappeared to prepare for their escape, Astrid tried to get some rest. Tossing and turning, she finally gave up. She needed to think about all that had happened.

Had it only been two days since she woke up expecting her beloved to come and tell her he changed his mind and still loved her, only to have that barbarian haul her out of her room? And one day since she'd been..? She couldn't finish that thought.

Contemplating what that disgusting man had done to her, the bruises, the pain the following morning, not only her body but down there, she just wanted to die. Who would want her now? Her face must be a mess. She'd seen the looks on people' when they saw it. Even though they must be used to quite a bit when it came to ugly scars from what she had seen so far, she needed to see what they saw.

Astrid searched for a mirror. Not finding one in the bedroom, she went through to a library crammed with books on every shelf. Any other time it would have been heaven. A large table was covered in maps and papers.

"Ah, you're up already. Would you like something to eat?"

Mallory had come into the room, carrying a bottle of wine teetering on a tray of pies.

"You could have one or two of these. The cook

was very generous when I told her I was hungry."

Astrid first thought she'd be too nervous to eat, but the delicious smell of the pies made her mouth water and persuaded her to try one. They were so good. She surprised herself by polishing off a second one. Except for the soup Jonah's mother had given her, she did not have much to eat. The boy had tried to share his rations with her, but Solo had kept a watchful eye on them, growling when he caught him, 'stop pampering the little bitch.'

Mallory nodded approvingly, happy to see his patient had regained her appetite. She would need all her strength tonight.

"Good girl. Make sure you drink some of that apple juice I left for you. I have to prepare the rest of these pies for the stable guards."

Seeing her look of surprise at his generosity, he told her he would put a strong sleeping draft in the pastries and the wine. Mattie, who had befriended most of the soldiers in the Fort, would bring them the refreshments under the pretence she wanted them to have something nice to eat as they couldn't go to the party.

"Knowing those scoundrels, they'll have no problem scoffing all the pies and the wine with it. They won't give us any grief after that."

It started to dawn on Astrid that Mallory must have been planning to escape his current master before today.

He hadn't come up with this plan just for Jonah and her. She looked up at the doctor, realising how lucky they were to have met this man at the right time.

"How did your talk with those minstrels go?"

"Peter and Jo were happy to help. Jo has taken quite a shine to you. He's the most sensitive of the two and can never resist anyone in trouble, and Peter will do anything for him. We have agreed they will perform the Apocalypse ballad when I have left the party. Do you know it?"

Astrid nodded enthusiastically. It was a favourite of hers as well. It told the story of how the earth nearly was destroyed before the Exodus.

"Yes, we had to learn the lyrics in school. The monks and nuns thought it would warn us to stick to their rules. I never heard it sung, though."

" That's a shame. It's a wonderful song, especially when sung by those two. Alas, you won't get to hear it tonight as we'll use their performance as a distraction to slip away. The song takes at least half an hour to perform. Maybe more with all the encores the people usually demand. Even if he did not love the song, Damien would never cut their concert short. People would get too upset, and fights would break out. He has let me know that he wants me to bring you downstairs near the end of the evening to pick the lottery ticket with yourself as the prize. It will be less risky for him to have the monks negotiate with your new owner, so he can pretend it is all out of his hands. He is meaner than the devil himself but clever with it."

Seeing the horror in her eyes, he realised how frightening it must all sound to her.

"Don't worry, dear. It will never come to that. We will be long gone before the lottery even starts. A little bird told me the negotiators from Luton will be arriving soon and hope to come up to the fort this evening to pay your ransom. Are you sure you don't want to wait for them? It might be your safest ticket out of here back to your family."

Astrid thought about what Solo had told her about being damaged goods, and when finding out, the Prior might not even want to waste any money on her release. She shook her head, wringing her hands.

"No, please. I want to go with you. I don't want people poking at me, asking questions. The Church is always so strict. They might decide I am not worth the ransom. My parents will pay anything to have me back no matter what. You will get me home, won't you?"

Mallory frowned and started to ask a question but thought the better of it.

"As much as I'd like to, I can't give you any guarantees. I will promise to do my utter best. There is one thing I will ask of you. If anything happens to me, please, look after Mattie for me. Take her to the mountain tribes in the Towers. I think she might have some relations there. I need to know someone will be watching over her besides me."

Astrid promised she would do what he asked.

Shuffling through the piles of papers lying on his desk, Mallory pulled a leather tube from under them. Out of the container came the most beautiful map Astrid had ever seen. Sweeping some papers to the ground, he rolled it out, securing its corners with some earthenware cups.

Despite being old, the colours were still as vibrant as if painted yesterday.

Mallory pointed out the route he planned to take.

"See this small fishing and mining town far south? That's Upavon, our final destination. My sister Plaxedes lives there. She was married to a miner who had the misfortune to die in a collapse. Even though it's only eighty miles from here as the crow flies, it will take us at least a month to get there if nothing gets in our way. Which would be a small miracle."

"Will everyone come with us?"

"Mattie and I definitely will, and Jonah, of course. The last thing I want is to hold you, young ones, back, though. If it comes to choosing between me or you three making it, you have to do the sensible thing. I've had a long and full life while you three are just starting yours."

He looked at her, his eyes shining with determination and stuck out his hand to confirm their pact with a handshake.

Deciding not to waste time trying to disagree, Astrid silently vowed that she would never let it come to that.

She gripped Mallory's hand firmly and solemnly shook it. She was sure Jonah and Mattie would agree they could never sacrifice this kind and generous man.

"Right, I think you need some warmer clothes for the trip. Let's find you some."

Looking much relieved at extracting her promise, Mallory started to busy himself with the rest of the preparations leaving Astrid to mull over all she had heard.

Chapter Twenty-four

Jonah wandered around the fort grounds going over the doctor's plans. He didn't want to go back to the stables because he didn't want anyone to remember him being anywhere near it. He felt a bit guilty for leaving his sister behind to face the consequences of their disappearance. She would just have to rely on Solo, who always landed on his feet no matter in what trouble he got himself.

After a while, he went back to the barracks. Peeking into the mess hall, he saw her and Solo playing cards with some other guests. He was glad they didn't notice him.

The place was heaving. Word had spread about the big party. A lot of men and women had come up from the town. Some were sailors from the ships anchored in the harbour and others shopkeepers and other dignitaries from White Fort village. Damien's parties were famous for their bountiful supply of food, drink and other substances.

Outside, servants were running around, attaching torches in their holders and setting down oil lamps on any surface that would hold them. Barrels of beer were being rolled to the main hall and set up inside on trestle tables.

Jonah followed to men to check out the room. Trays of food were making their way from the kitchen quarter and delivered at the Festival Hall. High up behind the dais, a balcony spanned the width of the hall. Musicians were tuning their instruments. There was a cacophony of sounds, drums, guitars and trumpets. To his relief, he saw there were enough exits to make a quick getaway later. He decided to see if his sister and Solo were ready to join him in finding a place to sit.

Solo seemed to be in a much better mood than when he left them a few hours ago.

"Hey, little brother, come and join us. Where have you been all this time?"

Good sleep combined with some food and, by the looks of it, a lot of beer had made him drunkenly affectionate. Yaya just glanced up from her cards and did not say anything. She was always a bit grumpy after having to spend too much time with Solo.

Jonah saw she was drinking wine like it would run out every moment and looked tired. He worried about her and wished she would take up with some decent guy instead of Solo. He decided to join their game. He would do anything to make the time go faster. To his surprise, Solo gave him some of his coins to play a few hands.

After a while, despite himself, Jonah enjoyed himself as he had an excellent memory and had no trouble remembering which cards everybody had drawn. He made sure to lose now and then in order not to get into trouble and attract attention. Some of these men were very sore losers.

When the evening started to draw in, the mess hall

began to empty. People were making their way to the main building in small groups, laughing and talking, undoubtedly looking forward to the upcoming bash.

In the soft, yellow light of the oil lamps, everything looked quite magical. Torches made the shadows jump about as if already dancing to the merry tunes coming from inside the house.

Solo, happy to have won more than he lost, gave Yaya a sloppy smack on the lips and pushed himself up from the table. He seemed to be a bit unsteady on his feet. She got up just in time to stop him colliding with some rough-looking types. His sister appeared determined this night was not going to end in yet another brawl.

Jonah followed them, staying close, doing his best to shepherd them to a table as near as possible to a side door.

Wild, thumping sound of drums and piercing thrills of flutes were whipping up the crowd of party-goers. The music was deafening but not enough to drown out the noise of about sixty men and women talking with loud voices interspersing it with laughs and screams.

Solo had fallen silent and seemed satisfied to continue drinking while eating copious amounts of food and watching others having fun. Many of the guests were already whirling around the floor, kept clear for that purpose, jumping crazily to the rhythm of the drums.

At the echoing sound of an enormous gong set up

behind the dais, the music stopped instantly. One after the other, the revellers sat down. Within a few minutes, you could hear a pin drop.

A hidden door at the back of the hall opened, and out came Damien with his twelve so-called Angels, their faces painted to represent various insects or reptiles. The vibrant colours on their faces were in sharp contrast to their pitch-black clothes: skin-tight trousers and shirts made of a shimmering material. Silver chains adorned every part of their bodies. No one dared to laugh or make a lewd comment. The solemn-looking young men took their place behind an enormous, winged throne covered in gold cloth. Another sonorous boing resonated from the giant gong.

Damien ascended the dais and, with a big grunt, sat down in his chair. He had exchanged his usual silver-grey robes for a flashy white suit covered in diamonds reminding Jonah of a puffer fish he once caught. It nearly made your eyes hurt to look at him. In contrast, he was wearing a black peaked cap with gold symbols on the front.

The large man's eyes swept over his guests. In the continuing silence, he didn't have to raise his shrill voice to be heard.

"My dear, dear fellows. Nice to see you all enjoying yourselves tonight. For the past three months, everyone has worked hard for our community. To honour that, I decided to throw you a big party. Cheers."

He raised his glass and saluted the crowd, which resulted in a roar of approval. People were shouting, clapping, and stamping their feet until Damien held up his hands. The noise stopped immediately.

"Besides good food and wine, I have more treats for you in-store tonight, my friends. Our beloved minstrels, Jo and Peter, will perform for us tonight. Before that starts, we will name a fine young fellow, stand up boy. Let's all give him a hand."

After a push from Solo, Jonah, his face gone red and white, had no choice but to stand up. He felt like disappearing into the ground. Everyone was looking at him and shouting lewd suggestions for the name he might choose. He gave a slight bow to Damien and sat down again as soon as he could. This kind of attention was the last thing he needed.

Damien, barely acknowledging Jonah's timidness, continued: "I haven't finished. There is another exciting thing in store for you tonight. Our man Solo there has managed to capture us, one of them Islander girls. And not just any girl but the daughter of that pain in my butt director of the Harrington Corporation. Instead of keeping this prize all to myself as many other bosses would have done, I've decided to allow one of you to be the lucky bastard to win the lottery with her ransom as the main prize. In a moment, my boys here will go round to sell tickets. For one Oro a piece, she could be yours to keep or to sell. But first, let's eat, drink."

The noise level after his announcement went through the roof. Damien nodded at his boys. They rose as one to go round the room, rattling their buckets selling tickets to all who wanted some.

Jonah saw Solo bought a handful too though it must be very sour for him to see his hard-won prize raffled away to all and sundry whose only contribution had been purchasing some pieces of paper with a number on it. He hoped his naming would be up soon, so he could make his exit before Damien sent Mallory to fetch Astrid.

He didn't have to wait long. When all the Angels sat down again, having sold every ticket, Damien rose. The excited chatter faded away.

"Just to leave you in suspense a bit longer, we will first get to the business of naming our brave young man. Come forward, boy."

This time Jonah couldn't get to the front of the room fast enough, eager to have his part over and done.

"Get right up here, boy. So, we can all see you."

Jonah was lifted onto the dais by some helpful men and tried not to stare at Damien like a frightened rabbit caught in the light of a torch. Up close, the man was even more repulsive.

"Come close so you can whisper your choice in my ear. I won't bite."

Damien leaned forward over the table, and Jonah

had no choice but to put his face next to Damien's and say:" I would like the name, Jonah, sir."

With a lecherous grin, Damien heaved himself out of his throne and came round the table. He grabbed Jonah's arm and stuck it into the air.

"From now on, his name is Jonah from West Drayton. Happy naming day, Jonah."

At which he planted a wet kiss on both of the boy's cheeks, looking him in the eyes and saying teasingly: "Are you sure you wouldn't like to join my Angels? There's always room for another beauty like you."

Trying not to show his horror at the idea, Jonah had his answer ready: "I'm very honoured, sir, but I have a girl at home who I promised to marry."

Jonah had been told by Mallory what to say in the event of a proposal like this. It seemed to have the required effect. The big man theatrically threw his hands up in the air.

"What a waste. I guess we need to create new boys and girls too. Tell her from me she's one lucky woman, and if you get fed up with her, there'll always be a place at my side. Now go and enjoy the rest of the evening."

Slapping Jonah playfully on his bottom, which nearly made him fall off the dais, Damien sent him back into the crowd.

On his way back to his table, people slapped him on his back and offered him to join them at their table for a drink. They were probably remembering their own naming day and feeling sentimental. Thanking them but refusing, Jonah quickly went back to join Solo and his sister. She hugged him fiercely.

"Happy Naming day, Jonah. Mum will be so happy when she hears you finally got your name. Especially this one. I love you, little brother."

Jonah hugged her back and felt touched by her happiness for him. It made him feel even worse about what he was going to do. It felt like such a betrayal to her and all the other people who loved him. She would get in terrible trouble. He would have to rely on Solo to protect her. Not a happy thought. Would he ever see her, his mother or Wulf again? He swallowed and tried to give a good impression of having no care in the world while enjoying a good party until he saw that Mallory had been called to the dais by one of the Angels.

Jonah tried to hear what they were saying over the din in the room. It was no good from where he was sitting, so he made the excuse of needing to pee and went to stand at the exit closest to the dais.

Chapter Twenty-five

Mallory stood in front of Damien, looking up without showing any fear or worry. Jonah admired him and was again grateful to have such a strong man on their side.

Damien spoke first: "The time has come to show these guys what they have bought with their tickets. Go and fetch the girl. I hope you make sure she looks as nice as possible. We don't want to disappoint this crowd."

Mallory asked: "Are we not going to wait until the monks get here?" Clever of him to put up some resistance in order not to look suspicious.

"No, I've decided it will be more fun to see those pious twits trying to haggle with one of those morons down there. The monks won't come until later tonight. I want to have the lottery over and done with before they arrive."

"I hope you know what you're doing, Damien. It is never a good idea to upset the Church." When Damien just shrugged his shoulders, Mallory sighed, saying, "Alright. I'll go and bring the girl down. Are you sure you can keep those yokels off her? You wouldn't want her to get damaged at the last minute, would you?"

"Are you suggesting I can't keep these bumpkins under control?" Damien's eyes turned into slivers of ice. He seemed ready to burst into one of his rages.

Mallory hastened to calm him. "I beg your pardon. I was only thinking about your interest. I'll go and get her right now."

Trying to look suitably repentant, Mallory scrambled off the dais and hurried to leave the hall. He made sure it was by the side door where Jonah was standing. Their eyes met for a moment. Mallory gave him an almost imperceptible nod. Jonah hid his relief by taking another swig from the beer he'd been nursing all evening.

Fortunately, Solo and Yaya had left their table to join the other dancers in the middle of the room. The music had swept to an even more frantic beat. Alcohol and drugs made sure that most of the onlookers were too incapacitated to notice him leave.

In the corridor, Jonah bumped into a few of the card players he met previously. They called out congratulations and invited him to come and have one at their table. Jonah mumbled something about having to piss and being right back and made his way to the stables as fast as his legs could carry him.

Mattie was already there and, with a flourish, showed him the guards, who were lying spreadeagled on the floor. She was jumping up and down with excitement.

"Look at these sweetlings sleeping like babies. Help me drag them into this empty box. Shit, they are heavy."

She seemed to be enjoying herself tremendously,

notwithstanding the danger. The ignorance of youth. Once they secured the men, she took him into a horse box right at the back. She had swept the straw to one side to reveal a large wooden hatch. The stable door creaked, letting in a gust of cold night air. They both looked up. Mallory stepped in accompanied by Astrid, who was wrapped in a cloak rather too big for her. Her face peeked out of the hood, pale as a ghost.

"Mattie, I take it there was no trouble getting the guards out of the way?"

His ward shook her head and proudly pointed at the box that held the sleeping men, putting her head sideways on both her hands closing her eyes.

"Right. Well done, my dear. I knew I could count on you. Let's get ourselves down below as soon as possible. But be careful."

Turning to him and the others, Mallory explained:" These corridors are from before the Exodus and will be wet in places. The lake has been seeping into them over the centuries. The fort has been built right on top of them. Damien is the only one who knows these tunnels exist and will do anything to keep them a secret in case he needs to get away one day. I don't think he will tell anybody, but I suppose he can always kill them afterwards to keep his secret safe. Shall we?."

One by one, Mattie first climbed down a long shaft using a rusty ladder stuck to the slimy green wall by even rustier nails. The little one scrambled down like a monkey and disappeared into the dark while the other three took it a bit slower. A foul stench of sewage in the back of his nose made Jonah retch.

"It will get better once we're at the lowest level, I promise."

Mallory didn't seem to be too much bothered by the smell. After they reached the bottom of the shaft, the child suddenly reappeared out of the gloom, looking worried.

"Doctor, they've closed the grate. Somebody put a big, fat lock on it."

Mallory didn't seem too perturbed by the news.

"It will be an iron one. I can open it. Don't worry. Let's continue."

Mattie must have sprinted very fast to the end and back as it took the rest some time to reach the grate she mentioned.

Mallory stepped forward and made a bright light appear out of nowhere. He heard him sigh.

"Thank the stars. It is iron. Stand back and don't breathe in too deeply."

He pulled a small, stoppered bottle out of his many pockets and poured a liquid over the lock. The metal immediately started to sizzle. An acrid fume filled the corridor making their eyes water. The bolt seemed to dissolve in front of their eyes.

"You must be a magician." Astrid gasped when

she could breathe again.

"No, my dear. As you will soon find out, science has its uses. Now let's climb down and carry on as fast as we safely can. Make sure you keep your eyes on the person in front of you. I can't keep this light on much longer. There'll be some areas we will have to wade through water, some of it quite deep. I take it everyone can swim?"

They all made confirming noises.

After that, no one had enough breath to do more than run and sometimes splash through the treacherous tunnels until they finally saw a circular light in the distance. It felt like they had been going for hours, though Mallory told them it was just a bit less than one. No one had time to wonder how he could be so sure.

Halfway through their flight, they had heard a loud rumbling above their heads, making the walls tremble. Mallory shouted not to worry as it was just the last train running close nearby.

They exited from a large stone cave covered in vines into a small clearing in some woods. Mallory turned to them.

"First part completed, but don't get too comfortable yet. We must get to the Badlands before we can have a proper rest. Midlanders are superstitious about entering that area. Damien will find it hard to convince his men to follow us in there no matter how much he threatens them."

Jonah had always heard that entering the Badlands would cause a person to erupt in blisters, followed by a terrible death, and felt slightly uncomfortable.

Mallory looked at them as if to explain why he knew it was safe to go there but shook his head. He hoisted his pack higher on his shoulders, setting off at a fast pace, calling out: "No time worrying about it. Once we're a whole lot further into the woods, we can rest briefly for a drink. After that, no more stopping. If any of you feels you can't keep up, let me know. I've got some herbs with me to help you. We will have to use them sparingly because once they stop working, you will have to sleep if you want it or not."

Millions of stars lit up the night sky but soon disappeared out of sight when they entered deeper into the woods. It felt like they were in a tunnel again: this time, one smelling of rotting leaves and pine.

Mallory took the lead, followed by Astrid, then Jonah, with Mattie making up the rear. It promised to be a long, exhausting night.

Chapter Twenty-six

The time had come for Nicholas and William to get into their canoes and make for the shore. They paddled away from the ship, aiming to land south from White Fort Harbour.

By the time they reached the pebbly beach surrounded by mangroves, the sun was low in the sky. They hid their canoes in some shrubs and unloaded their packs. William helped him to transform himself into a warrior monk.

Nicholas winced when his friend pulled the dry, soft, woollen tunic over his recently tattooed arm. After an excruciating session with the captain and his needle, it still looked inflamed and hurt like a bitch. By the time they would arrive in the fort, it would hopefully be too dark for anybody to see it.

He put the finishing touch to his outfit by putting the Warrior long sword, presented to him by the captain this morning, on his back. A sigh of awe from the crew had gone up.

Nicholas had held the sword, admiring the feel and balance of the unique weapon. The grip was engraved in pewter and gold with birds and symbols from the days before the Exodus. It was double-edged. The guard had a sharp, upturned point on each side handy to rip open your opponent's skin.

"I swear I will bring it back to you, sir. It's beautiful," he stammered.

"I hope it will save your life as many times as it

has done mine for more years than I can count. Now put it away before I change my mind." With these words, the captain had abruptly turned around and went down below.

Now this magnificent sword was resting on his back and made him feel a bit more confident.

William was wearing a Brother's outfit, having exchanged his white novice habit for a black one to demonstrate he was an ordained monk.

They found a small brook near their landing spot, where they took the opportunity to rinse off the salt and sweat from their journey and fill their bottles for their trek to White Fort town. Despite their nerves, the boys grinned at each other. What an adventure.

After they emerged from the smelly swamp between the mangroves, it was a relief to start climbing the steep cliff top path above the harbour, getting away from the hungry mosquitoes and the foul-smelling water. The wind was tugging at their clothes and smelt of salt, smoke, and fish. The ships down below looked like toys bobbing at their anchor. There were quite a few of them. The docks were teeming with activity. Good, it would make them less conspicuous.

On their way down, they were greeted by the impressive sight of a Midland steam train arriving at the station. It looked like a steel dragon breathing fire. Everybody had heard about it, but few got the chance to see it and even fewer to travel on it. That was reserved only for the very rich of the

Archipelago or for high clerics from the Church.

Witnessing this wonder with their own eyes, they momentarily forgot why they were there and behaved like any other boy seeing one of the miracles of his world for the first time. They whooped and clapped each other on the back, running down the path as fast as their legs could carry to see this monster from up close. Coming closer to the station yard, they could see clouds of steam still enveloping the carriages.

"Wow. I always wanted to see that. I never thought it would be this huge."

William seemed to have forgotten they should be as inconspicuous as possible and practically dragged him over to the platform. Lucky for them, everyone was too busy to see him completely forgetting his role as a seasoned monk travelling with his bodyguard.

Nicholas was just as impressed, but his worry about Astrid kept him a bit more focused on what they were supposed to be doing there.

"William. For goodness sake, pull yourself together. I bet real monks don't behave like country bumpkins who've never seen a train before. Let's have a drink in that inn opposite the station. We might learn some more about what's happening at the Fort."

Looking like a child whose favourite toy had been snatched away, William duly let Nicholas lead him to a dark, wooden building with a thatched roof. It was three stories high and had a large veranda in the front jam-packed with people. On the face, blackened by the smoke of trains, you could still make out the words: The Wagon Inn.

They entered the taproom and could barely see anything, the contrast between the bright wharf and the gloomy interior blinding them for a moment. As his sight adjusted, he saw the place packed with merchants, sailors, farmers, and unsavoury looking types bristling with weapons and their skins darkened or lit up by tattoos.

Trying to be heard over the din, William warned him: "Be careful. Those men in the back there look like they could be Damien's. Let's try to stay away from them. Go and order something to eat and drink for us while I find a table on the other side of the room. Be quick."

Seeing William disappearing into the gloom, Nicholas pulled made himself as tall as possible and tried to look as relaxed as he possibly could. He leaned one arm casually on the sticky surface of the bar. The innkeeper was barking orders at his barmaids and had his back to him.

"Exc.Hm, some food and drink for my patron and me." Nicholas tried to sound as commanding and haughty as he could.

The man, scars all over his face, looking like a survivor of many barroom brawls, turned around and looked at him as if he would sooner kill him than serve him. When he spoke, his voice rumbled, coming up from the bottom of his vast beer belly.

"We've got ale, whiskey and pasties. I might have some soup and bread. What will it be?"

Nicholas swallowed. "Two jugs of ale and two pasties. We are in that corner," pointing to William, who had managed to secure a small table tucked behind a large pillar.

The innkeeper hardly glanced at him and shouted to the girl standing nearest: "Angie, get your lazy ass over here. These gentlemen need serving."

He gave Nicholas a calculating look.

"She'll bring it round to your table."

He held up a large hairy hand.

"That'll be Five Oro's upfront."

It was an exorbitant sum for this little bit of food and drink, but Nicholas decided it was not worth drawing unwelcome attention by making a fuss about it and threw down the coins on the bar. He walked away without looking back.

William just stopped talking to some men at the table behind him and motioned him to sit.

"I just heard from these sailors there will be a big party in the Fort tonight. According to a local rumour, Damien is celebrating something. We might be able to join the crowds going there and get in without too many questions."

They were interrupted by the girl bringing their order, serving them the pasties accompanied with a large jug of the local ale. The food was delicious, and the ale better than they ever tasted on the Island. He wondered how these barbarians seemed to make it so good.

He swallowed his last bite and looked around the room catching sight of two rough-looking types leaving the inn through a dark passage at the back. The sign above the exit pointed to an outhouse.

He got up, shoving his seat backwards.

"I just saw two of what might be Damien's men go to the latrines. I want to go and see if I can find out more about that party tonight."

William shifted in his chair, looking a bit doubtful.

"Are you sure? What if they become suspicious? These men will kill you first before asking questions. We should just join one of the other groups."

"There will be more chance of getting into the Fort when we know what we might find there. I am going, don't worry."

He walked out through the passage, pretending to be a bit unsteady on his feet. It was dark, the courtyard only lit by one oil lamp swinging in the wind creating eerie shadows on the walls.

He was shocked to find the outhouse only consisted of a long wooden board with holes spaced closely together. It smelled like a pigsty which was probably an insult to pigs. He had to stop himself from gagging before he stepped in.

The men were quarrelling, standing side by side,

aiming in the direction of the holes, succeeding in splashing their pee all over the place. They were pretty drunk and talking loud.

"Hey, man. We'd better stop drinking now. Booze will be free tonight at Damien's. The guy is weird, but he does know how to give a good party."

"Don't you worry, buddy. It's still a few hours until it starts. If we stop now, we'll be practically sober by then. We can't have that, do we? Did you hear about Solo delivering this fancy package? He's such a lucky guy. And one of his crew will be named tonight. Fuck, the party will never end."

Nicholas settling for a spot out of the splashing zone, pretended he had trouble undoing his trousers.

One of the men gave the other one a push and pointed at him with his chin.

He pretended to whisper: "Hey Ricko, look who've we got here."

Then a lot louder, looking at Nicholas: "Are you allowed out by yourself, mate? Thought you always had to stick to your patrons like flies to a turd."

He cackled with laughter at his own joke.

His mate gave him a shove looking around nervously. He appeared less drunk than his companion. He spoke apologetically to Nicholas.

"Sorry, sir, he's not from here. Come on, Jazz. We're done here."

The first man was not planning to give in so easy.

"Shit, Ricko, I always heard you North Midlanders were a bit soft. Are you scared of that little twit? Look at him. He's just started to shave. That's a mighty big sword you got there, boy, I think a bit too good for such a brat. It'll be far more useful to an experienced fighter like me."

He tried to reach for the sword on Nicholas back, but his mate kicked him in the backside and told him to shut up.

"Don't be such an idiot, shit for brains. This guy is a warrior monk. They learn to kill from the moment they can walk. Damien doesn't want any shit tonight with any monks. He's expecting a whole delegation, I heard. When he finds out you've been bothering a man of the Church and ruined the negotiation, you'll spend tonight in his dungeons instead of a party but not before having your back whipped to shreds. Come on. Let's go back to the others."

Nicholas was happy he didn't have to put his fighting skills to the test. He could probably have gotten the better of the drunken hooligan, but it might have put their chances of getting into the Fort at risk.

He waited a bit to make sure the men had gone and then hastened back to tell William the excellent news. Astrid, for she must be that fancy package, was in the fort, and the real monks from Luton were coming for her. He felt as if a weight had been lifted from his shoulders.

Chapter Twenty-seven

Nicholas was panting when he came back. "We've got to leave right now. Monks from Luton are on their way. They will arrive tonight. Will they let us join them, you think? "

William got up, and they left the inn. He seemed to know where he was going, urging him to hurry as the delegation could be there already.

Nicholas was a bit puzzled. "Do you know how they can get here so fast? The Commander is waiting for us to come back and can't have alerted them. We didn't even know for sure if Astrid would be here. If Damien has sent them a bird, it should still take more time for a delegation from Luton to reach the Fort."

William looked uneasy.

"They can be here in such a short time because they come by air."

"By air. What magic is that?" Nicholas's eyes were gleaming.

"I'm telling you this in the greatest confidence. The monks use old tech devices, called zeppelins, which can rise in the air and fly to any destination they want. Until now, they've only used it around North Midland, as far as I know. For some reason, they don't want the Gen people to know. Maybe it comes too close to blasphemy for them. It's not exactly Elektrik, but it is old Tech. I've learned from Father Sirio they use them a lot more on the Continent."

Nicholas was a bit annoyed his friend had never trusted him enough to share this information. His generation always chafed under the multiple restrictions of the Church. Now the enforcers of those rules were using old forbidden knowledge for their own purposes. He felt let down.

"Man. You have known that people can fly like that all this time?"

William hastened to explain.

"The monks use them mainly to keep the Midlanders or, more specifically, Damien, under control. He is aware the Prior can knock him from his throne whenever he gets too rebellious. A lowly novice like me can never divulge anything about the Mysteries to laypeople. I would never see the Island again. People who don't stick to the rules have a habit of disappearing."

" You're telling me they can use all this power from the past to destroy whatever they want? Why do we need to go through all that trouble fighting the barbarians? What else can they do?"

" I don't know everything. Father Sirio is only allowed to reveal a few Mysteries before I take my final vows. Once I make my oath of dedication to the Church, I will go to Luton to learn more. After my initiation, I can never leave the Brotherhood even if I would change my mind about becoming a cleric."

He saw William shivering. His friend told him about when he had asked Father Sirio what would happen if he decided to leave the Academy and join his brothers in the army.

His friend started to walk faster. "We should hurry to the landing square if we want to watch the airship arrive. You'll love it. I have never seen one for real, but the pictures are magical."

On their way to an outcrop of rocky land north of White Lake, they had to watch their step as it was a new moon and the path itself unlit. When they came closer to their destination, William led them eastwards. The ground was sandy and dry. Bushes of gorse and broom growing everywhere made it difficult to stay on the path. Finally, they looked through two shimmering gates standing tall above them. William warned him not to touch them but did not explain why.

Judging by all the activity inside, they had arrived at the right time. Something looked about to happen soon. Lights pulsing, a strange green light were beaming from beacons set all around a square. A cloud of little bright sparkles lit up the night like fluttering fireflies.

William pulled Nicholas by his jacket.

"Let's first stay out of sight. I don't want the Keepers of the tower to spot us and start to ask questions. By the time we've explained ourselves, we might miss the landing. It will blow your mind to see one of those things descend."

"What's the tower for then? How do they stay in the air? When did they start using these zep-thingies? That cabin must be as light as a feather to be able to hang there without taking everything down."

"They're called Zeppelins. It is tech from way before the Exodus. Let me tell you about them. It is forbidden, but you will see it for yourself anyway. Just never tell anybody. The top bit, which we call the balloon, is made from very light wood in the shape of a big open cage. Inside that cage, there are bags with some sort of special air in them that keeps the whole thing afloat. The carriage dangling below is the cabin for the crew. More I can't tell you. I will be in great trouble if anyone finds out as it is."

Nicholas got the feeling William didn't know all the fine details himself.

But, Nicholas was getting more and more excited and curious.

"How do they steer that thing?"

"I think it's a bit like a sailing boat, with a rudder and vanes to catch the wind." William looked relieved when a loud siren sounded, making all further conversation impossible.

They both looked up and saw a large object with a smaller receptacle attached beneath it, obscuring the stars. With its tiny windows lit up and broad beams of light shining from beneath, the contraption, belying its size, slowly drifted downwards to the mast. For such a giant machine, it made practically no noise. It just sort of hummed like a swarm of angry bees.

Before they had a chance to close their mouths, ground personnel had the ship anchored and a platform shunted under it. While the Keepers were busy, they approached the tower without the men noticing them.

A party of five monks looking solemn and forbidding made their way towards a building besides the tower. They didn't talk or look around but went inside.

"Astrid's life must be very important for the Prior having sent a full Quintet," William was whispering.

"What do you mean? What's a Quintet?" Nicholas was speaking softly as well. His friend's deferential attitude was catching.

"The Priory has a Church Council of twenty-five monks, who are divided into five Quintets. Each Quintet comprises one representative from each of the five Arts of Knowledge. A full Quintet has the power to make decisions without deferring to the Prior first. When a new Prior is selected, or they have to make other vital decisions, they do not only need the majority of the single votes of all twenty-five, but they also need a majority of three or more Quintets to win."

Nicholas mind went numb with all these numbers. "When do you think we can go and introduce ourselves?"

"I think about now. If they haven't heard yet, we have to tell them what those Midlanders did at home and what we did about that village. It could make a difference with the negotiations."

The guards at the door refused to let them in until William showed them his father's letter. One of them went inside with it and returned with one of the monks. He greeted them. "Welcome. I read your letter, and I believe you got some information that might affect our mission. All we got from Damien is that the eldest daughter of Gregory Harrington is up for ransom. He kept vague about he got her in the first place. We already heard from Father Sirio of your Island Church what happened there. The Prior was not pleased by any of it, and now we hear of this unlawful culling. What was the Commander thinking?"

Before they could answer, the brother ushered the boys inside and sat them down in front of a large table. The room was only lit by a large fire, its flames throwing shadows over the four men already seated

"Let me introduce you. These are Brother Pieter, Brother Abraham, and Brother Jacob and Brother Lars." He pointed at each of the other monks, who were studying them with wooden faces. "My name is Brother Jeb. Tell them again in your own words what happened in Sevenoaks and West Drayton."

Nicholas left it to William to inform them about the attack, the aftermath with its casualties and what happened in their attempt to find out Astrid's whereabouts. The monks didn't look as surprised as much as they thought they would be. Having Damien as their neighbour, nothing must surprise them anymore.

One of their audience, introduced by Brother Jeb as Brother Abraham, an ascetic looking man, spoke first. "Let us hope Damien has not found out by now about the sacking of West Drayton, or his price for the Harrington girl will go up. The Prior has specifically told us we were not to pay above the price he set."

Nicholas, a bit troubled to hear them talking about bartering his best friend in such a cold and calculating way, was about to interrupt them.

William shot him a warning glance gripping his arm in a vice under the table to prevent Nicholas from making the colossal blunder of questioning a Quintet member, and quickly asked: "Why do you think Damien hasn't got news about West Drayton by now? Visitors from all over Midland come to this town every day. We saw many sailors in the inn. The train has arrived too"

Brother Abraham shook his head.

"No new ships are allowed to moor before tomorrow. When we spoke to him, Damien made no mention of West Drayton. If he knew, he would have used it to ask for a lot more. If we leave immediately for the Fort, we might close the deal before he gets wind of it and starts haggling."

"Sir, we heard there would be a big party tonight.

Some sort of feast? There will be a lot of people in the Fort. Won't that make it dangerous for us to go in with so few?" Nicholas wondered.

"No, less so. Knowing Damien, a big party with people fawning over him and the prospect of a large sum of money will put him in a good mood. The man's no better than a big malevolent child, but he has total control over his men. We will ask to see the girl first in order to determine if she is indeed your Astrid and not some random girl they took from somewhere. We need to confirm, too, if she hasn't been hurt or violated in any way. That would have far-fetched repercussions on our negotiations. If all is well, we will pay the ransom, and you will have your friend back."

"Will he just hand her over like that? He never struck me as a religious man from the stories I heard." Nicholas sounded a bit unsure about this whole plan. He thought they would be better off with a contingent of Warrior monks accompanying them to ensure they got Astrid back if all these talks came to nothing. How could these five learned men have enough power to make that evil man do anything? He felt out of his dept.

Brother Abraham assured him, "You don't have to be religious to worry about the Prior's wrath. He gave us a letter telling Damien what the ransom would be. Damien knows he won't get a better price elsewhere from anyone. Nobody outbids the Prior. It wouldn't be good for their health."

The monks nodded at each other, smiling a bit.

Increasingly Nicholas came to understand the absolute power the Prior. had in the Archipelago. Not only at home where the people lived by the strict rules of the Church, even here with these unbelievers. He started to feel closer to his goal of getting Astrid back to safety.

The monk named Brother Jacob, a short, rotund man without any of the jollity one usually associates with plump people, clapped his hands together and exclaimed they should at least have a bite to eat before they set out. They invited the boys to share their meal, an invitation they gratefully accepted.

Chapter Twenty-eight

Damien's head was swaying to the notes of the beautifully sung ballad. He might be a cruel man, but everyone knew he loved music. It seemed to make him forget being a monster for a bit. However, the moment the two lovely voices stopped their jubilant song, he started to look around the room. He called for Manuel, his right hand, and whispered something in his ear. Manuel's head shot up, and he jumped off the dais. Damien's eyes followed him as he went up to Solo, who was lying with his head on the table sunken in a drunken stupor. Manuel shook his shoulder, and Solo first tried to throw him off, but he was very persistent and kept shouting at him to come and speak with Damien now.

Yaya, soberer than her mate, wondered what was going on. She looked around for her brother but didn't see any sign of him. Doubt crept into her mind. She hoped the lad had not done something stupid. She got up and approached the high table herself, not bothering to see if Manuel succeeded in waking her companion.

Damien's eyes were boring into her. Yaya knew the man thought women were only good for two things and should be seen but not heard. Seeing him looking nervous and furious at the same time made her even more apprehensive. She still hoped her brother had just been kept talking on his way in and would be back shortly.

Damien did not take long to abuse her of that idea. He bent forward to her and hissed that he did not like to be played the fool in his own house. "Where's that brother of yours?"

"Last time I saw him, he went outside. He wasn't feeling well and needed some fresh air." Her mouth became dry. Oh shit, I hope he hasn't been dumb and gone to see that girl, she thought, trying frantically to come up with an excuse to go outside as quickly as possible to see if she could find him and drag him back before he did something that could get them all killed. "Shall I go and find him for you? He's probably passed out somewhere or might have gone back to the barracks."

But Damien was having none of it. "Don't bother. I've sent my boys. They'll find him if he's still in the compound. Go and help Manuel wake that lump, Solo. My medic Mallory seems to have disappeared as well. He was supposed to bring her down here ages ago. Maybe your brother is with him. Better pray it's only that old fool trying to be a hero. Doctor or not, when I find out he has slipped away taking her with him, I'll let him rue the day he was born. His dying will take a very long time. And your brother can join him if he is in any way involved with this shit."

Damien was practically foaming around the mouth with rage. He pointed with a trembling finger to the table where Manuel was still trying to wake up Solo. Yaya fled to help him.

While Damien had his rant, people had started to

look up, wondering what was going on. Yaya felt as if all eyes in the hall were following her. She pushed Manuel aside and smacked Solo over the head with his tankard, sloshing the content over his face. He swore, wiping the beer out of his face.

"What the fuck, woman. You better have an excellent reason to wake me."

He rubbed his head and spat on the floor.

Yaya told him what was going on, and Solo got up from the table so fast, the whole thing toppled over.

His face flushing bright red, he growled at her: "You and I both know that that stupid brat, who you convinced me to take with us, has gone and done something dumb. He's been making puppy eyes at that girl since we got her, Probably fancying himself a big man rescuing a lady in distress. You and your mum have always been too soft on him. Now I will have to go and sort this all out."

It hadn't taken Solo long to blame someone else. The room buzzing with rumours, he gripped Yaya's arm, half dragging her back to the dais. She saw he looked the nearly apoplectic Damien straight in the eye, determined not to show himself cowed by the man even though he knew what their ruler would do to people who upset him. 'Never show an animal that you're afraid' always was Solo's motto.

Damien sharply pointed at the chair next to him, all the while smiling at the crowd. He nodded with his head to tell Solo to do the same. He spitefully kept Yaya standing below the dais to show her her place. When he saw the men in the hall turn back to their party, he told Solo to start talking. The latter didn't need much encouragement and launched straight away into his defence.

"Look, I went to a lot of trouble getting you the girl. I handed her over. I can't be held responsible for your guys losing her. If your men are wasting time looking for Jonah, you can tell them to stop. I don't need to be a betting man to know that stupid son of a bitch has gone and taken the girl with him. Yaya told me you suspect that medic of yours to have been helping them get out of here?"

Damien just nodded.

Solo continued: "I don't know your guy, but you were the one who trusted him with the girl even though we all know these monks are as slippery as eels. Does he know how to get out of this place without going past security?"

Looking not a tiny bit calmer, Damien, his face flushing, slammed the table.

" Shit. Yes. I should have known the fucker would find out. Always sniffing around in my study, pretending to look for books on healing in my library. I'm warning you. I don't want anyone here to find out about this shit show. I will think of some excuse why we postpone picking the winning ticket. That will give you time to find them and get her back. I don't know which route they have taken. They can come out in two places, either next to the railway water tower or a cave on the edge of the forest northeast of here. I bet that they will try to go south. Go to the station and get on the train to the tower. You might catch them trying to hitch a ride. I will let the station master know. If they aren't there, come back, and I will send a few of my men the other way. Bring them back to me, dead or alive. Now go."

Solo got up without a word and strode to the door. Yaya had to run to keep up with him.

She furiously whispered: "Solo, you have to promise me to let me talk to Jonah first if we find them. Please, it will break my mother's heart to have anything happen to him. You can do with the rest what you want. I will send Jonah away and make him disappear. Damien will never hear or see him again. I swear to be yours for the rest of my life if you do this for me."

She tried to make Solo look at her and pulled at his shirt. He shrugged her hand off. "Stop moaning. Time is running out. If you can't do as I tell you, stay here. I don't need anybody slowing me down while I'm trying to catch a dumb boy, a stupid bitch, and some old fart. I'm not making any promises until we find them."

Yaya had no option but to follow him and pray she could do something to save her brother after Solo had calmed down a bit. Now he was too pissed about losing the girl and being blamed for it by Damien. They had made him look stupid in the eyes of the man he hoped to impress. With Solo, it was all about looking good and be in control.

After stocking up on water and food in the kitchen, they went on their way. Hurrying to the gates, she noticed they were already standing open. Manuel must have been a busy little man. They were walking so fast they barely noticed a small group of men approaching the fort on the other side of the road.

Chapter Twenty-nine

"I wonder why those two are in such a hurry?" one of the monks said as two shadowy figures shot past them in the direction of the station.

"Maybe they have to get back to their ship before it sails. But we have urgent business to attend to ourselves. Let's go inside," brother Jeb said.

He showed the guard at the gate their papers. They were immediately ushered inside and escorted to the great hall.

"Don't you find it weird it is so quiet? I thought there was a big party going on," Nicholas whispered to William.

The monks had noticed the absence of the expected racket as well. Walking towards the main hall, they passed small groups of people, who were on their way out softly, talking softly and looking very disappointed. No one was laughing or joking or seemed to give them much thought.

Brother Jeb was the first to speak up.

"I'm afraid the news about the sacking of West Drayton must have arrived before us and ruined the feast."

Brother Jacob stopped in his tracks.

"That's impossible. They don't have the tech in the rest of Midland to far speak. And to my knowledge, they don't have the patience to rear messenger birds. Besides, there is not much that will stop these people from having a party.

Something else must have happened. Good for us. It will mean we can have a quiet word with Damien. The only thing that concerns us is getting Astrid out of here as quickly as possible. Come, this way."

With these words, Brother Jacob pushed the doors to the big hall. The rest of his brethren followed close on his heels.

They found Damien on his throne, drinking a large tumbler of what looked to be wine, staring out over a silent, empty hall and tables littered with the leftovers of the big party.

Brother Abraham frowned. He mumbled to the rest of them that the sight of this man indulging himself in alcohol didn't bode very well. Damien hardly ever drank. His usual contingent of adoring young men seemed to be missing as well.

The tyrant looked up when they entered and dropped down from the dais. His face looking thunderous, he toddled up to them. They could all smell the alcohol on his breath.

"If you're coming for a party, you're too late. If you're coming for that Harrington wench, you are even more too late. That little birdie has flown the coop together with one of your old colleagues, the eminent doctor Mallory. I will tell you now, and you can let the Prior know that being a monk, even an ex-monk, won't save the bastard when I catch up with him. You lot have always been a treacherous bunch. I should kill all of you here and now just because it would make me feel better."

Nicholas and William looked wide-eyed at Brother Abraham, who seemed entirely unperturbed by Damien's rant. In a steady voice, as if to calm a rabid dog, he spoke: "I am very sorry to hear about your troubles, Damien, and so will be the Prior. How long has it been since they left? What have you done so far to recover them? Is there anything we can do to help ?"

"Are you fucking kidding me? You are in cahoots with that lot for all I know, and you are here to cover your tracks and find out what I am going to do about it. The Prior will do anything not to have to dig in his coffers for the ransom."

Brother Abraham bent his head and took a deep breath.

"As you well know, Damien, our Prior always keeps his word and would never behave like that. Why don't we wait here with you until they bring them back? Your men will undoubtedly catch up with them in no time. A young girl and an old man?"

"It is not just them. One of my guests, a young guy called Jonah, went with them. When we catch them, the prize for Harrington's daughter will have gone up to double your first offer for all the trouble they have caused. If you don't pay, she'll go to the highest bidder. I don't give a shit what the Prior thinks or wants," with these words, Damien turned his back on them and returned to his chair to continue drinking, refusing to even look at them.

When they didn't leave at once, he shouted: "Now

fuck off back to that stupid balloon of yours and tell your boss what I said. I will get compensation for this. I don't care from whom."

The other monks started to talk all at once, but Brother Abraham held up his hand to silence them and looked at the moping tyrant.

"We will go back to Luton as you wish but know that the Prior won't take this lying down. He has lost twenty-two of his best people, Islanders all, and wants reparation too. It might cost you more than you bargained for when you allowed those men to go and set foot on the Island to murder and burn innocent people. There is an explicit agreement about everyone's territory. You were the one to break it first. The Prior will not hesitate to make sure something like this will never happen again. The least you can do is to make sure the girl returns to us unharmed. You will be lucky to get a ransom instead of paying for your ignoring the Churches rules. Threatening or ignoring Prior Prendini has never been a healthy idea. For no one. You should know that better than anyone."

Damien seemed to sober up at once and looked at the fierce elder monk, all his chins trembling.

"What are you talking about? My guys were on a reconnaissance mission and were never to go onshore. I had no idea they were going to go inside Harrington House, let alone kidnap a girl. They acted without my approval. When I heard about what they did, I made sure they brought the Harrington brat to me. I was only trying to get her back to you. For a sum, I admit. But that is in our agreement too. The Prior can't hold me responsible for those people dying. I wasn't even there."

Brother Abraham shook his finger at him accusingly. "They were your men, Damien. They started the fires after the kidnap destroying a part of the house. We lost twenty-two fine people, amongst whom Master Gregory and his wife. John, their son and heir, is still lying in a coma, knocked out by one of your people. So, if you maintain you had no control over this, we might conclude you've lost your touch. The Prior might decide it is time to put a man in charge here who can restrain his people better."

Nicholas saw the man, known as one of the most dangerous criminals in Midland, positively shrink back into his chair. All his bluster was gone.

While motioning them to follow him, Brother Abraham turned on his heels at the door from where he took one last parting shot.

"Returning that girl unharmed to her home is now a top priority for the Prior, so you better get her to us pronto, or there will be consequences, and you won't like them."

Nicholas and his party were soon back at the balloon station. The monks didn't want to linger and called for their men to prepare the airship for take-off. They wanted to go back to Luton island and insisted the boys come with them.

"Couldn't we at least try to track down Astrid and

bring her home ourselves?" Nicholas couldn't believe they were just going to leave. He needed to do something now they knew his friend had left the White Fort not long ago. He might be able to catch up with them.

Brother Jacob put an arm around his shoulder. "Young man, it is now the business of the Priory. Midland is very large, and besides not knowing exactly where they have gone, you would be in the way of Damien's men. We don't want to lose two fine young men as well. Please leave it to us. Damien will have her found as he knows he has no other option to stay in power. We will take you to Luton and get you back on your ship. I heard the Commander is waiting before the coast here. We sent a message for them to sail to Luton when we heard from Sirio. He might be there before us. We don't want problems with the White Fort. We might lose the girl altogether. If she is with the same Mallory I know, she has an excellent chance of surviving. We expelled John from the Monastery for a reason, but he is the best tracker and swordsman I have ever met and a very smart man. He might contact us or manage to return her to you before Damien finds them. You two will be more useful, going home and helping your people restore the damage, believe me."

More familiar with the clerical authority, William persuaded Nicholas to accept the invitation of the monks. "We should talk with my father. He will know what to do."

The whole party stepped on the platform, which

lifted them to the contraption swinging gently under the flying machine. Once inside, seeing the fantastic interior, Nicholas could not believe his eyes. There were all sorts of wheels, dials, and other strange looking objects wherever he looked. Lights were sizzling behind glass windows. The front of the room consisted of a large, curved window from which they could see the fort winking in the distance.

The monks smiled at his wonder. The airship pilot kindly explained a little how Zeppelins worked.

"Isn't it dangerous to work here? Doesn't this tech make you ill?"

Seeing the lad's confusion, the pilot hastened to explain: "We're not using electricity to drive the Zeppelin, only wind and air. All parts of this ship are hand-made, using materials reclaimed from sites all over the Archipelago and the Mainland. The Prior has blessed the vessel. It is safe to travel in it without catching anything."

Nicholas still felt the explanation was a bit too easy. What was the source of all that light? He didn't see any candles or torches. He shook his head which had started to hurt a bit. He was too tired now. He would ask William about it later.

The crazy day was taking its toll, and they were nearly falling asleep where they were standing. Brother Jeb showed them to a small room in the back of the airship. Exhausted by all the new impressions, it didn't take them very long to be out like a light.

Chapter Thirty

White Fort town lay silent and dark, with just a few torches throwing long shadows along the alleys. Even the dogs did not make a sound at their passing.

At the station, the train's locomotive was already under steam. The stationmaster explained to Solo and Yaya it would only go as far as the water tower to drop them off and then return to town to reconnect with the waiting freight wagons.

Sightless by the steam and deafened by the thunder of its engine, they didn't notice a little messenger boy rushing towards them until he practically crashed into them. The lad's cheeks were bright red, his clouds of breath competing with the train.

She looked at Solo, wondering what the hell could be so important to have to send a messenger at this time of night.

"Sir, I have news from the south. I need to take it to the White Fort."

The lad had to take a few panting breaths before he could go on.

"I've come from Amersham. An army of Islanders has sacked the village of West Drayton. They torched it completely and killed everyone. Our mayor sent me to let

Damien know as soon as possible. What is the shortest way to the Fort?"

Yaya felt her legs give way and had to use all her strength not to collapse in a heap and scream.

Solo looked stunned but kept it together enough to start asking questions. "Are you sure it's West Drayton you're talking about? Were there no survivors?"

"Yes, sir. No, sir. I mean, as far as we know, in Amersham, no one has come out of West Drayton alive. Some fishermen from the next village saw the smoke and went to see if they could help. They only found ashes and loads of bodies too burnt to recognise."

His voice trembled, and sweat was pouring from his face.

The stationmaster, used to dealing with emergencies, calmly instructed the boy on the fastest route to the fort and sent him on his way.

Next, he turned to Solo and Yaya and said with a gentle voice: "I'm so sorry about your loss, but if you want to catch the fugitives, you have to board now. We will need the locomotive back before the first ride tomorrow."

The pair was too devastated to object and, holding each other up, followed him up to the engine. The station master assisted them up the steps onto the locomotive, where the fireman and the driver gave him a questioning look. He told them he would explain later, but now they needed to leave.

Yaya, too numb to say anything, just sat silently against the back of the cabin.

She was the first to speak: "I'm so sorry about Eric, Solo. My mother.." her voice broke, she had to swallow a few times to be able to continue, "My mother and all our friends will have their revenge."

She decided not to mention her worry about Jonah while Solo's grief was fresh. She'd never seen him so shattered as if he'd shrunk to half his size. She knew this wouldn't last long. Soon his anger would take over, and he would want to reckon with everyone even slightly connected to the tragedy. Her brother included.

The fact it had been all his own fault for taking the girl in the first place would never come up in Solo's mind. But she would be damned if she let that stupid decision harm the last person she had left in the world. She realised how strong her feelings were for her little brother, whose gentle nature she usually mocked and tried to remedy. Losing her mother made her realise she loved Jonah from the first day he was born.

She still remembered that day. She had only been thirteen at the time. The midwife had woken her in the middle of the night, ordering her to witness the whole thing. "One day, you'll have to do this yourself, girl. Better know what to expect."

Yaya had always sworn she would never have children, for she had seen what it did to women. Their freedom was gone. Their children made them vulnerable in a way she never wanted to be. She had worked too hard to stand on her own two feet.

That night it had not taken her mother long to give birth to the little one. Once he appeared, Yaya was shocked at how disgusting he looked, covered in mucus and blood. However, the moment the midwife had wiped him off and wrapped him tightly in a blanket, the woman had handed the little package to Yaya with the words: "Go and show your beautiful brother to your mother."

One look at the red, crumpled, little face, feeling the damp weight in her arms, was enough to melt all her carefully put up defences. So, this was what real love felt like. The child had looked straight at her with eyes as blue as the early morning sky. At that moment, he took her heart. Solo better watch his back.

Chapter Thirty-one

Sunk deep in her memories of Jonah, Yaya barely noticed the locomotive had reached the water tower. With a mighty jolt, the engine stopped right in front of it.

"Right, people, off you get. James, let's fill her up now. It'll save us doing a top-up when we come south again."

The engineer sounded relieved to get rid of them.

Yaya and Solo set off in the direction of the tunnel as instructed by Damien.

"We'll never find them here. They've had a head start while we were wasting time talking to Damien. This train ride might have won us some time, but not much." Solo sounded a bit like his old self again.

"If there is no sign of them here, I want us to go find the other entrance and see if there is a trail from there. Do you think we should tell Damien when we find nothing here? He will probably either punish us or, if we are lucky, let us go without paying us. Maybe we can do the deal ourselves."

"It's your decision," Yaya answered. It was always good to let Solo believe he was in charge. "Let's first check the tunnel near here."

Solo shook his head, pursing his lips. "Nah, it will be a total waste of time. If they came out here while we were faffing our time away at the Fort, they will be long gone."

Yaya countered quickly: "I don't think it would be

good for us to have to tell Damien we didn't check all exits, do you?"

She was terrified Solo wanted to go north straight away. She needed to stall him. Her brother would have chosen the least probable route to put the hunters on the wrong foot. He might not be the strongest or the most ruthless, her brother, but he was the cleverest.

Solo was a pig-headed bastard convinced his way was always best and would do the opposite of anything she suggested. Maybe she should show herself very keen to go east. She hoped it would have the desired effect.

While arguing, they were taken by surprise by the minstrels, Peter and Jo, popping up from where they had been lying low in a ditch.

"Hallo, we must stop meeting like this," Peter said, trying to lighten the mood.

But Solo wasn't having any of it.

" What the fuck are you two doing here? Did you happen to see her brother and that wench on your way down? Why are you here, anyway? The party seemed in full swing when we left"

"Answering your first question, my dear fellow, with the road so dark, we were happy to find our way here without falling from our horse. Our eyes were only on the trail, making it impossible to see anyone unless we tripped over them. As to your second question, we realised we had a performance planned in Amersham tomorrow or today by now. A wedding. The groom wanted to select the music and promised us a good meal if we came early. The party was dead anyway soon after you left."

It all rolled from his tongue like he had rehearsed it many times. He even managed to give Jo a naughty wink.

Solo gave them both a suspicious look. He was not completely stupid. She knew he'd noticed the attention Jo had given Astrid the first time they met.

"You better not be shitting me about. If I find out you did see them and didn't tell me, I'll track you down and kill you, both of you."

"Hey man, calm down. It's true that on top of having to play at that wedding in Amersham, we thought it might be a good idea to skedaddle before Damien's fury landed on our innocent heads. You know how he gets when he loses his temper. He'll look for a scapegoat, and when he doesn't find one, anyone will do. He'll select some unlucky bastard to vent his rage on. We were not planning to be there when that happened. No, thank you, sir."

Peter sounded very convincing. With a friendly smile, he asked Solo: "May we ask where you two lovely people are heading? Maybe we could travel together for a bit."

"We'll be travelling northeast until we reach the foot of the Towers. Damien has ordered us to find the fugitives, and their trail starts there."

Harbour Cities Midland

Seeing her looking surprised at this, Solo added: "Yes, I made up my mind. I am sure we missed them here. If we don't catch up with them before they disappear into the Towers, we will turn around and come back south to check out the harbours. It will give us a chance too to see what has become of West Drayton. I don't care what Damien thinks of it. Screw him. I'm not about to get myself killed by those savages in the mountains so he can get his revenge. You do want to know if anyone managed to survive, don't you?"

Peter asked, "So, you'll be going to the Towers, are you? Are you sure they went that way? With the Badlands and the Mountain people in their way? Seems highly unlikely to us."

Solo shook his head and growled, "It's none of your business where we go. Did you not hear what happened in our village? The bastards from the Island came and killed all our folk. When I find the girl, I will make her pay."

Both Peter and Jo stared at them with their mouth and eyes wide open, the latter saying," No, we hadn't heard. I am so sorry. Are you sure no one got out? I wouldn't be too harsh on the Harrington girl when you find her. First, she had nothing to do with that and second, you guys did kill twenty-two Islanders with your fires, amongst whom the girl's parents."

Yaya was taken aback by this news. They must have underestimated the speed with which the fires had spread. Lady, this many dead and the girl's parents too?

Looking unimpressed, Solo told them, "Well, I'll be happy to tell that Island brat, when I catch up with her, it was her pal Jonah's idea to set those fires. He might not have been there to light them personally, but the result was the same. See how much chance he will have with that bitch after that. If it weren't for that little cow, we would all be going home by now with a big bag of money. Good, we got at least a bunch of them. It didn't take very long, did it, for those Islander thugs to retaliate and murder all our folks. They're a bunch of snivelling, holier than thou criminals who think the only lives that matter are the ones written on their precious Tree. Scum. All of them. I bet those bloody monks knew all about it and gave them their blessing. May they rot in the Plague pits, all of them. Don't you two have a wedding to go to?"

The two troubadours looking sad, whistled for their horses. Everything was always such a mess. They said their farewell and went on their way.

Yaya shrugged her pack back on and trotted into the dark forest. Solo followed. They made their way northwest silently, both not speaking but walking with determined steps—each for their own reason.

Chapter Thirty-two

A strong humming sound nearly drowned out by voices calling out at each other woke the young men up out of a deep slumber. At first, Nicholas didn't realise where he was and why everything looked and smelled so different from home.

William, who was already up, reminded him, 'We must have arrived at Luton. I wonder if my father has already put up anchor here? Let's disembark and see if we can find him. I want to ask him what he thinks about this whole thing of leaving Astrid for that Damien to find."

Nicholas rubbed the sleep out of his eyes, "Surely the monks will send a search party? If they are so powerful, it shouldn't take them long to find out where she is. We can go and get her ourselves."

"It will all depend on what the Prior wants. Think for a moment what we did to that little village. Why did my father think he could do this? You told me about this culling. That doesn't make sense to me either. The Church of Light always taught us to respect all living creatures. There is much we need to find out before we can decide what to do. Let's first get back to our ship and speak with my father."

Nicholas threw his hands in the air, "I don't know how you can be so calm about all this. You saw that man Damien and heard what he said. Do you believe he will just hand her over when he finds her? He's a complete lunatic. Why do we even do business with such a creep? If anything needs wiping from the face of the earth, it is that degenerate and his men."

We, we .." Nicholas swallowed, his voice wavering," we just destroyed a whole village of what looked to me innocent women, children and old men. We are supposed to be the good guys. And for what? I bet the Prior knew already who was responsible and where they had taken Astrid. He seems to have a direct line to this guy in the White Fort. Couldn't he have let us know? We could have left those people alone. Why did Astrid not wait for us? I want answers, and if your father can't give them to me, I will have them from the Prior himself."

William tried to calm him, "No one ever gets to see the Prior face to face. The nearest you can get speaking to the man is by talking to his secretary, Father Macron. You are right. We need more answers, but we won't get them lying here."

Except for the pilot, the zeppelin was deserted. The man told them the other decided to let them sleep. They were expected in the Priory. He led the two young men to a hatch in the hull. A steep set of metal stairs led down to a broad balcony clinging precariously to a large building, perching on the high cliffs of Luton island. Another set of wider stairs led to the imposing Luton Priory, home to the most powerful man in the Archipelago.

The cry of sea birds circling the plateau and the loud whistling of the wind was deafening. Down, far below the balcony, they spotted a ship calmly floating next to a wooden pier. It was their ship. Nicholas sighed. Above their heads, the Zeppelin was dancing at its mooring lines. They could see and smell eye-watering smoke comes from two giant craters on the top of the wall. Gigantic multicoloured beacons attached to the building were pulsing with strange orange light.

Looking up, he saw the friendly monk, Jeb, beckoning them from an archway at the top of the stairs. After one more look around, William and Nicholas climbed up to the Priory, ready to find some answers and, at the same time, more about this place and its ruler.

Brother Jeb's face was beaming, "Welcome to my home. I will take you to the refectory to have some breakfast. We have sent word to your father, whose ship lies down below in the visitor's bay, you have arrived. He was quite worried about you two and will be happy to see you are still in one piece."

What looked like a forbidding, cold fortress on the outside now appeared to be a luxuriously decorated building inside. Despite the freezing morning winds, the place felt agreeably warm, and the boys were soon sweltering in their warm clothes and capes.

Seeing them trying to struggle out of them, their faces red and sweating, Jeb laughed kindly.

"An old invention from the time before. Central heating, it was called. Maybe you noticed the smoke outside? When the wind comes from the south, one can smell it on the landing stage. It comes from the large fires we keep burning under the rock to heat water fed through the whole building using metal pipes. One of the advantages of living in this place and having a boss who feels the cold," Jeb winked.

They continued up one wing of a set of stairs, seemingly made for giants. There were not many people about. "Where is everybody? I would think there would be more people living in such a big place?" Nicholas nearly whispered, impressed as he was with the vastness and silence of the palace.

Beautifully embroidered wall hangings strung up on every wall depicted lively scenes, some of which he recognised from his history books. Pictures of the sea flooding whole islands and fires devastating nature. Amongst it all strange looking machines and buildings.

Brother Jeb turned back to him, "We arrived early, and most of the brothers are still getting ready to start their day or are already about their chores. Then they have to go to the big assembly hall for a reading from the Book of Enlightenment. You will see more of them later at breakfast."

Reaching the top of the stairs, they were met by a loud buzz of voices now and then interspersed with a cheerful laugh.

Brother Jeb looked at the scene, a warm smile in

his eyes.

"I hear our students are already having breakfast. They are a loud bunch. William, you might enjoy meeting some of your peers. I heard you will be joining us this summer. You are the only novice from your Island, I think?"

William blushed and mumbled something unintelligible.

Nicholas stepped into a high vaulted space echoing with the voices of animatedly talking young men and stopped, forty or so young faces swivelled in their direction. The voices muted. Only some of the older monks went on eating without looking up.

He felt water run into his mouth from the delicious smells coming from a row of tables set out around the room. He was used to the bustling Harrington House meals and had no problem sitting down with a bunch of strangers without feeling too awkward. But he saw his friend blushing and hesitating to go on.

Monks garbed in white aprons, standing behind the food counter, were busy slapping food on everyone's plates. Other men, servants by the look of them, were filling cups from large steaming urns.

Brother Jeb told the boys to get something to eat and come and join him at his table. He would keep a place for them and order them a cup of mulled tea. Until then, they had not realised how hungry they were and didn't need much encouragement to have their plates filled to the rim.

Halfway through their meal, loud footsteps sounded outside the refectory. This time everyone stopped what they were doing as a large man, he immediately recognised as the Commander, came thundering into the room and, giving a joyous shout, proceeded to rush to their table. He lifted William from his seat, engulfing him in a hearty embrace, exclaiming: "My dear boy, you made it."

When he let go of him, he gave Nicholas the same treatment, leaving them both grinning widely but a little bit embarrassed as well.

Giving a slight bow, Brother Jeb introduced himself to the Commander. After exchanging greetings with some of the other brothers at their table, the Commander sat down beside Brother Jeb. He tried to disguise his outburst of feelings by immediately starting to question William and Nicholas about all that had occurred after leaving him on the ship. He seemed impressed with how well they had coped with the situation. Hearing about Astrid taking off with some Midlander strangers instead of waiting for the monks, the Commander looked bewildered.

"Why would she go with total strangers? The kidnap must have been a terrible experience. I know Damien would be enough to make anyone want to run as fast as they can, but why with those people? They probably didn't tell her the Monastery would come for her. We had abductions like hers before and were always able to solve them without anyone getting hurt. The monastery always made sure of that. An expensive solution, but no real harm done. We did always make sure, though, to let those Midlanders think twice before doing it again. You saw that yourself, Nicholas."

William winced. Nicholas' face went white, thinking back to his first culling. He tried to explain why he thought Astrid had fled.

"She didn't know the monks were coming to rescue her. We never heard about the Monastery doing business with those criminals, so how could she. They told us Damien had set up a lottery with Astrid as the main prize. That must have been enough to make her run for her life. The monks who brought us back said one of the people she escaped with is a former monk called John Mallory. He left the monastery under a cloud, but the brothers all spoke of him with respect. He trained as a warrior but later changed his vocation and became a medic. They told me that Astrid has an excellent chance to make it home with Mallory even without that Damien finding and returning her. You should have heard brother Abraham threaten Damien with what would happen if he didn't do his best to find Astrid and keep her unharmed. He told him he would risk the wrath of the Prior. It was epic."

The Commander looked at Brother Jeb, raising his eyebrows. "Is the Monastery planning to do anything about locating her? You can't possibly think we will just leave her to that scoundrel. The man is a lying bastard at the best of times. Why the Prior even does any business with that thug is beyond me. Why not eradicate that nest of vipers once and for all? If you don't have anything better to offer than to trust an animal like that to get her back, I'd rather take my men to Midland right now and bring her home myself. "He took a deep breath to continue his rant but was interrupted by a servant coming over to their table and whispering something in Brother Jeb's ear.

He stood up and motioned the Commander to do the same. "We have to go now. Father Macron is ready to see you, Commander. Nicholas and William, you are welcome to have a look around the monastery. I can ask one of our students to give you a tour if you want."

The Commander, still looking dissatisfied, got up. "I will see you, boys, later. There is a lot I need to talk about with Father Macron. We will discuss Astrid later after I have seen Macron."

With these words, the Commander left them, following Brother Jeb out of the room.

Chapter Thirty-three

Nicholas followed William around the vast building, his friend exclaiming everywhere how great it all looked and how exciting it would be to study here. A few times, they hit upon an area guarded by stern looking monks barring their way.

He was just starting to get tired and was about to suggest they turn back and see if they could find someone to take them to the Commander when a servant came up to them. The man asked them to follow and silently led them up yet another set of stairs leading to a vast, bright room entirely enclosed by glass panels, smelling of rich earth and feeling very warm and humid. The place smelt like a garden in Spring.

"Thank you, Marco." Turning to Nicholas and William, Jeb waved his muddy hands at the hundreds of plants around them, smiling a big happy smile. "Welcome to our Arboretum. I guess you want to know if the Commander has finished his talk?"

He spoke a few words into some kind of grill in the wall, then turned back to them, surprise registering on his face. "They have finished, and you are very fortunate. Father Macron wants to have a few words with both of you, so I am to escort you to his office. The Commander is still with him and will take you back with him afterwards."

Nicholas was relieved but a bit worried too. He

hoped to get the chance to plead with the man to help them find Astrid or at least give them permission to go out there and find her themselves, but why would this man, second in power only to the Prior, want to speak to two insignificant boys like them if he already had the chance to discuss Astrid with the Commander? Was it about the culling? Would he have to testify?

The Secretary's office lay not far from the Arboretum. Brother Jeb knocked softly on a thick oak door. A high voice told them to come in.

Entering, the first thing they saw was the Commander looking very red in the face. He was sitting on the edge of a straight-backed chair on one side of the vastest desk they had ever seen. The skinny, pale man nearly disappearing behind it did not look half as impressive. But one look from the man's sharp obsidian eyes changed his mind. The Secretary of the Prior looked like a serpent, ready to strike with the smile on his face doing nothing to make him feel more at ease. On the contrary, it made him realise he should be wary of what he said to the man. The defeated look on the face of the Commander, a man who struck fear in all his enemies, was enough to warn him to tread very carefully.

"Brother Jeb, you may leave us. So, Gerald, these are the young men you told me about. Tell me which one is which."

Nicholas opened his mouth immediately to feel

William pinching the back of his arm. The Commander quickly introduced them, "The one on the left is William, my youngest son, who will enter the university here this Summer to finish his studies. The other one is Nicholas Stewardson from the Harrington company. They were both very brave during our operation on Midland."

Father Macron looked them both up and down as if sizing them up for an auction. "William, let me will start with you. Your father and I have decided it will be best if you do not return home today but stay here at the Priory to begin your study a few months earlier. Count yourself lucky. As for you, Nicholas, you must go with Gerard and are ordered not to set foot on Midland until further notice. You can all leave now. I have work to do."

Not deigning to give them any further explanation, he dismissed them with a wave of his hand, hardly waiting for them to leave his office before bending over the papers on his desk as if they were not worth a second more of his attention.

Looking even more furious now, the Commander got up and returned the Secretary's incivility by turning his back on him without the usual salutations. He grabbed both boys by their arm and unceremoniously dragged them to the door. He tried to slam it but was frustrated in showing his anger by a spring that closed it softly behind them.

He shooed the boys back to the terrace from where they could see his ship already under sail bobbing in the bay.

The moment they were out of earshot from everybody, he burst loose.

"That bloody bastard. That man is getting too big for his shoes. The Prior is so busy sucking up to the Continent that he leaves everything to that weasel. If he couldn't make all of us disappear with the push of a button, I would have strangled him with his pompous manner. Better even, it should have happened in his cradle."

William's face blanched at the blasphemy his father was uttering on these hallowed premises. Nicholas didn't understand what just happened and stammered: "Sir, what was he talking about? Why does William have to stay here? Why can't I go to Midland? What are they planning to do about Astrid?"

The Commander, seeing his confusion, calmed down a bit. He explained that the Secretary had told him he would keep William here as security so the Commander would not take the law into his own hands again and go to Midland to get Astrid. As for what they were doing about her return, the only thing the secretary was willing to divulge was that he had taken care of it, and they shouldn't meddle in the Prior's business.

"There is nothing I can do about it now, but I intend to ask Father Sirio to help me launch a complaint with the Cathedral in Perris. William, you will have to start your studies here a bit earlier, son. Look out for yourself because I don't trust that man not to find reasons to find fault and use that against me. Keep your head down and try to learn about this lot and its powers as much as you can. It will come in useful one day. I will contact you through someone in this place I know and trust. He will make himself known to you in time. We have to go back now. Take care, my boy."

Nicholas did not know if to feel scared or excited for his friend and nodded, feeling a big lump in his throat. William embraced his father. The Commander held him tightly for a moment, cleared his throat and then released him, trying to look his usual forbidding self again. The two friends gave each other a big hug promising to keep in contact one way or the other. They both had tears in their eyes.

The Commander was silent on their way down. Nicholas felt sad to leave his friend behind. Looking up at the Priory one more time, he hoped it would not be the last time he saw him. He swore to himself he would not take the decision of the Secretary lying down. If they didn't return Astrid within the next few days, he promised, he would leave the Island to search for her himself.

Chapter Thirty-four

The moment they had boarded the ship, the Commander had stormed off to the captain's cabin, ordering Nicholas to go and get Henry. Henry was studying some papers, but his face lit up when he saw him.

"Back in one piece, I am glad to see. What happened? All I heard was we had to sail to Luton immediately. They told me you two had been taken there by the Prior's delegation. Any more news about Astrid?"

"The Commander would like you to come to the captain's cabin. He wants to have a word. William and I did not even get to see Astrid. She was gone when we arrived at the White Fort. The Prior's secretary has forbidden me to go and look for her" Nicholas' voice was trembling.

"Before I go and see the Commander, why don't you start telling me what happened from the beginning?"

The kindness of this man, who he so wanted to dislike, came as a surprise. He told Henry all that had befallen William and him until the moment he had to leave his friend behind.

"I don't understand why the Commander doesn't do anything. William is his son. They can't just keep him there. And why doesn't the Prior want us to look for Astrid? The more people who try to find her, the better, I would say. No one seems to care. Why are the monks doing this? Can't Father Sirio do something?" Nicholas slammed his fist on the wall of the cabin. He felt so frustrated.

"Why don't we both go to see the Commander. He will have a plan, I'm sure". Seeing Nicholas shaking his head, Henry continued," It will be fine. I will tell him I asked you to come. What you went through in the village makes you a full member of our Community, and you need to know some facts about our world. It might not do much about your worry, but it might make it easier to accept some of the decisions we have to make. I have no right here to do that, but I'm sure Gerald can enlighten you. I just had a letter from Father Sirio, and the news from home is not good either. We need to go back home as soon as possible. Are you coming?"

Henry stood up and opened the door of his cabin wide

Nicholas hoped Henry was right. He desperately wanted to understand what had happened these last few days and why. He ducked under Henry's arm and went up back to the Commander with Henry not far behind.

Gerald Selby growled, telling them to come in. They both entered the cabin. The Commander frowned when he saw Nicholas and looked at Henry, raising his eyebrows.

The latter raised his hands and said, "I think after all he went through, this lad deserves some answers, don't you? I've had some news from the Island. A bird came in while you were at the Priory."

Master Selby, Commander of the Harrington Company Army, leant back on the bench and dragged his hand over his face. He sighed deeply, worry lines etched on his face.

"I hope it is some good news for a change? Has the boy filled you in on what happened? Not only at the Fort but with that bastard Macron? The little weasel thinks he is the Prior already. "

The Commander's face had turned deep red. He was probably thinking back to his audience with the secretary. It must have been hard for this proud man to follow an order from a man he detested, added to the worry of leaving his son in the man's clutches.

Henry sat down and motioned Nicholas to do the same. He poured some wine for himself and topped the Commander's glass up. He tilted his head to one side and held the bottle up, looking at Nicholas, who put his hand above his glass and pulled a carafe of water to him.

"Nicholas told me what happened before he went to Luton and some of what was said when you spoke to Macron. What will the Priory do about Astrid if they don't want us to go and look for her? Did you have to leave William there? Don't tell me he was threatening again with his arsenal of weapons. We are not some uncivilised Midlander. We both know they would never destroy us. They are too far now. If we join our forces and ask for Kent's support, too, we can put pressure on those monks to give him back. They need us, too, even though they pretend they don't. Their program relies heavily on our cooperation. The news I got from home might give them some leverage to stop us from going against their plans. It's from Sirio. I'm afraid it isn't too good. John has been taken to London Monastery. We'll need the Prior's support to have him treated there and not on the Ship."

Nicholas saw the Commander sinking even deeper into his seat. He had never seen him so dejected. He knew the Churches' hospital in London was the best in the whole of Albion, but he thought only the clergy went there. The Sisters of Mercy treated the ailments of the rest of the inhabitants of their Archipelago. And what was so bad about that ship?

The Commander seeing him looking surprised, seemed to make a decision. "Right, let's start with the Church of Light. Have you ever been told about how our Island became separated from the rest of Albion?"

Nicholas shook his head, wondering what that had to do with all of this.

"What I'm going to tell you has to stay within these walls. If the Church finds out we told an unauthorised person, we could be in a lot of trouble. People who know too much have the habit of disappearing. As you know, priests always preach that technology ruins your soul and body. In the last two days, you've seen the monks don't practice what they preach when it suits their purpose. The Church is well aware there is nothing wrong with technology but has decided to keep that to themselves to control us better. And it seems to work. With the help of their friends on the Continent, they keep us on a tight rein. Not only through their false religion but also by the threat of the devastation they can unleash on any part of our isles with the press of a button. That's why I couldn't haul that snake Macron over his desk and beat the crap out of him and take William with me. We wouldn't have left the harbour without our ship being sunk, and William made to disappear. I comfort myself with the fact that he is a clever lad and will know how to survive. I have some people within those walls who will see to it".

Nicholas was felt even more confused. "What about Astrid? Why can't we go and get her? If they are so powerful, they must know where she is. And I don't understand why John going to this ship is so bad."

"Astrid has gone underground with an ex-monk, who is the best Warrior the Church ever had. If anyone can get her home, it will be him. She travelled with some Midlander scum before Mallory rescued her, and now the Church might forbid her to come back to the island. It might fit their purpose better were she to stay in Midland, and we forget about her". Looking more and more uncomfortable, the Commander quickly went on, "John had a nasty knock on his head during the attack and has still not gained consciousness. Without special equipment, he won't survive. He jas been transported to the London Hospital. If he can't be saved, the brothers there will let him serve the Project in another way. They will take him to a Continental ship lying far from our coast. No one is allowed to go there without the special dispensation from the Prior himself. Please don't ask me what they do there. The only thing we know is that no one ever comes back from that place. If you want to know about the Project, you better ask Father Sirio. He would be the better man to explain it. I've already told you more than is safe for both of us. The Prior will send his best tracker, Father Lucius, if Damien can't show them where Astrid is by next week. Macron told me they don't want us roaming around Midland stirring trouble. We have to stay in Gen territory. I'm sorry, but for now, you have to comply with his ruling, as do we. Go and rest. I have things to discuss with Henry."

      And just like that, Nicholas was dismissed. He felt bewildered. First the news from his mother and now all this about the Church. What else didn't he know? He swore to himself he would spend the coming weeks to find out. His first visit would be to Father Sirio. He would not give up this easily like the rest of them seemed to do.

Chapter Thirty-five

Making her way through the dense forest, the sounds and smells so different from those she remembered from the ones at home, Astrid missed her family so much it almost hurt. Was it only a few days ago that the only thing she had to worry about was her impending wedding to Henry? She would give anything to turn back the time to that morning five days ago when she was happily floating in the sea looking forward to choosing a puppy. She remembered the smell of smoke that terrible night. She had heard some men laughing about a diversion and taking care of the guards. Please, Lady. Let everyone be safe."

Wrapped up in her thoughts, she bumped into Mallory's back. He had stopped and thrown down his pack beside some fallen tree trunks. "Let us have a short rest here. I'm afraid we can't have a fire as it might give us away. Mattie, you know which bag contains our food. Everyone can have some bread and cheese and a sip of water. We have to be careful to drink it sparingly until we get to the Towers. We won't be able to refill our flasks before that."

With a sigh, Astrid dropped to the forest floor. Mattie, who didn't look tired at all, handed each of them some bread. She was such a resilient child. Astrid had never seen anybody with that remarkable colouring before. She wondered where she haled from.

After what seemed only a few minutes, Mallory urged them to get going again, setting a relentlessly fast pace as if to catch up for their short rest. It was getting light when they broke out of the dense forest and saw before them what looked like an enormous desert. Erratically curving hills of the whitest of sand rolled glittering before them in the early sunlight. Astrid saw large splashes of various shades of brilliant blue between the dunes, edged by black and green by all kinds of grasses.

Looking very pleased with himself, Mallory waved a hand over the wondrous landscape as if he had conjured it up by magic. "Welcome to the Badlands. The wet season is still on, I see. Has anyone of you heard about this area before?"

They all nodded their heads looking in awe at the majestic dunes. The stories had never done them justice. Some were more than twelve meters high and beautiful in their eerie emptiness. The contrast between the blue, green lagoons and the whiteness of the hills was mind-blowing. They had heard people describe the Badlands but never imagined it looking so beautiful. They usually spoke off this part of Midland with horror and warned you never to go there if you value your life. Three heads turned to Mallory with a worried look.

"You are probably wondering why we are here? The previous inhabitants have kept the stories about this place alive to stop people from coming here and bothering them. The Badlands has stopped being poisonous centuries ago and is fast healing from the terrible war that once raged here. Believe it or not, these lands were once the barren rocky shores of the Silver Sea. Constant western winds have blown the sands deposited here by two rivers, land inwards. The rock still hidden beneath the sand stops water from draining away and captures the spring rains to form these pockets of water. The rivers that used to come down from the Towers, containing melting water and debris from the peaks, have dried out, but I think they will be flowing here again to make this in a fertile area one day. The rainy season which will last until June, will keep filling these lakes and does a lot to make this land more habitable. We fish to get ourselves food, and there is plenty of fresh water."

Mallory sounded quite enthusiastic and was in full teaching mode. It was interesting, but now they wanted to sit down and have a well-earned rest instead of being lectured about history and nature. Exhausted as they were, Mallory still made them walk quite a bit further into the dunes until they were allowed to stop at a large patch of yellow-green grass bordered by some stunted trees on the edge of one of the lakes.

Some bright orange birds with long curved pointy beaks waded on the opposite side of the lake, but Astrid decided not to point them out not to unleash another detailed lesson about the local wildlife.

Mattie took one look at the sparkling water and tore off her travel-stained clothes, hurling them on the sand and, with a whoop of joy, ran straight into the sparkling water.

Within one second, she shrieked even louder and came running back as if being chased by a demon, dripping and shivering.

"It's ffffreezing," she said with chattering teeth.

"If you would have been a bit more patient, I could have told you that it is a bit too early in the morning to go in. This lake is very deep, as you can see by the dark colour in the middle. It stays freezing until much later in the season. Let's eat first, and then I will find you some shallower pools which will have a much pleasanter temperature," Mallory said, chuckling.

"Won't they catch up with us if we stay too long in one place?" Astrid looked in the direction they had just come from with a worried frown on her face.

Mallory put her mind at rest.

"The advantage of the Badlands is that there are still so many horror stories about it, we will be quite safe. On top of that, I made sure our trail would be difficult to follow. I know these dunes like the back of my hand. I grew up here. It is easy for strangers to get completely lost in these lands but not for me."

"You are from here?" Mattie looked around her at the seemingly empty space," What did you eat?"

"Oh, there's fish here, through all seasons if you know where to look. I'll show you later. There'll still be many who haven't reached the lake yet. There are lots of edible plants around here as well. We can stay here until it gets dark again and have a good rest. Now, who's for some breakfast?" With these words, Mallory opened his pack and took out some parcels wrapped in oilcloth.

"Why don't you, young people, go and find some dry wood. We will have some lovely warm food in our bellies this afternoon. It will make us all feel a whole lot better. As you are so keen on water, Mattie, go and fill our flasks. I intend to get to the foothills of the Towers by tomorrow morning. I, however, will get us some fresh fish." With these words, Mallory strode away into the dunes whistling a happy tune.

They did as he asked and went to look for firewood. When they arrived back at their camp, Mallory had not returned yet. Jonah told the girls to stay put and start the fire while he would see if he could find Mallory.

Like all Islanders, Astrid had learned to make camp from an early age and was happy to show herself useful for a change. She used two twigs and some dry grass and soon had a small fire going, which Mattie quickly fed the wood they had scavenged. The girls wrapped themselves in their cloaks and fell beside the flames, roasting their weary bodies. Astrid dozed off to the happy sound of Mattie chattering about anything and everything. For the moment, she was content to forget everything for a few hours. She needed a bit of respite from it all to be able to continue.

Chapter Thirty-six

Climbing a high dune not far from their encampment, Jonah saw the weirdest thing: Mallory on his knees with his hands stuck deep into the mud on the edge of one of the neighbouring pools. Had the man gone mad?

He called out to him, and to his surprise, Mallory suddenly stood up, a big fish wriggling in his sandy hands. His face was showing a wide grin when he looked up at Jonah. "I still haven't forgotten how to sandfish," he beamed, looking very pleased with himself.

When Jonah reached him, he saw Mallory was holding a peculiar-looking fish with black diamond markings over its whole body, making it look like it was wrapped in a net. The fish looked heavy, and its teeth quite ferocious. Mallory was panting a bit, trying to hold it aloft.

"We call this the Wolf Fish. At the height of the wet season, these fish usually all disappear into the lagoons. However, at the start of spring, you can catch some still hibernating in the mud, where they hide from the cold of winter. They were a delicacy in my youth. Let's go and eat, boy."

He pushed the slippery fish in Jonah's hands, slapped him on his back and laughed when he nearly toppled backwards.

"A nice fat one. We will eat well today."

On their return, Astrid and Mattie duly admired

the strange-looking creature and set to work preparing the rest of the meal. Jonah didn't need much time to clean the fish and hang it above the fire pit.

Soon, they were gorging themselves on the tasty, oily fish, grease dripping down their arms. They washed the food down with the fresh, clean water from the lagoon.

After everyone had had their fill, the doctor used the bread's empty wrappings to pack the rest of the fish. It would still be edible for another day. Rummaging in his backpack, he extracted a colourful sheet and put it on the sand, preventing it from blowing away by placing some rocks on the four corners.

"Gather round, my friends. I will show you which route we will be taking. Just in case anything happens to me, always try to hold on to this map. It is your best bet to get down south without getting lost. We will have to hide in these mountains for a while until our trail has grown sufficiently cold or Damien gives up on following us. This is how I plan to travel."

Three pairs of eyes were following his finger tracing the proposed route.

"Are the mountain people not going to be a problem? I heard they don't let outsiders anywhere near their villages," Jonah said.

He knew quite a bit of geography. Not many of his kind could read, but his mother had taught him at an early age.

"I hope not. We will have to take our chances with them. Better than being caught by Damien's guys and hauled back to the Fort. Besides, my folks used to have a treaty with the Dinali."

He looked up to see his young friends looking at him, waiting to continue his story. He shook the sand off the map and tucked it back in his pack.

"But that is a tale for another time. Once we get to the Dinali, I hope to persuade them we mean no harm and make them aware we share a common enemy. As they loath Damien, we better not tell them I lived in the Fort for all those years. They wouldn't understand. Better we say as little as possible about that."

"Why can't we stay with your people instead?" Mattie asked. Jonah had been wondering that too.

"They abandoned their farms in the Badlands a long time ago and moved across the Silver Sea to find arable land."

Mallory started busying himself before they could ask more questions, gathering his camping gear and stowing it away. He exhorted his companions to do the same. When all had finished packing, he clapped his hands together and said: "Who wants to go for a nice swim before we move on?"

Mattie didn't need more encouragement to let the subject drop, and, jumping up and down, she yelled:" Me, me, me." Her eagerness and joy were very infectious. They followed

Mallory to one of the smaller lagoons, and within a few moments, three of them, after shedding their clothes, were splashing around in the cool, clear water.

Jonah saw that Astrid hesitated. Maybe she didn't want to let the others see the extend of her bruises. They might tell everyone what had happened to her and raise awkward questions.

The cool water beckoning must have made up her mind for her, and Jonah saw her strip off her clothes as fast as she could and rush into the clean water plunging her head under again and again.

He noticed the others see her waver. They must have seen the damage, but as one decided not to mention it. It must be bad enough for her to have had to endure the abuse without having to explain to people what happened. When she was ready to tell them, they would listen.

Remembering the glorious vision that morning on the beach, Jonah felt sad, angry, and a bit guilty. It was him who had told the gang about the door into the castle. At the time, he thought it would only be a quick break-in to snatch the wedding presents. How could he have known Solo had a plan to abduct her? He should have known the guy would end up abusing Astrid given the opportunity. He felt so powerless. He swore to himself he would make it up to her by getting her home no matter the cost to himself.

Probably having seen far worse in the Fort, Mattie

didn't give the marks she saw on Astrid's body any special attention and had great fun trying to make everybody throw her around in the water and playing catch with her. Her joyous laughter was bouncing off the dunes and made everyone feel a bit lighter.

Afterwards, they all put on their spare clothes and washed the ones they had been travelling in for days. While those were drying, they sprawled on the hot sand and slept except for Mallory, who was keeping watch.

Chapter Thirty-seven

When Solo and Yaya arrived at the other exit, it was still dark. They spend quite some time rooting around trees and shrubs to find it. It was still pitch dark.

Yaya started to feel the exhaustion from being awake for a day and night and the stress of worrying about her brother. She only pretended to search while Solo was stomping around, messing up any trails the fugitives might have left behind. Finally, they discovered the tunnel's exit, but it was still too dark to see any footprints.

For, a little later, the morning sun was strong enough to filter through the leaves of the dense forest, and she heard Solo give a triumphant shout. "Here, I was right. They did go east. I can see their tracks."

Her heart sank. She couldn't help herself trying one more time to persuade Solo to leave it and go back to check on their village. She did not want to catch up with her brother. "Their trail will be cold by now. Are you sure we should keep following them? We both know what happens to people who run into the Dinali. None of them ever come back to tell the tale. Don't you think it more important to find out if Eric or my mum are still alive? They might need our help."

Solo didn't even deign to answer her but strode with renewed energy into the forest, leaving her no other option but to follow.

After a whole day of wrestling through the undergrowth, they made camp in a small clearing, both too tired to argue about the fruitlessness of their search to do more than eat some of their rations and fall asleep rolled up in their blankets.

Yaya felt she'd only been sleeping for a few minutes when she felt a hand clamped over her mouth, and before she could pull her knife, Solo whispered in her ear: "Quiet. I hear something. We are being followed."

She, now fully awake, immediately rolled off her blanket, took her bow and nocked an arrow, all the while keeping low and following Solo, who was crawling out of the clearing into the bushes. The latter had his axe in one hand and his gutting knife in the other, pushing himself forward on his elbows. He must have been sleeping with one ear open.

"They'll be coming from the other side of the clearing," he whispered, "Let's split up, so we can come at them from two sides."

After moving some distance apart, they each hid behind one of the many gigantic trees. They didn't have to wait too long before they caught sight of their nightly visitors. Four shadows appeared on the other side of the clearing. When their stalkers came closer, they saw that one of them was Marcel, one of Damien's inner circle and his right hand.

Yaya didn't think Damien had sent them to help

her and Solo with their search. It was more likely that after he'd calmed down a bit, Damien must have decided not to trust them after all and sent some of his men after them to make sure they did what they promised or to make them vanish. She looked in the direction Solo had gone and saw him making a throat slash with his hand nodding at the men. He must've come to the same conclusion.

Everything that had stood between them disappeared, and Solo and she moved in position. It was what they had trained for since they were children. She felt a calm coming over her and knew she was entering the state she would not come out of until the threat to herself and her friend was gone, or she died. In moments like this, she felt a strong bond with Solo, moving as one unit, both willing to go to the utmost to protect each other.

The idiots, blundering around the clearing, didn't seem to be worried about anyone hearing them coming. They must feel safe in the knowledge they were with double the numbers of their quarry. She wondered who the other three were. They sounded like a herd of swine. One of the four was complaining loudly about being tired and not having had anything to eat yet.

She heard Marcel, who was walking in front, whisper: "Stop your fucking moaning. We can't be far behind. They were lucky to hitch a ride with the train, but we made a good time using the underground route. You're making enough noise to wake up the dead. I want to surprise them, but they will hear you coming a mile away and will put up a fight. Those two will have you for breakfast. We need to surprise them because I don't want to die before my time if I can help it."

It confirmed what they both thought. After a glance at Solo, Yaya pulled back on her bow and let the first arrow fly. Even though it was still dark and the men were wearing dark clothes, she heard a thump and a gargle. She saw Marcel drop like a block of stone. An arrow was piercing his throat. In his vanity or stupidity, he had omitted to take off his brooch of office, which had caught what light there was, giving her the perfect target.

The other three froze for a second before scurrying back to the relative safety of the tree line. One had not been fast enough to stop Solo's axe from cutting his arm off at the elbow. Spurting blood everywhere, he fell not far from Marcel, crying and trying to stem the flow. It didn't take long for him to bleed out and stop moving.

Yaya and Solo both knew they would have to kill the other two too. They could not let them get back to report to Damien. He would undoubtedly call an all-out hunt for them before they had a chance to disappear, and then they were screwed.

Shooting a quick look at the bleeding man confirming he was a goner, she saw Solo already crashing ahead of her in the direction the men had taken. Shit. He never stopped to think first. For all she knew, those two could be waiting for him just behind the tree line. They had to stay together now the numbers were equal. The thought hadn't left her mind before she heard the unmistakable sounds of a fight. Forgetting her own advice, she ran to where she'd seen Solo disappear. Before she reached the trees, one of the men, a fat brute, came charging out of the woods right at her. He was waving a mace bellowing with rage.

  Yaya threw her bow down, no time to notch another arrow, and ran fast at her opponent, diving under the arm holding the weapon. He didn't expect that. Ducking past the big man, she stuck one of her knives in the armpit of the arm holding the mace. He dropped it with a confused look on his face. His hesitation would cost him his life.

  She knew most of Damien's bullies relied only on their strength during a fight and weren't inclined to use their brains. Always being smaller and lighter than the men she had sparred with at home, she had learnt to be smart and agile.

  Before her assailant had a chance to realise he had underestimated her, she turned quick as a flash and planted one knife deep in his neck, holding it while she cut his throat with the other. Without making another sound, he crashed to the forest floor. Hearing the sounds of weapons still clashing together from within the trees, Yaya pulled her knives out of the corpse and carefully approached the two men still fighting.

  Solo was a dangerous opponent, but like the man

she had just brought down, he trusted too much on his strength and made mistakes when letting his anger get the better of him. The man Solo was standing opposite was another brutish giant, though he seemed to be a bit wilier than her opponent had been.

Both men breathing hard were bleeding from various cuts and kept slashing at each other. Solo with his axe and knife, the other with a very dangerous looking scimitar. He must be a deserter from the Kent army. Those guys were renowned fighters and horsemen.

To her horror, she saw Solo was already limping. He had taken a deep cut in his upper thigh. She did not want to distract him, so she silently crept around them until she got behind Solo's adversary. Just after the man slashed another gash in Solo, this time cutting his chest, she yelled and jumped forward, neatly sticking her knives in both sides of the guy's torso. Before the man realised what happened, Solo sprung forward, decapitating him with his axe. He kicked the head away from the body for good measure and addressed her in his usual grumpy way.

"What was keeping you, woman?"

Yaya knew he probably felt a bit annoyed she had to come to his aid but decided she would wait forever if she wanted a thank you.

"I had a bit of clearing up to do myself, mate. Let me have a look at those wounds. A few of them will need stitching. I'll have to find clean water somewhere to wash them out before we can do anything else. These guys use their weapons for all sorts of shit. I didn't have time to bring my medicine bag with me, so I'll need to go and find some. Give me your bag and those weapons."

Too tired to resist, looking ready to faint, Solo, for once, didn't argue and just handed his stuff to Yaya.

Studying his wounds, she said, "I'll wash out your wounds with the water from our bottles for now. You should rest here while I'll look for the nearest brook. In the state you're in, we can't go on with our search. That would be plain stupid. You wouldn't get very far."

Solo looked up at her starting to say something but probably thought the better of it. She put his bag and blanket under his head and tended to his injuries. She wrapped the bandages she had made from one of his shirts as tightly as she could around his injuries in the hope it would stem the blood flow.

Tomorrow she would cut some oak bark to stem the bleeding. Thank the Lady, they were in a forest and not in some desert. She would treat that nasty cut on his leg with Goldenrod and some wild garlic if she could find it. She had to keep the wounds from getting infected, or he would die. She felt very grateful now for her mother's lessons.

The latter had been known in the village and beyond for her knowledge of herbal lore. Yaya had always protested how boring the sessions were and why couldn't she go outside and be with her friends. No one in their community had the money to pay the monks for treatment, so her mother's skills had been much in demand. Thinking back to her mother's never-ending love for her, even when she had been throwing it back in her face, Yaya had tears in her eyes. She wiped them away angrily. After she had made sure Solo would survive, she would head back to West Drayton. She had to know if her mother had survived the raid. Solo could do what he wanted, but she had made up her mind.

By killing Marcel and his men, they had more or less burned their bridges here in Midland. She needed to make sure if her mother was still alive or not before fleeing Damien's fury. The faster she did that, the better. If she found her alive, her mother would have to come with her. Damien would take it out on her family if he could not catch her.

Yaya hoped with all her heart Jonah would make it out too. It would be lovely to see him and know he was safe, no matter which stupid things he had done. She might try and find him before leaving Midland after she had made sure her mother was safe.

Having dealt with their latest threat, Yaya lay down close to Solo, who had already succumbed to deep sleep. His body felt hot to the touch. She hoped she could prevent a lethal infection by finding the necessary herbs. But that would have to wait until tomorrow. She put her arm around Solo and slept.

Chapter Thirty-eight

Astrid felt exhausted. For a few days, they travelled through the foothills of the Towers, with the road becoming ever more narrow and steep. Today was the fifth day of trudging uphill. She saw Mallory hold up his hand at a small stream bordered by tall grasses and pine trees. He gave them a stern look. "Right, now I need you three to listen to me carefully. The Dinali have already noticed that we are here."

Startled, they all started to ask questions simultaneously until Mallory raised his hand and told them to be quiet and listen.

"Only if you had lived here, you would have noticed the calls of birds that are not native to this area. The Dinali are warning each other there are strangers on their lands. We will stop here, and I will try to contact them. They make themselves known to us soon enough, and I rather would like it not to be by an arrow through our eye. They are very wary of outsiders since Damien rules Midland. He would send a band of his men over here to collect taxes as he did everywhere when he started. The Dinali sent parts of them back in the boxes they were carrying to collect their tariffs. Damien, furious, sent a larger group, this time accompanied by a small army. He never saw those back either. For the moment, Damien is leaving them alone. He knows the Dinali are too remote and too well hidden to be easy prey. Hopefully, he keeps doing so for the foreseeable future. It makes the Towers the safest place for us to rest for a bit before we go on."

"So why won't the Dinali kill us on sight? Why do we even want to travel through these harsh mountains? There must be a way around them?" Jonah gave voice to what they were all thinking.

Mallory answered: "We are just a small group. They might not immediately perceive us as a threat. I know some of their whistling codes and hope to communicate we don't mean them any harm. I hope to persuade them to let us stay for a while. It will be our best bet to stay out of Damien's reach until we can figure out how to get out of Midland. There is another reason why I need to speak to them, which I will explain after I have done so. I have to be certain my hunch is correct."

Once more, Mallory dug in his bag and pulled out a small bronze object, which looked like a folded piece of metal with two holes. He placed it in his mouth and blew. The air echoed with the most fantastic bird sounds. When he stopped, he turned to his young friends, who were looking at him open-mouthed.

"Most of the people here don't need a whistle. They just use their tongue or hands, but it has been a long time since I've tried this. This device makes it easier to make the whistles loud enough for them to hear. I just told them we mean no harm and that I have some good news for them."

They all wanted to hold the device and study it,

but Mallory didn't let them blow on it.

"Better not confuse them."

There was a crackle on the other side of the stream. A group of five people had appeared as out of nowhere, all holding bows with the arrows strung and pointing right at them. They had made absolutely no sound coming out of the woods. Their skins were dark, and their hair looked like spun gold except for a small woman whose hair looked like silver wire. She spoke first.

"Access to these lands is forbidden. What are you doing here? How do you know our code? You told us you come in peace, but everybody can claim that. You also spoke of news? We are not interested in what outlanders get up to. Tell me why we shouldn't shoot all four of you right now and be rid of you."

The man surrounding her all mumbled their agreement.

Mallory made a deep bow and tried to look as respectful as possible.

"My name is Mallory. I am a doctor. I know we are trespassing, but we had no choice. Damien, or to be precise, his men, are trying to apprehend us. We stole someone from him," pointing at Astrid, "this young lady, daughter of the Harrington family, your lifelong allies. The young man standing behind her aided us in escaping the White Fort and this child," he pulled Mattie to his side," I think she is one of yours."

On both sides of the creek, there was absolute

silence. The leader of the Dinali band did not seem convinced.

"How do you know she is one of us? She has our colouring, I'll give you that, but there are enough of our people who went to live outside the Towers in the past. How do I know if you are not using her to persuade us to take you in so you can tell Damien exactly how to get to our homes?"

"About eight years ago, this girl was found in the woods on the south side of the mountains near the rail tracks. I was working at the White Fort at that time.." Mallory stopped as an arrow was shot right beside his head to land in the tree behind him.

"Just what I thought, you work for that demon spawn, Damien," one of the men standing behind the old woman shouted while knocking the next arrow to his bow.

The elder, without looking back at him, her face a mask of fury, shouted: "Ronald, you stupid idiot. You shoot when I tell you to shoot. I want to hear more about the girl first. One more mistake like that, and you will never come on surveillance again, you oaf."

Breathing hard, she turned to Mallory: "Continue, old man," all the while staring at Mattie with a hopeful look in her eyes.

Not commenting on his near-death experience, Mallory put his arm around Mattie, walking her a bit closer to the creek.

"I've been looking after this young lady ever

since Damien's men brought her in. I was a prisoner at the Fort too. The only thing I know about her is her name: Mathilda. Does that mean anything to you?"

The woman on the other side of the creek staggered and nearly went on her knees was it not for the impetuous Ronald holding her up and steadying her. She looked shocked, too, but hopeful at the same time.

The old lady recovered her stance and ordered: "Men, put down your weapons. We are going to cross the creek. I want to ask this man some more questions."

Arriving on their side, she looked Mallory straight in the eye and said: "Why don't we all sit down except for the little one. I want to have a closer look at her."

Mattie balled her fists at hearing herself called little and was about to say something. Mallory grabbed her shoulder, telling her to be quiet.

The rest of the Dinali waded through the water, not letting the trespassers out of their sight. Mallory sat down and told Astrid and Jonah to do the same except for Mattie, whom he said to go up to the lady.

The woman studied Mattie's face and spoke to Mallory: "My name is Elder Jones, and as it happens, I am called Mathilda too, as is every first-born girl in our family. Eight years ago, my grandchild went with her parents to herd their goats in one of the outermost valleys. They never came back. We looked for them for days. Later we heard some of

Damien's tax collectors had been in the area. They must have run into them. A black day for our Tribe and especially for my family. Do you remember anything from before you came to the White Fort, my child?"

"She doesn't," Mallory interrupted, "the shock of being left to fend for herself must have wiped her memory. The mind can do that that when a particular memory is too harrowing."

Mathilda, nodding, addressed Mattie again.

"May I check something before I can be sure you are that girl? Would you let me look at your back, child?"

Astrid saw Mattie frowning furiously with all the talk about lost children and everybody telling her she was one of them

"I'm not your child. My name is Mattie. I am already twelve, Mallory says."

The elder got up and gave Mallory a beseeching look.

"Maybe you can help? Or do you already know what I'm looking for?"

"I think I do. Come on, Mattie, you're always so proud of them. Let the lady see them."

With a sigh, Mattie pulled her vest up to reveal her back. A colourful tattoo covered the top of it.

She wriggled about during their swim in the lake so much that Astrid and Jonah never noticed the details. They had been far too busy anyway to pretend not to be looking at each other's bodies. Mattie's shoulder blades showed a delicately drawn tattoo of a flock of butterflies in the brightest reds and blues, making them look nearly lifelike. That was not all. Above and below them were two small tattoos of a green and red mountain.

Tears started to roll down Mathilda's cheeks though her face was smiling. She called the other four to come closer and look. That was going a bit too far for Mattie, who pulled her shirt back down, determined not to be pawed by each and every one of these strange people. She sat down next to Astrid, her face looking like thunder, and crossed her arms in front of her chest.

Mathilda grabbed Mallory's hand, beaming.

"Thank you. We had lost all hope of ever finding her or her parents, for that matter. I wish they had made it back too and could see her now. She has become so tall and beautiful."

Her companions were looking at Mallory with something like awe now.

Astrid, who had been listening to the exchange, looked at Jonah, felt happy for her little friend and saw him smiling too.

The old woman, Mathilda, seemed to come to a decision: "Charles, why don't you run ahead to the house and tell everyone we have a big surprise. Ask the people on kitchen duty to prepare a feast for our guests. I bet they haven't seen a decent meal for a while. Am I right?"

This to Mallory, who nodded eagerly. One of her men whispered something in Mathilda's ear. She looked up, looking a bit uncomfortable.

"Before we go, I have to ask you to let us blindfold you. The rest of the tribe first has to agree to allow you in our village. If my people decide against it, they at least might let you leave unharmed if you don't know our location. They have learnt their lesson the hard way. My apologies."

Mallory assured her it was no problem at all. Only Mattie mumbled something about it being stupid. She only let them put the blindfold on after Mallory gave her a stern look.

Chapter Thirty-nine

Jonah thought their trip the last five days had been hard but soon found out that hiking up steep mountain paths without seeing was difficult on a whole different level. Fortunately, every time he stumbled or nearly walked into a bush, a helping hand shot out to guide him and keep him safe.

After what seemed like an endless climb, his legs burning, he finally heard the old woman calling them to a halt. Around him, he heard exclamations of wonder and anger. The air smelled of cooking fires and sweaty bodies.

His blindfold removed, Jonah blinked his eyes, blinded by the intense sunlight. He looked around, astonished at what he saw.

Into the mountain's rocky side, the Dinali people had carved out a complete village. The houses appeared to have melted halfway into the stone and were three or four stories high. They were looking out over a large lake bordered by towering mountains.

Mountain goats and sheep were milling around the square that lay in front of the dwellings. Shepherd boys were whistling for their dogs, trying to herd their flock to the stables. Pigs and chickens were completing the pandemonium of sounds.

He saw Mallory and the others looking around to find him. He waved at them and made his way to his friends.

Mathilda looked to be in a heated discussion with a grumpy looking man, gesticulating wildly. He did not seem too pleased with their arrival. The other villagers were just ogling them, murmuring amongst themselves.

"I thought that lady was glad to have found us. Why are they arguing?" Mattie was wondering out loud.

Bright as she was, she must have immediately picked up on the past tense when Mathilda mentioned her parents. She had told him she couldn't remember much about them, which sometimes made her sad, but when she saw some of the parents in the fort had treated their offspring, not that sad. She had said she had felt lucky to have had someone like Mallory looking after her. He was strict but never cruel.

Watching Mathilda, Mallory told them: "They must have had a lot of trouble with Damien. They seem very wary of outsiders. Let's hope Mathilda can change their minds about us. If she fails, we might have to leave sooner than we planned. But first, let's see what happens."

Jonah saw the old woman was motioning them to come over to where she was confronting the powerfully built, angry man. He was standing with his arms folded across his chest, his face set like a granite mask.

Pointing at him, Mathilda said: "This is Richard, our village leader. Richard, these are Doctor Mallory, his companions Astrid Harrington, and Jonah, from the village of West Drayton."

She drew in a big breath.

"And this," pointing at Mattie, "is my newly found granddaughter, Mathilde, who has been returned to us after eight long years, which should be cause for celebration, not for grumbling. They have recently escaped imprisonment by Damien and have been fleeing ever since. I want them to stay with my clan and me until I have figured out how I can help them. I will personally take full responsibility for them."

Despite Mathilda's promise, Richard did not look in any way resigned to their arrival. Ignoring the travellers, he told Mathilda: "The little girl, if she is truly one of your tribe, can stay. The others can't. My men will take them back to the foothills. They will make sure they leave our territory straight away and never come back. The risk of discovery by letting them wander about here is too great. I am not fooled as easily as you by their sob story. By their admission, they lived at the Fort for some time and can easily be Damien's spies. You're getting soft in old age, Mathilda. That monster will never give up trying to find us and get his revenge. This coincidence of bringing back your granddaughter would be just the thing he would cook up. We should never underestimate him. I hope you at least made sure they were blindfolded while coming up here? If you didn't, we can't let them go, and we don't need more hungry mouths to feed."

His determined look didn't leave Jonah in any doubt of what Richard's solution would be.

Mathilda hastened to confirm she had taken all precautions. She added: "I will take this issue to the council of the Elders. You might think you can boss me around, but the last time I looked, this was still a democracy."

Shaking with indignation, she continued: "It is getting too dark now to take them back. I will call for a meeting tomorrow morning. For the moment, I at least will show these people some hospitality. Tonight they can stay with me. When my husband was still alive, we always knew how to treat guests. Something you seem to have forgotten. We were making decisions like this for our people when you were still in your cradle, so you can stop trying to bully me around."

Leaving the irate looking clan chief to stew, she opened her arms to our friends.

"Now, my friends, come with me. We will give you a nice dinner, but first, I would recommend a visit to our bathing cave," she wrinkled her nose in a very suggestive way.

Mallory and the others followed Mathilda up to a brightly coloured house set into the mountain.

The old lady ushered them in and led them to a room where a huge fireplace was already heating a large copper pot whose delicious smells made their mouths water. A friendly smiling woman was stirring its contents gently.

"That is my son-in-law's sister Margie. I have brought you some guests. Would you be so kind as to take these good people to our bathing cave and make sure they have everything they need? I will hunt down some fresh clothes. I will explain everything later when we are all together."

The little, plump woman, her brown cheeks glowing with excitement, left the fire and beckoned them to follow her. Mathilda seemed to be able to make people obey her without any questions. Jonah hoped that she would do so tomorrow, too, when the elders would get together to decide their fate.

Walking them to the bathing house, Margie, glancing wide-eyed at Mattie, chatted nervously. But finally, not being able to stop herself, she blurted out: "Are you my niece?"

Mallory confirmed that her mother-in-law was sure about it, after which she squealed: "Now I will be a proper auntie. I'm so excited. Roland always looked up to his big brother John, Mattie's dad, and was inconsolable when he never returned to the village. Roland and I have never been blessed with children. It will be so nice to have a little girl in the family."

She looked so hopeful and happy that Mattie must have decided to let the 'little' remark go to everyone's relief.

Once in the bathhouse, Jonah and his friends took their clothes stained by days of travel off to slowly sink into a hot, steaming pool lying in a cave at the back of the house.

Margie meanwhile busied herself with soap and towels and then disappeared with their clothes only to arrive a little later with a pile of clean ones. After asking if she could do anything else for them, she left them to enjoy their first hot bath for over a week in peace.

"So, what do you think? Will they let us stay? What if they decide against it? "Jonah was worried. He knew they would have to hide out somewhere for more than a few weeks at least until their pursuers would be occupied with the usual summer raids or their crops and would not want to put much time and effort into finding them. Damien's promise of a reward would soon pale against the profits of a successful foray into the lands of their enemies. The enemy as in people who were willing to work hard and prosper. And crops waited for no man.

Mallory coming up from dunking his whole head in the fragrant water, looked at him: "Let's cross that bridge when we get to it. Mathilda seems to have a lot of influence. We should thank our lucky stars. I was right, and Mattie is a Dinali and one related to an important family. What I remember about these people is that they are very strict but very honourable too. The unfriendly way they treated us today stems from having to live in constant fear since Damien became the ruler. They must have heard the stories about his men extorting vast amounts of money from other communities and stealing their goods. Then when they cannot pay them, their children are hauled away to the slave markets. It takes a certain ruthlessness to keep your people safe under these circumstances. Let's hope the more tolerant people on the council can persuade Richard to take us in for at least a few days. We might have to promise to stay within the village's boundary or maybe even in this house. It will make it easier for them to be sure we don't know the exact location of their village before they let us go. So don't go, and try to be smart by sneaking off without telling me. Our lives will depend on it. I am looking at you, Mattie."

The girl looked at Mallory with her eyes flaming. "Okay, but I'll tell you right now, I'm not going to stay with these people, who treat me like a baby, who needs looking after. When you all leave, I'm coming with you."

"But, Mattie, these people are your family. They love you and will keep you out of danger. Keep you safe."

Astrid looked at the scowling young girl and then pointedly at Jonah.

"I don't understand why anybody would not rather be safe with their relatives than wandering about fleeing for their life. I would do anything to be with mine".

"They don't feel like family. Mallory is my family. They didn't keep me out of danger eight years ago, did they? That lady, who's supposed to be my grandmother, seems very nice and all that, but I will still die of boredom if I have to stay here cooped up between mountains and constantly looked after."

Mattie sounded more and more desperate. Her eyes were filling with tears, which she swiped away with an angry gesture trying to look defiant but looking more like a frightened child. She jumped out of the pool and tore a towel off the pile, grabbing one of the bundles of clothes her aunt had left behind before storming off.

Astrid wanted to go after Mattie, but Mallory put a restraining hand on her arm.

"Leave her. It must be an enormous shock for her to find out about her parents and finally meet her family. Mattie always imagined it very differently. She is a very resilient child. Once she has had the chance to get to know her family a bit better, she will change her mind. Mattie has never seen anything but violence and does not trust people easily. The Lady knows what happened to her before she came to me. I am getting out now and will see you in the main chamber."

With a groan, he got out and helped himself to a towel and another set of clothes, leaving Astrid and Jonah luxuriating in the warm bath.

Being alone for the first time in the past crazy week, Jonah felt awkward and busied himself washing his hair and rubbing the dirt off his body.

He was the first to break the silence.

"Maybe we should get out as well. But before we do, tell me, how are you feeling? Your face looks nearly normal again, and your other bruises seem to be healing well."

He blushed, realising his words meant he had been looking at Astrid's body.

Astrid quickly rose from the fragrant water to

cover herself with one of the large towels. Before she left, she did answer him, though.

"I feel much better. Thank you. The sight in my right eye is still blurry. Mallory said it might take longer to heal, or it could stay this way. The rest is not bothering me anymore. I'm going to look for Margie and see if I can help with something. Maybe you could find Mattie and persuade her to join us in the kitchen?"

At which point she fled the bathing chamber, leaving him with a whole bunch of confusing feelings.

Astrid had attracted him from the first moment he saw her on that beach. She had looked like a mermaid rising from the sea, her beautiful body all golden and glinting with seawater. He felt his body stirring at the thought and decided it was time for him to get out too and stop thinking about her in this manner. He refused to be like Solo. He felt Astrid was beginning to like him back a little. He hoped it would become more than that but did not believe it likely.

'We're from different worlds, so I better stop being a lovesick idiot. Yaya was right. I must have become soft in the head. I wonder where she and Solo are now? I hope Damien hasn't punished her for our escape. Solo deserves everything he gets, but Yaya is still my sister. Not much I can do about it now. Damn, I'm hungry.

He shrugged his shoulders, hauled himself out of the warm water and got dressed. There was a lot to sort out.

Harbour Cities Midland

Chapter Forty

In the kitchen, Jonah found Mathilda had not only invited her own family but many other Dinali friends for the evening meal. She must hope to persuade them to support her tomorrow.

The table was laden with food. Everybody was in a good mood and wanted to talk to the newcomers as it had become rare to have outsiders in their midst. They were jostling each other, keen to start a conversation with their guests. They wanted to know who they were and from where they had travelled. It seemed more like a big party than an assembly of people who would decide their fate tomorrow.

Jonah saw Astrid sitting at the far end of the big table surrounded by a group of young Dinali. He went to join them and, to be honest, to make sure none of the young men became too friendly with her. After what she had been through, she might feel vulnerable with strangers. He sat down right beside her, wriggling between her and some bold village lout.

Astrid gave him a grateful look and introduced him as 'my friend Jonah, who saved me from my captors', which gave him a warm glow inside. He did his best to make it look like he and Astrid belonged together, but that did not deter some of the Dinali girls from throwing him coy looks and attempting to get his attention under the ruse of offering him a drink or some food. He was not interested and politely waved them away, only having eyes for the lovely girl next to him.

Margie, who had spotted Jonah come in, brought him some food and winked at him pointing her chin at his table companion to let him know she knew what he was doing and had his back.

Astrid, who caught the exchange, took his hand under the table and squeezed it. Her cheeks were glowing. For the first time, with her eyes shining like emeralds, she didn't look exhausted or sad, just a young girl enjoying herself. She looked at him and smiled.

Jonah's breath caught in his throat at the beauty of her. He vowed to himself he would do everything in his power to keep that smile on her face. He owed it to her.

He looked over at Mallory, who was sitting next to Mattie, surrounded by her new relatives. He didn't know if the good doctor was protecting the girl from their overwhelming attention or them from her puncturing holes in them if they got on her nerves.

Mallory stood up and went to Mathilda to whisper something in her ear. She rang a small bell and, in the ensuing silence, addressed the whole company.

"Good people. Tomorrow will be an important day for us all. I know we have suffered at the hands of outsiders over the past years, and I am sure Richard is just trying to keep us safe, but I hope too that we have not forgotten our laws of hospitality and decency. Our guests here have brought my granddaughter Mathilde, Mattie, back to us with danger to their own lives. In return, the only thing they ask is a few weeks of respite by being allowed to stay in our community. I should be able to give them that for a few days at the very least. Tomorrow I will put my request to the vote in the village council meeting. I hope you will all support me and acknowledge what these people did for my family and me by returning my granddaughter. Please, show them that the Dinali know how to treat people in a civilised way. Now let us all bid each other goodnight. I will see you tomorrow at noon when the elders decide if I can keep these people safe for a while. I hope you will not let me down. Thank you."

Margie came up to them and asked them to follow her. She led them to a large bedroom on the first floor. Mattie had more or less politely declined Mathilda's offer to sleep with her cousins in the nursery. She dangled on Astrid's arm, begging her to share with her and no one else.

The room looked very comfortable, with one large bed and two smaller couches draped in colourful plaids. There was still a small fire crackling in the hearth. Hidden behind a beautifully embroidered screen, they found a small washroom supplied with everything they needed to refresh themselves.

The men left the double bed to Astrid and Mattie and made themselves comfortable on the couches. After all the excitement, even Mallory's loud snoring could not keep the others awake.

Jonah, seeing that Mattie and Astrid had fallen fast asleep as soon as their heads hit their pillow, gave a deep sigh of contentment and followed their example.

Chapter Forty-one

Astrid woke up with a jolt. She desperately needed to pee. Mattie had already disappeared to somewhere. She saw Jonah and Mallory still fast asleep and did not want to disturb them by using the privy in their room. She silently slid out of bed, got dressed and found her way downstairs.

She followed the delicious smell of freshly baked bread to the kitchen, where Margie, Mathilda, and two other women were busy preparing breakfast.

Mathilda looked up, smiling at her:" Young Mattie was up early and has eaten with the children. Most of our men are still taking care of the animals. The girls are collecting eggs. They will all join us for breakfast. Are the other two awake too?"

Astrid shook her head and shyly asked where she could find the washroom as she'd forgotten where it was, being too tired last night to pay attention.

"Oh dear, yes, yesterday and the days before must have been exhausting. Margie here will take you. This place is a maze for people who didn't grow up here."

Margie dried her hands on her apron and motioned Astrid to follow her. Mattie's aunt seemed such a sweet woman, going out of her way to make them feel at home. She showed Astrid where to relieve herself and stayed around while the latter washed her hands and face and tried rather unsuccessfully to comb the tangles out of her hair. It was a mess after not having been brushed for nearly a week. It was almost impossible to get a comb through it. Chattering throughout about nothing and everything, Margie stopped and offered to do brush Astrid's hair.

Stroking it, she sighed: "It's so lovely. I bet you never had it cut. The colours remind me of autumn leaves. I wish my hair was like that."

Astrid glanced up at her, taking in the homely figure with above it the kindest face she'd ever seen and said generously: "Your hair is beautiful too. That golden-white, in contrast with your dark complexion, is awesome. I've never seen anything like it."

Margie laughed.

"Well, you are too kind. You must have noticed there's nothing special about it here. Everyone's hair and skin are like mine. It's probably why your doctor guessed Mattie belonged with us. Lucky for her, she has the beauty of her mother to go with it. Joan was an exquisite looking woman, and she and my brother Paul made such a beautiful couple. Joan was Mathilde's only daughter.

Astrid, nearly lulled into sleep again by the gentle combing of her hair and the soft voice of Margie, suddenly felt sick in her stomach and flew up. She ran over to the sink and stood there retching.

"I'm sorry," she gasped, "must've been all the rich

food yesterday. Drinking all that cider hasn't helped either, I think. I am not used anymore to eating so much. The last few days, we've been surviving on what we could find in the fields."

She kept heaving until she felt she was empty down to her toes. Margie was studying her intensely with a slight frown on her face.

"Have you been feeling sick like this before?"

"Well, before in my old life, only after eating something that had gone off. But you mean recently? No, this is the first time. Why do you ask?"

Margie suddenly busied herself with the wet towels and didn't look her in her eyes, mumbling: "Never mind. You are right. It was probably all the rich food. You're not used to the spices we use either. Let me give you some fennel tea to settle your stomach. Make sure you have a light breakfast this morning. You'll soon feel as right as rain again."

Astrid straightening up, felt rather hungry even though she'd just been sick. She rinsed her mouth and followed Margie back to the dining room.

Jonah and Mallory were already helping themselves to large quantities of the warm crusty bread topped with homemade cheese washing it all down with the blackest of teas. They made room for her between them.

Astrid decided to heed Margie's advice and ate only a little. She drank the soothing fennel tea, grateful that the kind woman did not mention her nausea. While sipping it, she wondered aloud where Mattie was.

Standing at the stove, one of the women called over her shoulder the girl had gone outside with some of her cousins. They wanted to show her their dogs and cats. Even at the ripe old age of twelve, Mattie had not been able to resist the chance of having a good cuddle with some furry animals.

Hearing this, Mallory explained: "I could never let her have a cat or dog of her own while we were living in the fort. Some of the children could be very cruel. It would have meant terrible heartache if something horrible had happened to a pet of hers. Let's leave her with her friends for now. We will see her later in the square. I have told her yesterday not to wander outside the village perimeter and hope she will heed me. I made it clear to her she would endanger us all if she did not listen."

After breakfast, all three offered to help clear up the kitchen but were shooed away by the women, who probably wanted to have a lovely natter about their mysterious guests. Before leaving the house, Mathilda insisted they put on some warm, colourful felt coats. Outside, they were grateful for them. This high up in the mountains was very chilly this early, even with the sun brightening up the sky.

They found Mattie surrounded by a gaggle of children, who, she told them, were going to show her the view from the highest window in the village.

"They said we could see the whole valley from there. Even what's outside the village without going there.

Please come with us. Please?"

Astrid and the others decided it would be good to get some exercise after all that food and get their bearings. They followed Mattie and her cousins, who were chattering like a flock of little birds. It was satisfying to see Mattie looking so free, not continually looking over her shoulder for danger. She was just having fun like any other child.

After quite a bit of a climb, which made their sore muscles felt, they took in the magnificent view towards the mountain ranges all over the high valley. They could see the village lay at the bottom of a rocky bowl. On three sides, they noticed houses hewn out of the grey, lichen-streaked rocks. Across, they could see a large, cobalt blue lake, fed by many streams burbling down from the surrounding mountains that hovered over them like giant sentinels. Their peaks shone golden in the morning sun

"I wondered how Mathilda manages to have such a marvellous supply of clean running water. They must have rigged up some pumping system to get it up here from those waterfalls," Mallory mused aloud. He was always interested in how things worked.

Though the village itself was on a very high altitude, there were even higher mountains towering over it, providing a natural barrier to keep the Dinali out of sight of the outside world. Looking down in the square, Astrid could see a large crowd gathering, which reminded her that they should make their way back down to be on time for the meeting. It would decide their fate, and she hoped it would turn out to be in their favour.

Mallory seemed to have had the same thought and shooed them downstairs.

Chapter Forty-two

They pushed through the crowd to get in front of a high dais constructed on one side of the square. On it, she saw five people seated behind an intricately carved table with Mathilda amongst them. Mattie's grandmother gave them an encouraging smile.

Seated in the middle, Richard was already very red in the face and whispering to his neighbour, an ancient wrinkly man. Silence fell when a man standing beside the dais hit a drum, the deep sound echoing between the mountains.

Astrid felt all eyes directed at her and her friends. It made her feel uncomfortable. Jonah, noticing, took her hand and squeezed it as if to say:" I'm here, don't worry." She pressed closer to him.

Mallory looked as unperturbed as always and had positioned himself right before the five elders as if to show their judges he had nothing to hide. Seeing many friendly faces from yesterday around her gave her hope they would come out of this meeting unscathed. It all depended on how much clout Mathilda had with the other council members.

Richard rose from his seat and pointed at his unwanted guests.

"Here before you, you see four people from outside our borders who claim sanctuary. They say they are on the run from Damien, the monster from the North. One of them is an Islander girl, and one is a monk, the other a Midlander and the little one, according to Mathilda, is Dinali and her granddaughter. Our honourable friend claims she is the girl stolen from the Butterfly clan all those years ago when Damien's thugs were harassing us. We lost many lives, and the only way we've survived since is by not letting anyone trespass on our territory, with no exception. It would take only one person to tell the world about us, and we are doomed to pay crippling taxes and live in poverty, slowly being exterminated by that monster. Our children will be led away into slavery. I swore never to allow that to happen. Therefore I want to propose to let Mathilde keep the child. Hopefully, we can still retrain her. The other three, we should put to death. That is the law. They must be in cahoots with Damien. How else did the girl end up in their company? It would be the perfect ruse, pretending they want to return her, to make us trust them, and then leave here to go back and tell that villain where we live. As this is a crucially important decision for our whole community, I want to let every adult in our compound vote on our decision instead of the Council of Elders."

This announcement made the other council members sit up straight, looking around, startled by Robert's proposition.

Mathilda rose from her seat and, shaking with anger, spoke: "As much as I respect the opinion of my fellow board member, Robert, I want to remind everyone this is a matter of life and death. Never before has such an important decision been dependent on the whim of the general populace. These three people have risked their lives and suffered great hardship to return my granddaughter to me. I am one hundred per cent sure she belongs to my family. I've seen the proof. She has our family's totem on her back. Look at her. Have you ever seen hair and skin like that on outsiders? I have listened to these people and seen the scars Damien and his minions have given them with my own eyes. The eldest is a doctor who once worked in the monastery and who has been instrumental in the little one's safe return. That young woman over there is the eldest daughter of the Harrington family. Even here in our remote village, we know that honourable name. The young man travelling with them? Yes, he is a Midlander, but," and here she stopped to silence the grumbles at her admission Jonah was one of their enemies with an impatient gesture, "he is a simple fisherman. He got caught up in this situation and has given up everything he holds dear to help the others survive. It will cost him his life if he ever has to go back to his people. They all have too much to lose, to go back and betray us. I vote to let the elders decide on their fate because I take it they still represent the will of our people."

After Mathilda sat down again, breathing hard, Astrid heard many discussions starting behind them until Richard stood up and called for quiet.

"The council shall first decide if we're going to

have a general ballot or if they will decide I trust my fellow council members to do their best for all of you and not just for their own family." here, looking pointedly at Mathilda.

"Do you want to be safe and live a good life? Vote to have these liars put to death for trespassing our territory. Do you want to risk your family's future and every day look over your shoulder for Damien's men to come and destroy us? Let them stay, and I assure you that will happen. I want to remind our esteemed council members to think hard about the risks of taking the wrong decision. Their family's lives might depend on it. I, Richard, think it would be better to leave it up to every man and woman of our clan to decide on this issue, but I'll let you honourable members decide if you choose to take the matter into your own hands."

The elders, except for Mathilda and the ancient man beside Robert, looked very uncomfortable. They could hear a lot of people yelling "we want to decide" or " we have a right to make this decision" or just chanting "ballot. ballot."

Robert smiled and looked very satisfied with himself.

Mathilda had not seen this coming and was expecting the worst. She rose from her chair to add some more arguments to her speech.

Before she could repeat her appeal, the old council member sitting next to her rose from his seat, he looked very frail but surprised our friends by bellowing with a booming voice: "I have never heard such balderdash in my life even though I've been around longer than any of you. As Mathilda here just said, the elders always decide when it is a question of life and death. When a decision does not affect one family but the whole community, we will not set a precedent by leaving judgement to the general people as much as I respect you. We might as well do away with this council altogether. No, as the eldest on the committee, I have two votes, which I will cast now in favour of keeping these fugitives alive and give them temporary sanctuary. If Mathilda believes the girl is her granddaughter, I see no problem welcoming her back into our tribe. About the others, though, and here I must side with caution, they can stay here until they are ready to travel again. We will then blindfold them and bring them to the Silver Falls, where they can continue south. Or have we become mindless animals like Damien and his ilk to kill fellow beings at will? I trust my other colleagues here on the council to agree with me and decide likewise."

He sat down after giving everyone on the assembly a stern look.

Mallory turned to Astrid and Jonah, looking more relaxed:" Let's hope the old boy can convince the others. I don't know if a general ballot would have gone in our favour. Too many families have lost dear ones to outsiders. Richard won't give up his power on the council by abolishing it. The chairman cleverly played that. Now we can only wait. Mathilda explained to me the council members have to put a black or white marble in a bag. If black wins, we die. If white wins, the rest of us, except Mattie, will have to leave here sooner than I hoped. At least Mattie will be safe."

Mattie, who'd been listening, pulled him down by his sleeve and whispered loudly in his ear: "I will NOT stay here."

He stroked her hair and whispered back: "Shall we first see what the verdict is? We can cross that bridge when we get to it."

Astrid pulled the girl in front of her and put her arms around her to calm her.

One of the villagers reached out to the judges with a red velvet bag dangling from a long pole. Each of the councillors dropped their ballot into the bag without showing anybody the colour. The decision would be final. After collecting the votes, the same man took the pouch off the pole and handed it to the village elder.

In front of the councillors stood a clear glass bowl. One by one, the elder took the marbles from the bag and, proclaiming its colour, put it into the bowl. There was a general gasp from the public when they saw all the balls were white except for one, no guesses whose it was.

With the same booming voice, the chairman proclaimed the result of the ballot.

"Five white, one black. The council has spoken. I

won't have to tell Mathilda that these people will be her full responsibility while staying in our village. I think three days should suffice to have these people ready to travel again. I will appoint the men and women who will escort them to our border at the Silver Falls. Her granddaughter can stay."

Looking down at Mallory and his companions:" We hope we haven't put our trust in you only for you to betray it later. Once you leave our borders, you can never return. Next time I will give the order to kill you myself. And you, little lady, your grandmother is one of the bravest and kindest people in our tribe. Obey her, and she will make sure you will make an excellent addition to our community."

Before Mattie could say anything about the subject, Mallory bowed and thanked him. He shooed the cross looking girl back to Mathilde's house. People made way for him, some clapping him on his shoulder, congratulating him and others muttering, looking disgruntled.

He told Astrid and Jonah he needed to have a serious talk with Mattie back at the house. They should go and make themselves scarce for a bit.

"Make sure you take one of Mathilda's relatives with you if you want to go out of sight of the village. I don't trust Richard and his followers not to take the law into their own hands. You might conveniently end up having an accident."

Chapter Forty-three

"Shall we have a look at the lake?" Astrid looked at Jonah, hoping he would join her. She needed some fresh air as she still felt a bit queasy but didn't want to go out by herself, followed by this Roderick guy.

Jonah readily agreed, and they set off in the direction of the lake. It wasn't hard to find. From every street of the village, you could see it shimmering far below.

A wide path wound its way leisurely to the bottom of the valley. After a short stroll downhill, they found themselves admiring the expanse of crystal clear water. Across the lake, they could see a jumble of waterfalls tumbling down the sun, painting rainbows in their spray.

"It's called the Chilly Lake" Roderick seemed to have got up the courage to say something. He was a skinny young man, about their age, and one of the large brood of children of Mathilda's clan.

"In the time before, there used to be low hills here called the Chilterns, and the water stays ice-cold even in the summer."

He blushed and looked nervously at them as if hoping he had not spoken out of turn. Feeling a bit sorry for him, they asked him a few more questions about the village and the valley, which seemed to put him more at ease. Soon the conversation petered out, and Roderick sat down on the edge of the boardwalk dangling his feet above the water, pretending he wasn't keeping an eye on them.

Spotting a bench slightly higher up on the bank, Astrid sat down, not quite sure what to say to her companion. Before the silence became too awkward, she started. "Do you miss your family? I mean, why did you come with us? You could've just stayed with your sister and her friend."

Jonah swallowed a few times. Astrid gave him an encouraging smile which seemed to prompt him to answer.

"It wasn't an easy decision. You've met my whole family. I do miss my mum. I even miss my sister, whom you've only seen from her worst side. Since my dad died she looked after my mum and me, ensuring the other clan people left us alone. She loves us but at the same time hates us as she thinks her feelings for us make her vulnerable. Solo has that effect on her. She just wants to show him she can be as tough as he is. My mother and I always wonder why Yaya chose that guy as her mate."

He looked out over the water as if to find inspiration. "All my life, I've felt I didn't belong in West Drayton. I was the only one in our village who wanted to know what lay beyond it. I wanted to do more with my life than just fight and fish. The villagers often called my mum a witch because she knew all about herbs and their uses. Being her son wasn't easy. If not for my best friend Wulf, the other children would have bullied me every day of my life just for being different. I miss him too. You would have liked him," he turned to look at her, his eyes crinkling with a smile, thinking of his friend.

"But you wanted to know why I came with you? I feel I have to make up for what we did to you by taking you from your home and letting Solo hurt you. I am guilty because I was there and didn't protect you. Nothing I do can change what happened to you, but I hope and will try my utmost to make sure nothing bad happens to you ever again. I swear on my father's grave that I'll do everything in my power to help you to return home again. It's the least I can do," his eyes were bright with tears and burning with a fire she had not seen in them before. He sounded so sincere. His story touched Astrid, and she felt something dissolving in her.

She took a deep breath. Somebody must have seen Marion and her leaving the basement door open in their hurry to get back to the house that morning. She needed to know if that was the reason her life had started to go so horribly wrong. She did share a part of the guilt.

"How did you manage to get in? There were soldiers everywhere, and the walls are too high to climb without being spotted ."

Looking very uncomfortable, Jonah gave a deep sigh: "I saw you and your friend on the beach and told the others about the door. When we came back that evening, the door was still open. I thought it would stop anyone from getting hurt if we could walk in, steal what we could and get out without anyone having to start a fight. I was wrong."

And here it was. He is responsible for what happened. If he hadn't told anyone, things would not have turned out the way they did. But she was just as guilty. If not for her, that gate would have been closed securely. Nothing would have happened.

She wasn't finished yet. There was one more thing that had been going through her head these last few days. "When they took me, I smelt smoke. Do you know what happened?"

Jonah shuffled his feet on his side of the bench and sat with his head down, clasping his hands.

"I'm not sure. I stayed with the boat. Solo needed me to pilot the boat through the straights, or I wouldn't have even been there. Yaya didn't say anything either. Everyone told me things had gone as planned and that no one would be quick to pursue us."

Astrid wanted to believe him. She desperately needed a friend. Jonah had only shown her kindness ever since she found herself in that boat. He saved her from drowning. He gave up his family for her to go back to hers. She looked aside at him, seeing an earnest young man, who seemed very sorry about his part in her abduction and following troubles. Still, it could all be a lie.

She needed to talk with someone who hadn't been part of her abduction. She decided to discuss her doubts with Mallory after dinner. He would know if she could trust Jonah.

She stood up and straightened her clothes.

"We'd better get back and give that poor boy a break. He must be so bored by now. I want to ask Mallory how his talk with Mattie went." Astrid hurried off, followed immediately by Roderick before Jonah had a chance to ask her if she believed him.

Chapter Forty-four

As the evenings were still cold this early in the season, there was a pleasant fire burning in Father Sirio's rooms. He preferred his cosy apartment in Harrington House to his cold chambers under the cathedral in Sevenoaks.

He was finishing his notes for his next meeting with Luton when he heard a loud rapping on the door. He called out to come in. One of the young apprentices from the harbourmaster entered, still breathing hard from running or from excitement or both.

"The ships are coming back," he said, bouncing from foot to foot as if to make ready to rush off again.

"Thank you, Simon, isn't it?" Sirio prided himself to know most of the people in Sevenoaks. He reached into his pocket and flicked half an Oro at the boy. "Here's something for your trouble. Go back to your master and tell him I'll be right over."

"Wow. Thanks. I will", and away the lad shot.

Father Sirio called for his assistant to tell him he would go and welcome the Commander's party at the harbour.

Tell mistress Judith. She'll want to prepare some rooms and dinner for our men. Make sure she will let Marion know. The poor girl has been pining since John was taken to London. But make sure she doesn't follow me. The news is not good. Astrid has not been found yet, and her brother has been confined to the Priory in Luton. Tell her I will send for her when we are back at the house."

Shrugging on his woollen coat, he thought about yesterday's conversation with the Prior's secretary, Macron. The man had looked so smug telling him about what had been said in his meeting with Gerald Selby. He told him too that Astrid had left with Mallory. "You two used to be quite close, weren't you? Never thought the bastard would hide in the Fort."

Macron had given him the new directives for the Island Project, for which he, Sirio, was going to be held fully responsible. The Harrington boy had been assessed and would be sent to the Hospital Ship. No one was to leave Gen territory to find the girl. Brother Lucius would take care of the Midland situation if Damien didn't do so by next week.

Father Sirio shivered. Lucius had studied at Luton at the same time as Mallory and himself. The man was a great scout but a complete psycho with it. Lucius had always enjoyed throwing his weight around with people weaker than himself. And John being put on the Ship. He would have to tell the family about this new blow. And Marion would be even more devastated.

He had been convinced they had kept their plans to discredit the Prior from the eyes of the Church. It had taken some time for Harrington to join them. Henry marrying into his family would have consolidated their position on the Island.

Sirio was certain the Prior had been behind the attack and the abduction. Damien wouldn't have dared to let any of his people go so drastically every law of the Church. When he had enough proof, it might be enough to overthrow the bastard and make the other monks join them. Most of them had no clue what their leader was up to. He had to be careful not to alarm the allies of Pendrini on the Continent. His thoughts were interrupted by a loud buzz of voices.

On the quay, news about the impending arrival of the ships had drawn a large crowd to welcome the arrivals. Sirio walked to the landing area, the people giving him a wide berth.

They were always a bit wary of any high ranking clergy. And they had a good right to be.

The main ship bumped into place, and he saw Gerard Selby come down the gangway, his face looking like thunder. He'd better stop him from starting a whole tirade in front of his flock. Henry noticed his nod and overtook the Commander, laying a hand on his arm, whispering in his ear. It seemed to do the trick.

Nicholas brought up the rear. The boy looked changed, somehow older than when he left. The responsibility he had been given on the trip and his terrible experience with West Drayton seemed to have aged him. Well, there would be more in store for the lad. Thank the Lady, Trudy had told the boy about his father. It would make things less complicated.

"Dear Gerald, good to see you all made it back in one piece. Shall we convene in my rooms at Harrington House this evening? It will be more private. There are a lot of things we need to discuss. Nicholas, maybe you can come by before that."

Nicholas nodded and left them to see his mother. He agreed to meet with Sirio before dinner.

After he left, Sirio pulled the other two close and, in a low voice, told them about the decision of London Hospital to send John to the Hospital Ship. The men froze. They both knew it meant they had lost another friend to the scheming of the Church.

Harbour Cities Midland

The Commander growled he had had enough and would see them tonight. He added that he would inform his daughter himself. Henry thanked Sirio for telling them and suggested he would accompany Father Sirio back to Harrington House. Henry reported that they had to enlighten Nicholas about some of the things playing in the Archipelago. They were silent for the rest of the walk. Sirio saw Henry averting his eyes from the blackened tower that had taken the brunt of the fires.

He sighed and returned to his rooms to eat and prepare for the meeting.

When Sirio had finished his dinner when there was a light rap on the door, Nicholas came in looking a whole lot cleaner, his hair still dripping. The boy's face looked grim. There wasn't much left from the eager young man who left them a few days to have his adventure.

Nicholas opened his mouth as soon as he had sat down, but Sirio put up his hand. "Before you start to ask me the many questions you undoubtedly have, let me say a few things first. I heard from Henry they told you a little about why we can't go and find Astrid ourselves. Commander Selby, Henry and many others in our territories have decided that we have had enough of the Priory pulling our strings. There is also something brewing on the Continent that might be dangerous for all of us on the Archipelago.

We have united under The Order of the True Earth. Most of the Gen countries, but Midland too, want to free themselves from the tyranny of the Priory. The Church of Light is a good institution but has slowly been taken over by a group of people who only want to enrich themselves and keep the rest as their willing servants. Those who don't comply will be terminated. The Continent is involved too.

You, my boy, I would like to go abroad and find out what is going on. You will not be going alone. Henry will be coming with you."

Nicholas's mouth was opening and closing. He looked very pale and was frantically shaking his head. "How can we go? We would kill everyone abroad by just being in the same room with them. Why me? I understand about Henry, he has a lot of experience, but I know nothing. How long will we be away? Astrid will need me here if she comes back."

"It's a shock, I know, but you are chosen as you are un known to the Church. You don't belong to one of the leading Houses. As you correctly mentioned, Henry will have the experience to keep you safe. You will travel as a Tech salesman. It might surprise you that Henry has been dabbling in Tech since he was a boy. I was his tutor and have inspired him to look around and see the corruption of the Church. As for the Plague, you will both take medicines to ensure that you'll not be contagious. You can only take these for a short while as they appear to be very bad for your heart., You will have to come back within a month. I hope to contact Mallory to see what I can do to help him get Astrid home. It will take time as we have to move with extreme caution. Please, think about it and let us know this evening at the meeting. Go and spend some time with Marion. She had news about John, and it wasn't good. She will need a friend. I will let her tell you herself."

Sirio got up and opened the door to show Nicholas out, patting him on his shoulder. He felt sorry that he had to spring his plan on the lad, but they had to move faster now. The attack and abduction had thrown a spanner in their plans. It looked like the Prior was beginning to sense there was something brewing, and it wouldn't take long for the man to find out who was behind it. Pendrini had shown his hand by moving John to the ship and keeping William hostage. They had to get to Astrid before he added her to the cards he was holding.

Sirio stretched down on his cot to rest and ponder all the ramifications of the latest developments.

Chapter Forty-five

Astrid was helping the women in the kitchen when she heard excited voices clamouring outside. She glanced at the others who seemed to have noticed the racket as well. They all stopped what they were doing and, as one, agreed to go outside and find out what was going on. They wiped their hands and went outside. A group of villagers were clustered a tall figure calling out questions.

Astrid couldn't see who it was. She did see Mathilda and Mallory coming outside, looking worried. Maybe there was news about Damien. He might have gotten word about them staying with the Dinali, And they would have to flee again. She very much hoped not. They were just recovering from their gruelling flight from the Fort. She hoped Damien would get bored and find something else to occupy his mind. Though Mallory had told them, oceans would dry up before that happened.

"I know no one as vindictive as this man. It's what makes people so afraid to cross him. He would sacrifice everybody and everything to get his vengeance on anyone who dared to disrespect him. I've seen enough examples of it while living in the fort."

Astrid always wondered why Mallory had stayed for such a long time. When they questioned him about his living in the shadow of a man he despised for such a long time, he abruptly changed the subject.

When the crowd parted a bit, she could see Mathilda talking with an exhausted-looking woman carrying an enormous pack on her back. Mallory stood silently beside them. When he looked up, he tapped Mathilda on her shoulder as if to warn her of Astrid's arrival. They both looked at her with great pity in their eyes. Mathilda sent the woman on her way with a few more words and walked up to Astrid with Mallory not far behind.

"We just heard from one of our messengers. Let's go inside to my rooms where it's less noisy as the message concerns your family."

Judging by her serious demeanour, it didn't look to be good news.

Astrid froze, then stumbled, when she tried to follow Mathilda fast as possible. Mallory sat down next to her on a couch beside her in Mathilda's private quarters.

Mathilda, who was already seated, her face looking drawn, spoke: "I will come out with it straight: the night when they took you, your abductors set fires to delay any pursuit. Twenty-two people died as a result. They managed to burn down one of the towers of Harrington house completely. Quite a few were wounded. It is with deep sadness I have to tell you your father and mother were amongst the victims."

Astrid felt all the blood was draining from her body which became numb all over. Her head was spinning. This could not be happening to her. Just when she started to feel hopeful about getting home back with her loved ones. She must have heard wrong. It could not be possible she would never see her parents again. It was all her fault. Jonah told her how they had seen them on the beach that day and found out about the basement entry door. But he never said anything about any fire. He had looked shifty when she asked him about the smoke.

With a trembling voice, Astrid asked:" What about the others? You said quite a few. How many? Who? One of the towers? You mean the rest of my family is alright?"

She was feeling more and more afraid she wouldn't like the answers.

"Dori, the messenger you just saw me talking to, said she heard your brother was hurt badly too and taken to London. She wasn't sure what exactly happened to him. As far as she knows, the others who got hurt were all staying in the only tower that burned down. We don't know their names. She also told us your fiancée, with the help of your grandfather, had taken control of your family's firm for the moment. A fleet has been sent looking for you, but we don't know where they are at the moment."

"You said, messengers. Is there any way I can contact my family through them?"

Astrid felt angry at herself, cowardly running away from the monks. She had the chance to get home so much sooner and didn't take it. Why had she cared so much about what people would say about her? They would be happy to know she was alive. Being forced to become a nun seemed the least of her worries now. She prayed someone was looking after her sister. Nicholas, Marion, what were they doing? Neither had been staying at the House that night. Lily had been in her, Astrid's, bed in the Eastern Tower and hopefully staid there. John must have come back from the Commander's house because he was going to stay in town with Marion. He'd probably been worried about his dogs. The thought of anything horrible happening to those sweet puppies strangely made her realise the enormity of it all. She trembled all over.

Mallory poured her a cup of Tatra, a strong alcoholic drink, and she gratefully took a big sip. It went some way to melt the ice she felt all over her body. She finished the rest in one swallow and looked at Mathilda.

The latter hastened to answer her question: "We can try, but a messenger will never get to the Island and back before you have to leave here. The girls regularly fly down to the desert with their kites and can leave a message with one of the Sinese caravans heading for Reading station. From there, it would go on the next boat to your Island. All in all, it could take a few weeks for an answer to get back to us. I can't give you that time. Why don't you write your message down anyway? We will send it with the messenger. At least it will let your people know you are still alive."

Mallory leant over to take Astrid's hand, looking

worried.

"Why don't you do that, my dear? Maybe we can depart a bit sooner? That would make it easier not only for you but you too, Mathilda. Half of the Dinali wants us gone anyway. Less hassle for your family."

Mathilda nodded, but with her voice trembling, wondered: "Do you think that would be wise? You will still have to worry about Damien looking for revenge. The longer you stay here, the better. You will have to take the western route. He has less power along that coast, and your chance of reaching Upavon will be considerably higher. Don't worry about my people. I can take care of them. After hearing about Astrid's terrible loss, they will feel more predisposed to let you stay here for a few more days. They are decent people but often let fear rule their hearts. Dear girl, could you find it in your heart to stay the three days we agreed on, so I will have a better chance of persuading Mattie to stay with us."

Astrid, having just lost her dear ones, felt how important it was for Mathilda. She had heard from Mallory about his conversation with Mattie that morning.

She had followed Mallory upstairs, her face looking like a thunder cloud. The decision of the council had not been to her liking. Mallory had sat her down and tried to explain, "Right, I understand you want to have some say about what's going to happen to you when we leave here," holding up his hand when he saw that Mattie immediately wanted to say something," Wait. I have not finished yet. You know I've always looked out for you since Damien brought you to me. You were so small but still managed to survive for weeks on your own. It took me a long time to make you speak to me, let alone trust me. I've tried to raise you to be a good human being. Not easy in that place. If you stay here, I will miss you very much, but I will never forget you. I think you are fortunate to have found your kin. Now you will have the opportunity to grow up to become the beautiful and decent woman I know you can be. Your grandmother is respected here. Life will be better for you than it has been before, and you will never want for anything.

     Most importantly, you will be safe. I can't offer you any of that on the road ahead of us. Jonah and I need to get Astrid home, which will make this trip very dangerous and our lives uncertain. I sometimes fear none of us will come out of this alive. Knowing you to be safe will make it much easier for me to keep going. I don't care much about saving my own skin, but the thought of one day having to choose between your safety or that of Astrid or Jonah makes me sick. Please don't think you have to decide now what you want to do. We have three days before our welcome runs out. I was hoping you could do me a favour and join your cousins. Try to get to know them and your grandmother, aunt and uncle a bit better. These people love you very much too. They have suffered a lot in the past years, not knowing where you were or what had happened to you. Can you at least give it a try? I promise before we leave, we will have another talk, and you can tell me if you still want to come with us. If you do, I will not stop you."

During his speech, Mattie's face had relaxed, her body slumping. When he had finished, she had given him a big hug and promised she would do what he asked.

"But if I want to come, you'll let me, won't you?"

She still hadn't been sure, though she wanted to believe him.

He had answered, "Definitely. I've never lied to you and am not going to start now. Go and see if you can find your friends while I will let your grandmother know what we have discussed. I hope I can convince her you are mature enough to make this decision for yourself."

Astrid felt that to delay going home by even one minute, nearly impossible. At the same time, she understood Mathilda's fear of being robbed of her grandchild again. You only realise what family means to you after you have lost them. Mathilda had lived so long, believing she would never see her son and his family again. If they all left now, she risked losing her granddaughter all over again.

Astrid looked at Mallory, torn between asking him to leave as soon as possible or, which would be the kind and sensible thing to do, agreeing to delay their departure for at least one or two more days to give Mattie a chance to find out what she meant to these people.

His voice was gentle when he spoke: "Child, I know you're hurting and would like nothing more than to go home straight away and be with the rest of your family. We do have to get provisions together, and, as Mathilda says, we can't take a direct route to Reading Station from here. Damien's watchdogs will be watching it. We have constantly been travelling and still have a long way to go. One more day should not make a big difference to us but would mean the world to Mathilda, who has been so good to us."

Feeling exhausted, the alcohol stopping her thinking clearly, Astrid slumped back against the couch. It was all too much at the moment. She felt sick again. The room seemed to be closing in on her. She did not have the willpower to resist anymore.

"I guess we can stay a bit longer. I would like to be alone now, please. I need to think. I don't feel very well and want to lie down for a bit."

"That sounds like a good plan. Shall we wake you when dinner is ready, dear?" the old woman sounded relieved.

Feeling she would never be able to eat anything ever, Astrid declined. She needed solitude.

Mallory and Mathilda got up and went downstairs. Probably to discuss the news that everyone would've heard of by now.

She went back to the room they had stayed in the night before. Throwing herself on the bed, she sobbed with her head buried in the pillows. The kidnapping had been a shock. When Solo had hurt her, she felt destroyed. Finding out her eyesight would never be the same again, and the desperate flight from that evil man nearly had finished her. Still, she had always been able to go on not giving in to the despair she felt at times. The hope of returning home and seeing her family again had always kept her from completely falling apart. But this. It was as if the last drop of her courage was draining away with her tears.

Memories of her parents and the love they had always showed her were flooding her mind. They had such a good time the evening before it happened. Her father, proud that she had been so graceful in accepting his decision and her mother, so happy to see her daughter marrying a good man. Whatever she had wanted to do, they had always been there to give her advice and keep her safe. She had been such a silly girl moping around because Nicholas turned her down. That all seemed so childish now. At least her Dadi was in charge at home. He would take good care of her little sister. Henry was supporting him so the firm would be in capable hands. After what happened with Solo, she could forget ever marrying him or anyone else for that matter. Oh, Lady. They always say, 'beware what you wish for, and she had passionately wished her marriage not to take place? What about Nicholas? He would keep looking for her no matter what had happened between them. She was sure of it. If only she had taken her chances with the monks while she was at the fort.

And Jonah. Had he known about the fires? Was that why he had been so kind to her? He told her down by the lake he had stayed with the boat. Was that the truth, or had he just been trying to cover his part in the raid? People had been right all along. All Midlanders were scum. Why should she believe him? Mallory should never have agreed to take him along. He might betray them and side with his sister.

Astrid turned her wet pillow around and put her head down again. She wondered if she would be able to sleep with all those thoughts making her head spin. Eventually, she did fall into a deep, troubled sleep, not waking when the others crept in many hours later.

Chapter Forty-six

The morning after their fight with Damien's henchmen, Yaya woke up, her body aching all over. She hated to think how Solo must be feeling. She saw he was still asleep. His face was ashen, and he moaned when he tried to turn over. Covering him with her blanket, she went to find the herbs she needed to tend to his wounds before he woke up.

The bandages she had put on last night had stemmed the worst of the blood flow, but she was worried when she saw the one on his leg saturated with blood. She needed to change that dressing as soon as possible.

She walked silently away from their camp. The loud birdsong on this early, bright morning sounded so cheerful. It made her smile despite her worries. It was so different from the screeching of the sea birds in West Drayton.

Yaya didn't have to walk far before she heard the sound of running water. It was like music to her ears. She pushed through some undergrowth, following the bubbling melody. A tiny stream was struggling to make its way through the forest. Around its border, she saw an explosion of beautiful colours. The day suddenly felt so much better. Her trained eye soon found the Blue Flag Water Iris, good for reducing inflammation, waving gaily in the breeze. And there were some Lotus flowers which her mother told her could stop any kind of bleeding. This place was a treasure trove for any medicine woman. Her mother would love this place.

Yaya felt her throat closing at the thought her mother might never enjoy a place like this again. They must go back as soon as Solo was able to walk again. The uncertainty was killing her.

She should try to take him to this place. It would be much easier to fix him up with all these herbs and running water within reach. She had better get back. Solo might think she had left him there and gone home without him. He trusted other people as he trusted himself.

Gathering as many herbs as she could hold in her pack and filling the water bottles she had brought, she set off back to see to her mate feeling slightly more optimistic.

Solo was awake and unsuccessfully trying to get on his feet, muttering to himself. He looked up, his face relaxing a bit. Yaya knew he would never admit it, but he must have been worried if she would return. He was not used to people staying around when the going got rough. She knelt at his side and gently pushed him down again.

"How are you feeling? Don't try to get up yet. It will just reopen that wound in your leg. I'll make some crutches after I've prepared a new bandage. I found this great place quite close by having all we need to get you up and going again. First, I'll make us some hot tea with these herbs I found."

Proudly she pulled them out of her bag.

"Going to try and poison me now?" he tried to

look as if he wasn't hurting like a bitch. Knowing him better than he knew himself, she laughed.

"Come on. You know, as well as I do, my mother knows all about healing. Count yourself lucky she thought it would be a good idea to teach me. I don't know as much as her, but she was adamant that it would come in handy one day if I had at least some knowledge about treating injuries. Now relax while I boil some water. I'll need it to soak off the bandage I put on yesterday. I won't touch the smaller cuts in your arm and face as they seem superficial. That Kentish beast must have been off his game yesterday. Encountering one of those madmen usually makes you end up looking like minced meat. If you're planning to walk any far distance, you must rest that leg for a few days and ensure there'll be no infection. We all know what gangrene can do. Do I have to remind you of David?"

Solo, who had started to open his mouth to complain, closed it again. His friend had taken a long time to die, and the end had been horrible. They'd been out on their boat when one of the tackles got caught in his thigh. David never had a chance as they had been too far from shore to get him to her mother on time. They tried amputation, but being on a small boat without the right medicines, Solo had had to watch his friend die in agony.

Satisfied she had scared the shit out of him so he would listen, Yaya set about making a fire and treating his wounds. She offered Solo one of the pies, but he wasn't hungry.

She told him to try to eat it anyway because he needed his strength to make it to the brook.

Using the crutch Yaya had made him and leaning heavily on her, Solo slowly made it to the bank of the creek. He lay down, exhausted from that little walk. Leaving him to rest, Yaya went back to the corpses of the men they slew yesterday and stripped them of anything useful. The coolness of the forest had prevented them from starting to smell too badly. Still, she covered her face with her scarf. Flies were having a feast, and judging by the gaping sockets, so had the birds. They were too heavy to move them on her own, so she covered them with branches and mulch leaving nature to do its work to make them disappear.

By the time Yaya had finished, she was sweating profusely. The generously filled packs of food from the fort they had been carrying at least freed her from having to waste time hunting for a while. She doubted she would be able to convince Solo to stay for longer than two days.

"What did you bring?" he stretched his hands out to her haul.

Happy to let it keep him busy for a while, she dropped her prize next to him and set off immediately. Before they continued their trip, she wanted to collect as many herbs as she could. Seeing Solo looking disgusted at the bloody shirts she had taken off the men, she explained: "They will make good bandages after I have rinsed them out and dried them. Knowing you'll want to walk far too soon, we'll need plenty of those."

"You got that damn right. I don't want to leave here later than tomorrow morning. You'll be glad to hear I've decided to go home. Jonah and his buddies are too far ahead of us now to catch up with them. And by what happened to us yesterday, Damien wants us dead. Our village is gone. You were right. We must find out who survived and then leave. Eric never had a chance if they caught him in the village. I still hope, though, he might have been on one of his freaky wanderings in the marshes when it happened. If he's still alive, he will be so scared. Fuck knows what could happen to him."

Solo looked up at Yaya, his eyes wide with worry. For the first time since she had known him, he looked afraid. The bond with his older brother was the only thing that told her Solo could love somebody else besides himself. His parents perished during a shipwreck before the shore of Diggers Peninsula not far from their village. They had been set adrift in an unseaworthy vessel from an Islander ship. The Midlander fishermen who rescued the two brothers still talked about seeing this Solo swimming with all his might with his much bigger brother clinging to his back.

Yaya always felt Solo had hooked up with her because Eric had taken such a shine to her. The man-child followed her like a puppy. She had come to love the gentle giant too. It was as if all goodness in the world had gone into Eric, leaving very little for his brother.

Her feelings for Solo always had been ambiguous. When they were alone and in a good mood, he could be fun to be with. To his brother, he was generous and loving to a fault. To other people, herself included, he could be surly, always suspicious someone was trying to cheat him. When he had been drinking, his rages made most people fear him and would be the main reason she would leave him despite the attraction she felt.

Until now, she needed the protection he offered her and her family. Besides, the sex was fantastic. Her body flushed, just thinking about it.

Seeing how frightened he was for his brother, she tried to make him understand that they could not leave straight away. "We'll have to wait and see. I think tomorrow will be far too soon. You have to try to keep off that leg for at least a few days longer, or else you will be of no use to anyone. It will give me time to collect more herbs before we set off. I'm glad you changed your mind about going home. It's the right decision if you ask me. We can always decide what to do about the situation with Damien and Jonah when we get there and have more information."

Before she left him, Yaya helped Solo to a bush to relieve himself. When he came back to his bedroll, his face was a mask of pain. He stretched his body on the soft moss and was soon asleep again. Even this short walk and their conversation had worn him out completely. It would be a miracle if he would be well enough to travel tomorrow. They would be here for quite a while longer.

        She would use the time to decide what to do about her brother. With a sigh, she marched off to go and collect the plants she needed.

Chapter Forty-seven

Astrid wasn't sure what caused her to wake up. Next to her, Mattie lay curled up like a kitten, only her hair sticking out from under the covers. The familiar sound of Mallory's snoring gave her a few precious moments of thinking that everything was normal.

Then, all that had happened the day before hit her anew like a sledgehammer. She inhaled sharply. Was it true?? Or had it just been a nightmare? Her eyes, sore from crying, and the pain she felt in her whole body, belied that. She had never known grief would hurt physically. She dragged herself from the bed, careful not to disturb Mattie or the others.

She looked outside and saw it was pitch dark. The ashes in the hearth were still glowing a bit. She would go down to the kitchen and make herself a cup of tea. Her mouth felt parched. It would be nice to sit quietly by the fire downstairs to contemplate what she wanted to do.

She remembered promising Mathilda and Mallory to stay a bit longer and didn't think she could do it. Everything inside her screamed to get home as soon as possible. She craved to be amongst her own people. She replayed her conversation with Jonah the evening before, and a terrible bitterness came over her.

I'm such a gullible idiot. He must have known

about the fires. He was there. The others must have talked about it on the way back. I smelt the smoke when they carried me out. He must've seen something while they were getting away. You can see the towers of Harrington House from miles away. I never want to be anywhere near him again. Let him go back to his murdering people. To think, I started to believe he wanted to help me and liked me. He's probably just waiting until he's gained my trust to lead me in some kind of trap. He must have wanted to prevent the monks from finding us at the Fort. Damien is probably in on it and ordered him to keep us away for a good while until everyone assumed I was dead. Then he would sell me to the highest bidder without the Prior being any the wiser. And what about Mallory? Was he in on it too?

The more she thought about it, the more she felt she had to get away as soon as possible. She could trust no one.

Astrid collected her clothes and felt her way to the door. Stepping through it, she spotted the Midland map on a table next to the couch Mallory was sleeping on. Remembering his words, she grabbed it and tucked it into her tunic.

Downstairs she found the kitchen empty, but the fire in the grate gave enough light to search for some food to take with her. She hurriedly put the rest of her clothes on. Their bags lay piled in a heap in one corner of the kitchen. She picked up her own and found someone had put some clean clothes in it, probably Margie. She felt like a criminal sneaking away like a thief in the night. Thinking about how she was repaying the kindness of that good woman and her family, she felt ashamed. But she had no choice, did she?

She pulled on the coat Mathilda had given her and carefully opened the front door in the hall. Before stepping outside, she looked around the square to see if someone was watching the house. But the place lay silent and completely deserted in front of her. Her guards must have thought that after all the trouble Mathilda went through to let Mallory and his group stay a few days, none of her guests would try and leave earlier than they had to.

She took the stairs to the jetty two at a time, not hindered by the dark night. She vaguely remembered seeing a small sailboat tied at the very end of it. Despite the ice-cold wind, her fear of being caught made her sweat. She heaved a sigh of relief. There it was, a grey shape bobbing lightly on the dark water. It looked similar to her boat at home. She would have no problems managing it on the calm lake. She got in and, in no time had it rigged it up before sailing away from the village.

Astrid soon put a fair distance between her and the shore, taking advantage of the constant wind coming from the east. She had no clue where she was heading as it was too dark to take the map out, but the wind blew her west, and that was where she intended to go. Hopefully, it would take the Dinali a while before they discovered her gone and came after her.

Lady, she had to pee like mad. She had wanted to

go the moment she woke, but it would have been too risky to spend precious minutes going to the bathroom before she left. Her bladder felt like bursting. Tying the sail to the rudder, she felt around the bilge and found the bucket every boat had on board if it needed baling. It would have to do for now.

Feeling much relieved, Astrid was overwhelmed by an incredible feeling of freedom. Being here on this beautiful lake all on her own felt like bliss. Sailing had always been her escape from reality, just like swimming. Handling the ropes and the sail all felt familiar and nearly made her forget why she was there. But not for long. The wind and the cold radiating from the freezing lake conspired to make her shiver. She huddled deeper into the lovely warm coat she had taken from the house.

After what felt like hours, the dark was dissipating, and though the sun was still behind the mountains, it became light enough to see she had sailed far enough away from the village that she could see hardly see it anymore. Good. That meant they could not see her either. The light also brought the realisation of what she had done. If they caught her now, it would mean certain death. With a slight pang of remorse, she thought about the others. Her departure could mean their death penalty. She might have lost them the little bit of goodwill Mathilda had got them with the Dinali.

Too late to worry about that now. She was sure they could look after themselves. Mallory could talk his way out of any trouble, and Jonah deserved anything he got. Being one of their own and a child to boot, Mattie would be spared from any repercussions her flight would have. She trusted Mathilda to make sure of that.

A sound like soft thunder shook her out of her reverie. There was now enough light to see she was heading straight to a cloud of mist. A steady current was fighting the wind, keeping her boat nearly stationary. She opened her bag and looked at the map. Oh shit. It showed her she was heading for a colossal waterfall called the Clearwater Falls. She must have come further than she thought and was sailing straight for it.

Getting a bit closer, she could see a wall of water tumbling down from hundreds of metres above her. If she kept on this course, the torrents of water would shatter her boat to smithereens.

In one instinctive move, she tacked around sharply and let the now ever more powerful growing stream take her rapidly to the left bank of the lake. She would have to abandon the boat here for the Dinali to find. Giving it up so soon would mean a much longer track through steep mountainous terrain on foot to reach her goal, the Silver River. There should be somewhere to cross it to the other side, after which she should be safe to continue without being followed.

While sailing, Astrid had decided to take the longer, but safer route via Midland's east coast like Mallory had shown her. Her first instinct had been to head the other way as it would be shorter, but even if she didn't know if she could trust Mallory, she did believe him when he said the chance of being recaptured would be less by travelling east. He had planned to take them to a small town called Sinatown and get help from an old friend to get them to a harbour on the south coast safely. That option was not open to her now. She would have to make her own way. She had enough food with her for a few days. After that, she would have to rely on the goodwill of the people she met on her way. She might even get someone to take a message to a travelling monk.

Her boat bumped against the bank knocking her nearly from her bench. She stretched her stiff limbs and jumped ashore, making sure to keep holding the line attached to the front.

She tied the boat to one of the trees hanging over the water. Someone might find it and return it. She did not want to prove the Dinali right in thinking they were a group of scoundrels who stole their possessions.

She shrugged her backpack higher on her shoulders and started the next part of her journey, the steep track over the Dark Towers.

Chapter Forty-eight

Jonah felt like he had been sucking a dead animal. Fuck. That Dinali booze was strong stuff. He had needed it after hearing the news from Harrington House. Mallory had told him how devastated Astrid was and had stopped him from going to her.

"I don't think you are her favourite person at the moment. It will not help keep her to her decision to stay here a few more days."

Mallory had confirmed that Astrid had agreed to remain with the Dinaly for the entire three days they were allowed to stay so Mathilda could work on Mattie in the hope the girl would want to stay with her family.

Jonah got up to get himself a cup of water. In passing, he looked at the bed they had given up to the girls and noticed Astrid's side empty. She must have gotten up already after going to bed so early last night. She would be downstairs having something to eat.

He hoped she had slept a bit after the terrible news she had to process. Life had not been kind to her lately. He better leave her to herself. Maybe he could have a look at Mallory's map downstairs somewhere, where he wouldn't disturb her.

Jonah felt for the map beside Mallory's bed. Strange, it wasn't there. Maybe he left it under his clothes? He went to the chair where he had seen the doctor throw his clothes but found nothing there either. It could be downstairs in Mallory's bag. The doctor might have started packing last night. Jonah rapidly got dressed and, in his hurry, toppled a stool against one of the couches. Mallory shot up. Mattie was sticking her head up out of the bedclothes.

"What are you doing?" their mentor said.

"Sorry. I am just getting dressed to go downstairs. Astrid has gone down, and I think she took your map. Did one of you take it?"

They both looked a bit confused and shook their heads.

"Why do you think she took it downstairs?"

Jonah, who had felt Astrid's grief and despair profoundly and had been willing to leave with her the next day if she only asked him, started to feel worried. He was wide awake now. Mallory had started to get up as well. Mattie was already tugging on her clothes.

The doctor tried to calm everyone down: "Let's not start to think the worst. I will go downstairs and check on Astrid. She must have been hungry, missing the evening meal and is probably eating a very early breakfast. I don't want to wake the whole house up. Just in case she did a runner, get dressed but stay in this room. I will let you know if I find her."

He was saying aloud what the other two were already thinking.

"You think Astrid left us behind? What would happen if she did? Shouldn't we all go downstairs and see where she is?" Mattie sounded very young.

Jonah tried to think of an explanation, "She was devastated by her parents 'death and wanted to go home as soon as possible. She promised your grandmother last night she was willing to wait a few days before leaving. She might have changed her mind when she woke up this morning and thought about it again. I do hope she didn't."

Mallory was beginning to have some doubts, too.

"Maybe you're right. Mattie, Jonah and I will both go downstairs. If Astrid, on an impulse, has decided to leave, we can't stay around either. The Dinali would kill us without giving it a second thought. But Mattie, they would never harm you. I beg you to go back to bed and pretend you never saw or heard us. You would be safe with your family."

"No. You are my only real family. My parents are gone. I don't know these people. I don't like them if they want to hurt you."

Mattie's voice wobbled.

Jonah felt they were wasting time while they could be on their way, saving Astrid from herself. His gut was telling him she had left them. He didn't know if she knew how to survive on her own in these rugged mountains. "Mallory, I could go and check on Astrid. You could stay here with Mattie."

"That is not an option, Jonah. The Dinali would

make me pay for our breach of promise. Please, Mattie. Are you sure?"

Jonah knew they did not have much time before someone would find them gone and raise the alarm. He hoped they had all got it wrong, and he would find Astrid quietly sitting in the kitchen having some tea.

All three collected their belongings and tiptoed downstairs. One look into the empty, cold kitchen told them what they feared had happened. Astrid was gone.

"Let's pack what food we can and leave straight away. Astrid must have taken my map, but I know how we can get out of the valley undetected."

"We need to get our weapons," Jonah whispered," Do you have any idea where they put them?"

Mattie put her hand up, saying softly, "I know. They are in a chest in the pantry. I'll get them."

Before he could stop her, she shot away and, a few minutes later, returned, triumphantly clutching all their armour. Just as they were about to leave, Margie came out of the back. The poor woman eyes stared at them when she saw them all dressed to go. She did not make a sound, just stood there frozen. Mattie ran to her and threw her arms around her aunt's waist.

"Please, Aunt Margie, we have to go. I do love you and my grandmother, but our friend Astrid has left so we can't stay here. We need to follow her and protect her. I need to go with Mallory. I love him, and he is the only father I know.

Please, don't call the others, I beg you."

Margie looked at the grown-ups and down at the child. She had come to adore her little niece in the short time she got to know her. The kind woman would have loved to look after the girl, cherish her, and have her be the daughter she never had. She felt her eyes tearing up.

Kissing Mattie on her head while embracing her tightly, she made her decision:" The others will be up in about two hours. Go now. Don't tell me where you're going. Sweetling, I love you too much to have you unhappy. Promise me one thing, though. If you ever get the chance, send us a message to let us know you are safe. We have worried about you for such a long time. Please don't let us have to go through that again. Did you get provisions? I will go and prepare breakfast as I usually do, and I never saw you."

Margie looked at the other two, who nodded and both hugged her before they slipped out of the door as silently as possible.

Mallory didn't take them to the village's outskirts, as they thought he would, but took them up a steep mountain trail behind Mathilda's house. Even though it was still dark, he seemed to know where he was going.

After a lot of scrambling, following a narrow goat path through scraggly trees and bushes, he stopped before a colossal Hawthorne bush. Looking down at the village in the first light of day, he did not see anyone stirring. Margie must have held her word.

He turned to his fellow travellers: "We are going through here, and it will hurt a bit. Try to cover your face and arms as much as possible. It doesn't look like anyone has been here for ages. Hold your pack in front of you when you push through the thorns. We don't want to disturb the bush too much, or people might notice where we went through."

Mallory was last pushing himself past the thorns, following the two young people. After fighting their way through the dense shrub, they had to worm their way through a narrow crevice. Mattie made it through first. Her small body a better fit for the narrow fissure. They emerged in a small cave from where a low tunnel made its way deeper into the mountain. It was pitch dark. Mallory's voice sounded a bit breathless.

"There won't be a lot of space in some places, and we can't make a light yet. Just follow me and make sure you keep your eyes on the person in front of you."

Mallory had been right. Jonah thought he would be stuck in the darkness forever. He was a strong, stocky lad, and his broad shoulders were scraped raw by the narrow tunnel. After what seemed like an eternity of crawling, half crouching and here and there, thank the Lady, walking upright, the group emerged from the other side of the mountain.

He looked up at a dizzyingly high granite wall forming a natural obstacle to anyone wanting to get to the village. Before him, he saw a narrow river winding its way through the lowlands.

Mallory's chest was heaving from the exertion, and he was clutching his back. He grimaced, massaging his back and shoulders. He pointed down the mountain.

"We will cross the river down there, where it is at its narrowest. We are near the source of the Silver River. It flows to the Cascades. I doubt we will be followed by the Dinali this far from their valley. I fear Astrid went by the lake. She must have gone a few hours before us, and with the winds in her favour, she will have a few hours advantage on any pursuers. If Astrid makes it safely past the falls on the other side of the lake, she will have a good climb before reaching this same river. She will come out a long way further downstream, closer to the Cascades. It will be impossible to cross there. She will have to follow the river south first, which will bring her dangerously close to the Ravines. Have you heard about them?"

Jonah had never heard or read anything about these Ravines. He raised his eyebrows, shaking his head. Mattie, who had never been a great reader at the best of times and found geography lessons always the most boring, shook her head as well.

"While we're having a little breather up here before we descend, I will tell you something about them. During and after the Exodus, many of the people left behind fought each other for arable land. A group called the Military was still in possession of old weapons capable of destroying everything in sight and not afraid to use them. It resulted in a large area of the land imploding and becoming infertile. Now it is a desert where nothing much grows. But that is not the only problem. Hiding under the rocks and sand are deep ravines. No one can cross that area without either dying from poisonous fumes or being in danger of plunging to the bottom of mile-deep crevices."

"Where are those Military now?' Mattie suddenly looked very interested. Any mention of fighting or disasters still had a great appeal for her.

"The monks dealt with them. One day they were there, and the next, they had all disappeared. No one but the Order knows what happened to them. I always wondered about it. That information was never given to the monks who were not part of the higher orders. But enough talking. Let's climb down and cross to the other side. Then we can have some food and fill our water bottles. We have a long way to go before we reach Sinatown. It is the only place where we can be safe for the moment. I never thought Astrid would leave us. She must have been so desperate. She doesn't strike me as a person who treats people who try to help her so callously. If I had not woken in time, we could have been in a lot of trouble."

Mallory sounded very disappointed and a bit indignant.

Jonah immediately felt he had to defend Astrid. Mallory didn't know what had happened to Astrid in Amersham. It had all been downhill from the moment he told

Solo about the entrance.

"She's been through a lot these last few weeks for a girl who's only ever known an easy life. She can't have been thinking clearly, or she would never have left us."

After that, all deep in their thoughts, none of them spoke.

Chapter Forty-nine

They stripped and put their clothes on a small raft they made from the abundance of driftwood lying on the banks. The water was still freezing. They tried to keep their body out of the water as much as they could. They all helped push the raft across with their legs while fighting to keep it straight against the strong currents.

Jonah saw that Mallory was suffering the worst from the exertion. When they reached the other side, they practically had to drag themselves out of the water.

They were safe from immediate danger, and Mallory told them they could make a small fire. "Let's keep the food packed by Margie for another time. There is enough wildlife around here to provide us with dinner. You two go out to shoot us some dinner while I get some more wood. "

Mattie didn't need much encouragement, and they soon returned with two rabbits, which Mallory skinned, cleaned, and roasted. It tasted amazing after living on dried food.

Pointing a bone dripping with fat at the river, Mallory spoke, "We will get ourselves as quickly as possible down to the Cascades. Let's pray Astrid can join us somewhere close by. It won't take long before The Dinali see that one of their sailboats is missing. They might think she has left with us if Margie kept her word. Thank the Lady they are a people of shepherds and not soldiers. They might be discouraged from wandering too far from their valley, risking exposure of their whole community. We'd better keep our eyes open, just in case I'm wrong."

None of them had much energy left to talk after their exhausting crawl through the mountain, followed by a swim in freezing water. They quietly followed the river on its way further west.

The sun was right above them when a roaring sound became louder and louder. Ever denser vegetation made it harder to navigate their way down. The air was beginning to have a very damp feel to it. Soon a fine spray of mist surrounded them.

The quiet, narrow river they had been travelling along had gradually become a vast expanse of foaming water. Suddenly it seemed to stop in mid-air. Looking left at where the river seemed to have disappeared, Jonah carefully looked over the edge of the path and saw an array of waterfalls dropping vigorously down to a lagoon very far below. It was a breathtaking sight. The water, coming from many rivers like the one they had been travelling along, hurled down with enormous force, spreading over ever-widening terraces, to end up in a pool as vast as a small lake. They could barely hear each other over the deafening sound of all that water eagerly throwing itself down over the rocky ledges.

Mallory motioned him to step away from the edge.

He pointed to a crooked path that led further down and told them it would lead to a lagoon at the bottom of the waterfall. Only when they had reached its shore, Jonah realised how wide it was. He could just about see the other side. Astrid would never be able to cross here. He looked up again and, despite his worries, felt awed by the magnificent sight of the lush, green platforms overflowing from one to the other with all that white-blue water. He sank gratefully onto the soft sand of the beach. The rest followed his example. Mallory told them they would have to keep a lookout for Astrid, and for the eventual event, the Dinali would still be following them.

   Jonah offered to keep the first watch and promised to wake the next person in a few hours. His fear of never seeing Astrid safe and sound again would prevent him from sleeping anyway, as tired as he was.

   Nearly dozing off, he saw movement on the other side of the lagoon. A small, familiar figure that he would have recognised anywhere had appeared on the other side of the lagoon. Rubbing his eyes to make sure he wasn't dreaming, he looked again. He felt a jolt of happiness go through him. It was her, Astrid. Keeping his eyes trained on that dear image, he shouted to the others: "Mallory, Mattie, wake up. It's Astrid. She made it."

   The others shot up. They all stood on their little beach, waving their arms and jumping up and down, trying to get Astrid to notice them. They saw her jumping in and heading towards them, clinging to a tree branch. Behind her, they noticed a small band of people streaming onto the beach. The Dinali had followed, after all.

"I wonder why she keeps standing there?" Mattie wondered.

"Maybe she's too tired or too afraid to cross here. She must've been going all day" Mallory sounded very worried. Hearing this, Jonah stripped off his clothes. He threw himself into the freezing water and began to swim faster than he ever had in his life. He would have crossed oceans to save Astrid and be with her again. She could hate him all she liked, but he just needed to speak to her at least one more time to explain.

Chapter Fifty

Astrid had been continuously climbing uphill. After what seemed like forever, her legs trembling, she had arrived on a small plateau near the top of the mountain. With the sun already high up in the sky, she was dripping with sweat. She stopped for a moment to take most of her clothes off, stuffing them into her pack.

She was relieved the flies had finally given up on her. She scanned her surroundings and could see the lake she had left that morning far below. To her shock, she spotted a band of Dinali arriving in a large canoe on the shore just where she had left her boat. She saw them pointing at it and then up to the mountain. They must have found her tracks. She had not done much to hide them feeling too tired and under pressure to get away from the lake as fast as she could. Her pursuers started up the same track she had been climbing the last few hours.

On her other side, she saw a steep rock face with the tiniest hint of a path, more of a goat trail, carving its way down to a river. It seemed to be flowing west. She took out Mallory's map and traced it as a narrow river running west towards yet another waterfall. She had no choice but to follow the path in that direction. It might be easier to lose the Dinali there if she could find a good place to cross. She was at a disadvantage of staying ahead of them for much longer as they were used to these mountains and had a good night's sleep while she was dead on her feet. Despite her tiredness, she picked up her pace and hurriedly scrambled down the narrow path.

As a child, she loved to climb. Walls, trees, and vertical cliffs, nothing could scare her. It took her only half the time it had taken her to get up the mountain to get herself down it.

Reaching the river and seeing she was not far from the falls, Astrid saw to her horror that swimming across at this point would be impossible. She had not reckoned with the enormous speed the water was hurtling along pulled forwards by the waterfall.

One glance up the path behind her was enough to see the Dinali were already beginning their descent. They must have spotted her too, as she could hear them shouting and see them pointing at her.

She had to get herself to the other side. The only way she could see was to clamber down beside the waterfall to see if she could cross further down the river. Looking back again, she saw the men were already halfway down, and her fear gave her strength to make a final effort to escape them. More falling than walking, she hurtled down the path beside the thunderous falls to find herself at last at the shore of a vast lagoon foaming with the multitude of rivers pouring down in it from various heights. The water looked very turbulent, and the distance to the other side enormous.

With a sinking feeling, she realised she

didn't have enough energy left to swim across. She had to decide. She didn't know if she would make it to the other side, but she had no choice. The men already gaining on her, it was too late to try and outrun them. The Lady thank her brother for teaching her to be a strong swimmer.

From far too close, she heard the excited voices of the men hunting her. Frantically looking around, she spotted a sturdy branch of driftwood. She dragged the wood closer to the water, and with a hefty push, managed to get it in. She had to cling to her raft for dear life in order not to let it go as the pull downstream by the masses of water plunging into the lagoon felt like she was pushed downriver by a giant monster. In a few seconds, the torrents swept her away from the beach and, thankfully, from the men following her. She started to furiously push the trunk with her legs towards the other shore.

The foaming water made a bubble around her head, making it nearly impossible to breathe. She prayed it would hide her from the men. The wet backpack weighed like a ton of bricks, but she had had no time to undo the straps. Despairing if she would ever have the strength to reach the other shore, Astrid felt something punch her back. They were shooting at her. Her backpack had saved her. She tried to push harder with her legs but felt herself grow weaker. Lack of sleep, the exhausting climb and the ice-cold water were all starting to take their toll.

'Mum, Dad, I might be seeing you soon, after all,"

was her last thought as she felt herself slipping away from the log, her arms and legs feeling like lead. She closed her eyes and let go. It felt strangely peaceful.

"Astrid. Hold on. I'll tie you to me." never was she happier to hear the sound of his voice. Vaguely she remembered there was a reason she shouldn't be, but the feel of a pair of strong arms holding her up and pulling her along away from danger made it all irrelevant. She passed out.

Chapter Fifty-one

When Astrid opened her eyes, it was to find three pairs of them staring down at her with a mixture of wonder and worry.

"Welcome back, my dear" Mallory's smile was beaming at her.

Hearing that voice and seeing his kind face made tears come to her eyes. What had she been thinking, leaving them, her only friends in this land, behind? The shock of finding out about the horrible events at home must have driven her momentarily insane. She had only been able to think about getting home as soon as possible. She felt ashamed of having put her friends, who had already done so much for her, in danger. And here they were saving her again.

"How long have I been out?"

"Not very long. Why don't you try to sit up, so we can get you out of those wet clothes? Your things are still wet, but some of Jonah's stuff will fit you. Then you should have something warm to drink. You must be cold. You'll be happy to hear the Dinali men gave up and seemed to have disappeared. For good, I hope."

It was as if a weight lifted from her shoulders. She looked up at the doctor, who did not sound angry at all.

"Are you not mad at me? I only left because I thought they wouldn't harm you after the council had spoken. I just wasn't thinking, I..," here, Mallory put his hand on her arm.

"All three of us realise what a shock the news about your parents and the other people must have been for you. Let's not waste time looking back. We have to concentrate now on getting you home safely. Maybe not as fast as you want," here he smiled and winked at her, "but we will get you there in the end. Now eat this while I can have a look at that map that you have been keeping safe for me."

Feeling a little ashamed by their forgiveness, she first opened her backpack and took everything out to let it dry in the sun. Wordlessly she handed the tube that contained Mallory's map to him.

It appeared not to have suffered much, but, to her dismay, there were several small holes in the tube and the map. They must be from the arrows puncturing her pack while she was swimming away.

"Saved by a map. That must be a first. Don't worry, Astrid, it is still perfectly readable," Mallory laughed, taking it out of her hands and spreading it out on the sand.

"Lucky it is a plestik one. The old ones worshipped this stuff as it is waterproof and lasts forever. Later they found it had some nasty side effects. They got rid of most of it when they found out. You can still find pottery, utensils and even clothes made of the stuff. We used them in the fort."

"But isn't that forbidden?"

Astrid had finished her meal and looked more

alert.

"I am afraid that differs from where you live. Life here in Midland is a lot harder than on your beautiful isle. We use whatever we can find. For some reason, the monks leave it to Damien to make Midland keep to the law. They don't seem to care how he does it or how strict he is. As long as no one stops them from doing what they are here for. In my opinion, the Church made a pact with a monster. I know all about it as I had to do the same when they evicted me from the Order."

Mallory looked around at the surprised faces of his little band.

"Yes, my friends, one day I will tell you how that came about, but then I want to start at the beginning. I'm afraid we just don't have the time. We should be past the Ravines and sheltering in the forest before nightfall. We still have Damien to worry about. Let's pack up and get going. Astrid, are you up to it? We won't have to walk so fast if we leave now. But first, go and put those dry clothes on before you catch something."

Astrid assured him she was ready and keen to be on her way again. The fear of being caught by the Dinali had not left her just yet. She accepted the clothes Jonah handed her, thanking him with a smile.

Their route took them via a small stand of trees into a very desolate area. A yellow-brown, smelly smoke hung in the air making their eyes water.

"Sulphur," Mallory said, "the wars raging here in

the past have left the earth crust very brittle, resulting in cracks going down further than we can fathom. Right at the bottom, there seems to be a permanent fire raging. We don't know what causes it to keep burning over all that time, but we do know that inhaling the smoke for too long can make you very ill."

None of them needed much encouragement to pick up their pace. Covering their faces with scarves, the travellers practically ran for the green line of trees and shrubs beckoning them in the distance.

The unpolluted air and the welcome shade of the forest was a relief. Everyone seemed to pick up their pace. Feeling Jonah's eyes pricking in her back, Astrid turned to give him an intense stare upon which he dropped down on his knee, pretending to remove a pebble from his shoe.

She knew he had saved her yet again, but she still found it hard to forgive him for having been part of the men who destroyed her home and killed her loved ones. How did one ever get over that? Maybe he had not been lying when he told her he had no part in the arson and the following disaster. She would like to believe it.

She felt a strong attraction to that brave and kind-hearted boy. His strong features surrounded by a mane of tawny hair, going riot in every which way, had become dear to her in ways she could not explain. When he smiled, his bright blue eyes sparkled with mischief, making you want to smile back. All her life, she thought she could only love Nicholas. After all that had happened, she now realised she had been a silly girl in love with being in love. She thought of Jonah's strong arms carrying her on land twice, first when they landed at Amersham and secondly when he saved her from certain death in the lake by the falls. He had made her feel so safe despite the dangers everywhere. She shivered, thinking back at that moment when she had been ready to let go and sink to oblivion.

"Are you cold? Would you like my coat? I'm too warm anyway" Jonah touched her arm, practically begging her to let him do something for her. She relented and shrugged his coat on. It was one of the beautiful woollen ones Mathilda had given them. Sadly, she had to leave hers behind on the shore of the lagoon. His smelt of sweat and grass and was still warm from his body. It did give her the same feeling of comfort as when he was holding her in his arms. She blushed.

"Thanks," she mumbled, not looking at him and walked briskly to the front to join Mattie, who, as per usual, was more skipping than walking in front of them.

The woods were far less dense than the ones in the north, and there was enough light coming through the trees during the day to give grasses and a multitude of bushes the chance to thrive. Mattie had a wonderful time collecting fresh berries and stuffing her mouth as full as she could. She had been running ahead of them and back again like a young puppy, covering more than twice the distance the others did. Her exuberance lifted everyone's spirits to the point they all sang along with her when Mattie started to belt out an utterly inappropriate tavern song.

When night fell, they made camp and ate some of the food Margie had provided them with. After, Astrid was happy to join Mattie beside the fire to get some long-awaited sleep.

She felt safe with Mallory keeping watch. "I'm an old man. We don't sleep a lot anyway. You three better get your beauty sleep."

Soon the campsite was quiet except for the rustle and small sounds of a forest at night-time.

Astrid woke from the low rumble of voices. She froze but then realised it was Mallory talking to Jonah, who must have gotten up to relieve him from his watch.

She heard Mallory say, "Give it time, my boy, she will come round." "Do you think she'll ever believe I had nothing to do with kidnapping her? Or was even aware of Solo planning it?" Jonah sounded so despondent.

"Just keep looking out for her as you've been doing all along, and I'm certain if you give her enough time, she will realise you always have her best interest at heart. Even if that could one day mean letting her go," Mallory answered. She heard Jonah sighing and heard Mallory lying down. She lifted her head and saw the light of the fire throwing shadows on Jonah's face. He was looking into the glowing embers as if he would find all the answers in there. Had he been telling the truth to Mallory? The doctor seemed to believe him. Maybe it was time for her to do the same.

Chapter Fifty-two

It had taken three days before Solo was ready to travel. He was the worst patient ever. Yaya was glad when she could declare the wound in his leg healed enough to walk on it. Thank the Lady, Solo mended so fast, or she would have finished where the scimitar wielding fiend had left off.

They stayed off the beaten track as much as possible to avoid meeting anyone who could report to the fort they were still alive. Many people would be happy to turn them in as there was no doubt a fair sum of money on their heads. The last thing Damien would expect them to do was to return home. He must know there wasn't much left of their village. But she was damned sure he had everyone still keeping an eye out for them as well as for Jonah and his friends. Hell had no fury like a Damien thwarted.

After carefully skirting around Amersham, they felt a bit more at ease when they reached Diggers Peninsula. Most people here were not very fond of the Monster in the North, as they called Damien. Having lived in Diggers all their lives, they knew every little hidden trail to get to their destination unseen.

Solo, having the constitution of an ox, was walking with greater ease each day. The herbs and his innate strength had done the trick. When he lay with her at night, he seemed not just to seek physical relief. Yaya doubted this behaviour would last. It was nice while it did, though.

Close to their village, they could smell it. The onslaught had happened nearly two weeks ago, but the smell of smoke and ashes was still everywhere. Unwilling to have their fears confirmed too soon, they walked ever slower. Yaya grabbed Solo's hand when she first laid eyes on what the Islanders had done to her home. She gasped and clutched her throat. All around them, they could see nothing but the black skeletons of the yurts and the burnt trees and shrubs. And there, in the middle of it all, was the pile of horrifying remains from what used to be their community.

Scraping all her courage together, Yaya walked slowly through the devastation, only one thought playing through her mind. Who could have possibly survived this?

She heard Solo say something but was too taken in by the sight to make out what he said. Stepping closer and shaking her arm, he repeated, "I just found something or better did not find something."

She looked at him, tears in her eyes, wondering what the idiot had found to grin about.

"What? Besides that, it's all gone?"

"It is gone. I buried all my savings, and it is gone."

"Have you gone mad? They are all dead, and you are talking about your money? Don't you even care that Eric is gone?." Yaya's voice trembled.

"I do, but I think, no, I know, he survived."

"What are you on about?"

Yaya gaped at Solo, feeling herself becoming worried. Maybe his grief over Eric had removed his sanity.

"No, I didn't lose my mind, woman. I buried my savings, and only Eric knew where to find it. I told him to take it in case something happened."

Yaya didn't dare to hope but felt herself breathing more freely.

Solo explained, "If they got away, there is only one place he could have gone to be safe. You would know it too if you think about it."

His eyes shining, Solo willed her to come to the same conclusion he had. He was waiting for her to confirm his hope. Yaya swallowed, her throat feeling dry.

"Wakeware?" she whispered.

"Yeah, I know what you're going to say. We never mixed with those freaks, but even Damien, let alone those fucking islanders, would risk trying to travel through their domain. Besides, no one knows how to get through those bogs."

"So, how would Eric know?"

She had no idea why Solo thought Eric could have made that dangerous trip. The boy was sweet but could barely look after himself. Solo's fever must have come back after looking at all the ravages around them. He was talking nonsense.

Solo grabbed her impatiently by her arms, "Eric used to wander off all the time and never wanted to tell me where he went. So, one day I stayed at home without him knowing and followed him. He went to the edge of the Bog and started to whistle like some bird. He did it a few times, every time waiting for a bit. When I was about to go and get him to tell him off for going to such a dangerous place, this person appeared covered in grey rags. They were talking and laughing. Eric followed it right into the Bog. Before I could call him back, they were gone. I had to wait nearly the whole day before Eric came back. I was very angry with him and told him never to go into the swamp again as it was too dangerous. He usually listens to me, but this time, Eric told me he would do what he wanted as Tish was his friend. She made the swamp safe for him. He tried to explain to me that those swampers, he called them Bunyip, are nice. They didn't treat him like an abomination, like he wasn't normal. I had to let it go and was glad he had come to no harm. Somehow, I don't know how. He must have gotten away taking my bag. He must have remembered the swamp was safe for him. There could be others with him."

It started to dawn on Yaya why Solo looked so relieved. He hoped that Eric had used his connection with the swamp people to get himself to safety. She worried he was clutching on straws, but she felt a bit of hope creeping up.

"Let's go and try to get to Wakeware then. There is nothing here for us. Do you really think there could be more who have survived? Can you remember how to do that call?"

Yaya was bursting with renewed energy, thinking of the possibility her mother and other friends might have made it out. "Let me look at your wound and try to cover it with something to stop water getting in. Those bogs are poisonous, I heard."Solo was so excited he hardly sat still long enough for her to change his bandages. His leg wound seemed to be healing at an extraordinary speed.

They reached the edge of the Bog of Wakeware, a vast area filled with rust-red water and the stunted growth of the trees and bushes, draped with strings of yellow moss. It smelt like an open sewer. There was a rumour amongst the Midlanders that the people of the remote fishing village of Wakeware were scary-looking monsters. They were the only ones who knew how to travel over the small islets and narrow footpaths crisscrossing this dismal land.

Solo stopped right where the murky water started. "Here is where I found him that time. Let's hope they keep an eye on their borders."

He formed a funnel of his hands and let out a long hard ululating call. It rang out across the still waters and seemed to reverberate against the trees surrounding them. A deafening silence met it. They waited. Nothing stirred.

"What do we do now?" Yaya said when there was no reaction whatsoever after a few more calls.

"Now we wait some more." Solo sat down and

started to root in his bag for his water bottle.

Yaya did not feel comfortable being so exposed so close to the edge of the swamp. She made sure she had her bow within easy reach and leaned against a large green willow tree, which looked rather out of place between its deformed bald relatives.

The sound of loud splashing ruptured the silence. Solo stood up, staring in the direction where it came from. A familiar yell of delight rang out. There was Eric, his face split by the happiest smile ever, running at them with his arms spread wide. He was followed more sedately by a slight figure covered from head to toe in orange drapes. Only her eyes were visible, peeking above a strange contraption masking nearly all her face. She was holding a similar one, which Eric, in his joy, had ripped off his face.

The brothers embraced each other, laughing with such joy that Yaya felt a smile coming on her face. Before she knew it, Eric was wrapping his big arms around her neck as well, giving her loud smacks on her cheeks. He kept saying her name with each kiss. Solo, tears rolling down his cheeks, looked enormously relieved. Yaya, yet again, understood how deep his feelings for his brother, this big man child, went.

The girl accompanying Eric had been silent all the while watching them closely. When Eric let go of Solo and Yaya, she spoke, her voice sounding a bit muffled behind her mask.

"Welcome, siblings of our friend Eric. My name is Tish from the Bunyip clan."

Looking at Solo, she went on, "You are Eric's little brother, no? You look very big to me."

Eric, looking at her with complete devotion, shouted, "And this is Yaya, his girlfriend and my best friend too." Suddenly, he seemed very nervous, looking away from Yaya. He pulled at his brother's arm, bringing his mouth close to his ear whispering something in it. Yaya saw Solo's body stiffen.

He stepped in front of her, gripping her arms so tight it hurt, saying without any preamble: "I better tell it to you straight. Your mother didn't make it out of the village. Eric just told me only he, Wulf, Freya and a few others managed to survive, as they were not at home during the attack. Eric, Wulf and Freya were gathering berries in the forest. The others were fishing. Those fuckers have a lot to answer for."

Yaya was trying her utmost to hold it together screams striving to escape her mouth. She knew if she started, she would never be able to stop. She felt a tiny hand creep under her arm. Small as she was, the little woman managed to hold her up when she finally crumpled like a wet piece of paper.

The first time she heard about the destruction of her village, she was devastated. Though in the back of her mind, a little voice had kept saying, maybe mum made it? Listening to Solo, she had stupidly dared to hope again. Now, her worst fear was confirmed. Her mother was gone. Thinking of Jonah having to hear this devastating news while he was amongst strangers, she decided there and then, she had to be the one to tell him. It was that thought that kept her from completely falling apart and made her stand up.

All the while, the swamp girl held her tight, cooing soft words in a strange dialect. It felt strangely comforting. Gathering herself, Yaya gently removed the girl's hands and straightened her shoulders. She would find Jonah. That is what she would live for now. Nothing and nobody would stop her. Her new purpose gave her the strength to push all her grief deep inside her. Now wasn't the time to mourn her mother. She had work to do, find her brother and keep him safe.

The girl called Tish spoke softly to Eric, sounding quite urgent. The latter stood close to his brother, holding on to his hand looking worriedly at Yaya. He told his brother that Tish said they had to follow her if they wanted to cross the bog before high tide made it impassable.

Tish nodded, and Eric added: "A lot of the paths will be underwater soon. We'll have to hurry. We brought you some masks to wear. I have been coming here every day to wait for you. I knew you would come back. Just like you always do."

"I'll never leave you, big brother. What do I always say?"

"I'll always come for you no matter the cost," Eric proudly recited.

Solo clapped him on his back. "Now, let's follow your friend Tish."

The girl had already taken the masks out of her sack and helped them adjust the straps. She set a quick pace, clearly very worried about the tide cutting them off from her village.

Yaya felt Eric large hand taking hold of her own. "It will be alright, Yaya," he said. He must feel how the news had broken her and was trying to comfort her. It gave her the will to go on.

Chapter Fifty-three

After crossing the swamp, Tish and her charges reached a mangrove forest. The sea was not far away as they could hear the screams of seagulls and roaring of the surf. The air had taken on a briny smell, which was a significant improvement to the bog's putrid smell. It was a relief to get away from the swarms of hungry mosquitoes becoming more and more of a nuisance the higher the sun rose.

Their masks had not done a lot to stop the stink filling their noses and throats. By the time they got out of the marsh, Yaya and Solo were both coughing, tears streaming down their faces. Eric and the girl were not affected by the inhospitality of the terrain breathing the clean air from their tanks. Yaya understood now why no one in their right mind ever tried to cross this marsh on their own. Without Tish's guidance, they would never have made it.

Solo just kept slapping his arms and face and complaining about having to cross a fucking swamp to get eaten alive by those bloody mosquitoes. He had already forgotten how lucky he was to have found his brother alive. Not to mention a safe place to hide from Damien.

Tish and Eric stopped when they reached the white sands of a beach.

Yaya gratefully removed the sweaty mask and,

with great gulps, breathed in the clean sea air. Swamp dwellers, all wrapped from head to toe in multicoloured rags, flocked around them. It was impossible to make out if they were men or women. Even the tinier figures, which Yaya assumed to be children, were all covered with swathes of material in various shades of red and orange. It was like standing in a field of rusty marigolds.

She saw Tish searching the crowd of onlookers. Then, seeming to find who she was looking for, she waved to a tall figure making his way towards them. Telling them to wait, Tish went up to the man and started talking to him, now and then looking and pointing at Yaya and Solo. The tall, dignified looking man, who seemed to be in charge, approached and addressed the new arrivals in halting Midlands.

"Welcome to our Bunyip community, brother and friend of Eric. My name is Pinnodh, the community eldest. I'm sorry Tish and Eric had to bring you such sad news. Losing one of your family is one of the heaviest burdens to bear. May their way to the next life be easy. Grief shared is grief halved, so maybe it would be best if we head back to our village to reunite you with your other friends. They have been anxiously waiting for you and praying for your safe return. Our friend Eric here never doubted his brother would return to him. He's been keeping his vigil at our border every day since he arrived. We are very happy for him that his faith has been rewarded. Stay with your fellow countrymen at our village guest house as long as you need. We hardly ever get guests nowadays but have not forgotten how to treat them."

Yaya was lost for words. Why had Eric not told her there were more survivors? Solo must have had the same thought because his hand gripped his brother's arm, shaking him a little.

Instead of looking guilty, Eric just laughed loudly, clapping his hands. "Do you like my surprise?"

He looked so proud. They didn't have the heart to tell him off. And it was great to hear more of their village had gotten away. When they asked Eric, he refused to say who they were, saying, "Surprise, surprise".

The Bunyip had been listening as if understanding every word they heard. Later Yaya would find out all had to learn Universal in the hope of being accepted again by the other Midlanders one day.

Following their leader and his guests, the crowd trooped to a large village house, looming high over the beach. It was held up by bamboo poles and built out of palm leaves and grass

Word must have reached the people who had stayed behind to expect guests as she saw villagers busy setting out a meal in the shade under the building. Cocos mats and colourful pillows lay scattered around the cool sand.

Pinnodh motioned Yaya and Solo to sit down on either side of him. The others sat down in a circle, pretending not to be looking at them and failing miserably. The glimmering of multiple pairs of eyes was visible between their face coverings.

"Apology for the staring," Pinnodh said, glaring around him, "They hardly ever see outsiders. And now, two new ones following the first lot in such a short time has made them forget their manners. Please help yourself with the food. You must be hungry after your track over here. When you finish, I hope you will regale us with the stories of your travels. We love tales about the outside. We don't get to hear them very often. Most people are so frightened of us they either want to kill us or drive us away."

He sounded more or less resigned to it.

Yaya saw some of the little ones starting to unwrap their veils. A short, abrupt command from Pinnodh in their language was enough to stop them.

Pinnodh looked at Eric, "Will your companions be fine to see our faces?"

Before Eric could answer, two familiar figures appeared under the canopy of the house. Yaya, enveloped by the soft, warm arms of Freya, felt her grief overwhelming her again. She hid her face in the ample bosom of the woman, who had been her mother's best friend and a second mum to her children.

"My sweet girl," Freya said, stroking her hair as if she was a small child, "Your mother was the bravest and loveliest woman I will ever know. Hearing of her passing broke my heart. The Islanders caught her trying to save some of the children, the bastards. But so typical of her to try. I'm happy you and your brother were away when they came. No one understands why the Islanders went this far. We heard you and your friends took one of their children, but it isn't the first time we seized one of them. We always returned them. Never before did they slaughter a whole village for that reason. Since Damien took over, something must have changed. Solo, do you know why the islanders came to West Drayton instead of dealing with the Fort? You took her there, Didn't you. Did Damien or her priest not alert the Prior?"

Solo had the decency to look ashamed, knowing quite well he'd been the instigator of all their grief. He and his scouts had started this whole sorry sequence of events. Setting the fires might not have been his idea, but making sure they did as much damage as they did, had. Abducting the Harrington girl must have added to the fury of the Islanders. He pretended not to have heard Freya's question.

Wulf glared at Solo and quietly shook his head as if to warn him not to say anything about that night. Yaya didn't think he cared what his mother thought about Solo, but he probably didn't want Freya to know that it had been her brother's idea to use fire as their diversion tactic. It had resulted in many deaths and, in the end, the Islanders' revenge.

His eyes on Yaya but addressing Solo, Wulf now spoke: "Do you two know where the boy is? And the girl? Your mother told us you went to the White Fort to hand her over to Damien.."

Solo, shifting uncomfortably on his pillow, answered before Yaya could say anything.

"We lost Harrington's brat in the Fort. Some old guy, who used to be a monk, decided it would be a great idea to escape taking her with him. I don't understand why she didn't wait for her people to pay the ransom. He would've returned her to her island, and everything would have been fine. Damien never got the chance. She was gone by the time the intermediaries from the monastery reached the White Fort. Damien, blaming us, sent us after them to bring them back. He didn't want anyone else to find out. Afterwards, he must have thought Yaya and I were in some way involved in their escape. We had to kill the cut-throats he sent after us. Now we can't stay in Midland anymore. You know what Damien is like. He would make us all suffer."

A gasp of alarm went through his listeners. A storm of whispers erupted until Pinnodh held up his hand, and they all went quiet again. Even amongst this remote tribe, the fear of Damien was so ingrained the sheer mention of doing something so undoubtedly sure to incur his wrath was enough to shock every one of them.

Starting to fear the worst, Wulf asked: "What does this have to do with the boy? Why did he not stay with you two? Where is he? Has Damien still got him? Yaya, you wouldn't be here if you knew he was in trouble. Please tell me he didn't do anything stupid?"

Yaya, who had managed to pull herself together, wiped her wet face. Her eyes flashing, she nearly shouted at Wulf: "You of all people should know I would never in a million years leave my brother behind. No, you are right. He did something stupid like deciding to be the hero of the day and save the girl. He went with the monk and the Harrington brat. We don't know where they are, but the last thing we know is that they went into the Dark Towers. And as to calling him Boy, he did manage to get himself named before he ran off. His name is Jonah."

Looking from one to the other, Freya gave a delighted whoop of joy, ignoring the first part of the story.

"Your father's name. Yaya, my girl, your dear mother, would have been so happy to hear that. She missed your father so much. If only she could be here with us." Her voice started to tremble.

When she saw how much her mother's death had touched Freya, Yaya went on in a much quieter voice, "Jonah and his friends have taken the long way around the Westcoast. They probably hope that Damien will find something else to be outraged about in the time it will take them to reach a southern harbour. Fat chance, I'd say. Still, by the end of the day, they will have to find a harbour. The girl will want to return to her island, and there are no harbours in the west. Jonah will not be able to go to the Island with her. Her people never allow outsiders on their island, let alone be friends with one of their daughters. Everyone who doesn't come from their bloody Tree is not better than an animal in their eyes. No, if he's clever, he will try to get to London. He always wanted to go there, and Damien has no influence there. I am going to find him before he makes the crossing to keep him safe. He is all I have left." Yaya looked at Solo to see if he would offer to come along.

He stopped eating for a moment to growl, "I'm not going to waste any more of my time on those idiots. I've already made an enemy out of the most powerful man in Midland. I've saved enough to pay for our fare to London. Eric, did you go to our secret place to get our things before you ran away, as I always taught you? I saw they were gone."

Eric dug in his backpack and proudly produced a dirty bag covered in mud. He handed it to his brother, who patted him on the head and looked inside. Solo smiled at seeing the content and clapped his brother on the back.

"Eric, we're going to London."

Turning to the others: "I have to take Eric to London to see a doctor. We have been waiting too long already. Freya, do you and Wulf want to join us? If need be, I'll lend you the money. You can pay me back later. There is enough work for anyone who wants to make a living in London. Yaya, it will be better if you stay with us instead of going on some wild goose chase for Jonah. Midland is too dangerous for us at the moment. We can be sure he will get himself there on his own if he is as clever as you always say."

Before Yaya could answer, Wulf interrupted her.

"Yaya, if you want to go and find Jonah, I will join you if you let me. I can help you track down your brother. He might need both our help getting out of Midland. We can take him to London as long as Solo will promise to keep my mother safe until I come back."

Solo's face nearly went purple, the veins standing out on his forehead.

Yaya, who had already made up her mind to go and find her brother, was glad to have someone else supporting her. Ignoring Solo's dark looks, staring her lover straight in the eye, she said: "I'll be happy for you to join me, Wulf. I will not be sitting around waiting for Jonah to come to London when I can do something to make it happen. No one in Midland connects you to any that's happened, but there is a price on Solo's and my head. You could do all the asking around while I can cover your back when needed. I want to leave as soon as possible."

With everyone, even the villagers, waiting for him to try and change her mind, Solo threw his hands up in the air. "If that's what you two want to do, it's fine by me. I don't care if you two want to get yourselves killed for nothing. I'll take Eric and Freya with me to London. I will see you there, but I won't be holding my breath."

He abruptly stood up and walked to the sea to stand there, staring out over its glinting water. He did not look very happy with Yaya's decision.

Chapter Fifty-four

Pinnodh clapped his hands together and got up too. He said a few things in Bunyip. All the villagers got up as one and started to drift away from the meeting. He turned to his guests and promised them he would help them get to London on one condition.

"It would be a great service to me if you could take my granddaughter Tish to London. She's one of the Pura, the untouched. They have to leave our lands for a few years to study in the outside world to become our ambassadors. Most of us can't leave the village and mix with the rest of the Archipelagos people."

He explained that Tish was one of those few exceptions born to their tribe without facial or bodily mutations. "She looks just like everyone else outside Wakeland. She will leave to get an education. We need people like her to communicate with the rest of the Archipelago. Eric accepts us as we are. Others who see our true faces turn away in disgust or fear. In the beginning, we tried to maintain contact with other islands but were only met with hate. Some of us, when caught, were burned alive. They thought we would be contagious."

Pinnodh's eyes looked very sad. Tish, who had been sitting beside Eric, took off her headscarf and veil.

Yaya was stunned to see her uncover a face of

nearly impossible beauty. Tish's eyes commanding her whole face were grey and blue, like the sea behind her. The kindness in them lent her look even more grace. Her lips were full and pink, and her skin was of the palest bronze without even one blemish. She looked at her tattooed arms and, for the first time, felt something like regret.

Wulf could only stare open-mouthed. Lady. The boy was practically drooling. She had to admit to herself, though, Tish looked stunning. However, beauty like that would be a liability for the others hoping to keep a low profile in London. Everyone who saw that face would not easily forget her nor her companions. She would stand out, and you did not want that when you were in hiding.

Pinnodh smiled at their wonder.

"Yes, my friends, the ones who the Curse spared, were given a big blessing. The Pura still cover themselves in public in solidarity with their kin. Outside our borders, it might be a good idea to continue doing this not to attract unwanted attention." He must have read Yaya's mind.

Pinnodh took his head covering off as well. Yaya saw a very handsome older man with even features marred only by an enormous swelling under his chin.

"I am one of the more fortunate amongst my people. Some of us wouldn't be so easy for you to look at. The Bunyip are all lovely, talented human beings, but alas, society judges first on how you look."

Eric, not paying any attention to the conversation until Pinnodh mentioned his wish for Tish to go to London, pulled Freya's arm and kept shouting," Tish must come, Tish, must come." making them all smile.

Wulf encouraged the others to give the village elder his wish. He probably was already planning to get to know Tish better after he found Jonah.

Solo, when he heard Eric shouting, had returned to see what the commotion was about. He grudgingly agreed to take Tish to London. Pinnodh told him he could arrange for them to leave for London the very next day, and he would pay him handsomely to take his granddaughter. Pinnodh added, he would contact one of their traders to make his trip to London a few weeks earlier than planned.

Seeing Solo looking more convinced after this generous offer and not giving him the chance to change his mind, Freya answered for all of them: "We'll be honoured to do you this service. You've been so hospitable and helped us in so many ways. I'm happy to return some of your kindness. I promise to look after Tish as if she were my own daughter."

With Solo not daring to contradict her, Freya told Pinnodh, they would not think of accepting any payment. They would look after Tish and deliver her safely to where ever she needed to be. It was the least they could do.

Pinnodh looked relieved but, to put their minds at rest, added, "The Bunyip have a long-standing arrangement with the Buddhists in London town to accept our children in their academy. You will only have to escort her there. You won't have to carry the responsibility for her safety on your shoulders for long. I insist on paying something for your trouble."

Freya refused again to take any of his money. After that, Pinnodh and his granddaughter left the friends to talk some more and plan their respective journeys.

Chapter Fifty-five

A long day of walking through trees and prickly shrubs brought Astrid and her companions facing a vast grassy plain. On the far side of it, she saw a tall gate flanked by bright red walls stretching as far as she could see.

"We have arrived. That is the gate to Sinatown or Silk town, as some call it. The people who live here have kept the art of producing silk alive. The town is known to be one of the most beautiful in Midland."

Mallory looked as proud as if he built the place himself.

Jonah said that he had never seen silk but had heard of it.

Astrid, forgetting herself for a moment, told them her wedding dress had been of Sinise silk and that it had been the most magnificent stuff she had ever seen and felt.

Mattie immediately bombarded her with questions such as 'who were you going to marry?', 'When were you going to?', which made the rest of them feel rather uncomfortable as it reminded them why the wedding never took place and why she might never get to marry anyone in a silk dress or otherwise.

Astrid knew she had to tell her something to stop all the questions and patiently told her about Henry and that it would have been right before she left her home. She tried not to look at Jonah, who was also studiously looking elsewhere.

Mallory cut in, stopping Mattie from grilling Astrid relentlessly about the event. "I have friends in Sinatown who can help us get to Upavon, where my sister lives. Last I heard of her, she was working as a midwife. It should be no problem to find you a passage home from the harbour there, Astrid. There is no suitable one on this coast as the sea here isn't deep enough for ships to come near. Many obstacles from the time before are still lying hidden underwater. The Sinise transported their silk via the Red River to Upavon to load it onto trader ships. Since Damien has built an ore mine on the river, it is now too hazardous to go that way. The Sinise have started to take the desert route to bring their silk to the markets. My friend will shelter us until we can join their next caravan to Upavon. It will give us some respite from our travelling looking over our shoulder for Damien's men."

To her relief, his words succeeded in drawing his ward's attention away from Astrid.

Mattie started to bombard Mallory now with questions about the Sinise and caravans. He patiently tried to answer them all while marching through the high grasses towards the town's gate.

When they arrived, they saw a colossal portal with its gateposts encircled by the tails of two very lifelike, copper creatures. Mallory called them 'dragons'. They seemed to be guarding the entrance with their fierce look and large fangs. Mallory told them they would have to get off the plains as dusk was falling, and wild creatures would come out as soon as it got dark.

He knocked with his staff on a small door set into the gate. Immediately, they heard a man's voice from above: "Who goes there? The town is closed for today. Come back tomorrow at dawn."

A large smile lighting up his face, Mallory shouted to the invisible guard above: "Hey Cheng, I've been looking forward to finally drinking that wine you owe me from our last chess game. Are you sure you want to let your old friend Mallory stand outside all night to be devoured by the wild things?"

Astrid heard some loud swearing. A few moments later, the door was thrown open, and a short brown figure, his long plait of hair streaming behind him, pelted out to throw himself on Mallory, giving him two big smacks on his cheeks and hugging him fiercely.

"Mall, my dear friend. I never thought I would see you again at this side of the pearly gates. My shift is nearly over. Come and keep me company for the last half hour, and then we'll celebrate."

Spotting Astrid and the others peeking around Mallory, he stopped in his tracks.

"And who are these young lads? You old goat, did you finally manage to convince some poor woman to take you on and give you some children to support you in your old age?"

"My dear Cheng, if you wouldn't be so vain and wear your glasses, you would see I brought two lovely ladies and one nice young man. Fortune has brought them on my path. Let me introduce them."

He pointed at each one of them and told the little man their names.

"But are you going to let us in or not? It's getting dark. I've heard it wouldn't be wise to stay on this plain at night-time. I will explain why we are here while hopefully having a nice warm meal and a drink. Take us to a cheap inn, so we can freshen up before having that drink."

"Don't even think of it. You will all come to my house and be my guests. My wife, Anna, will be delighted to meet you, as will be my son, mmm, daughter. I keep forgetting. Come, I will ask the other guard to finish my watch. Follow me."

Cheng ushered them through the door, taking great care at closing it and securing the entrance with a metal crossbar. He whistled and told the man who appeared he had to go home straight away and would explain tomorrow.

Astrid had not seen Mallory in such high spirits before, as if he had won the lottery. He sounded decades younger, walking in front of them, joking and chatting with his friend.

Cheng was updating Mallory on all his adventures since their paths had split up. He told Mallory how one day, on a visit to his birthplace, he met his wife. They married and had a child, which had kept him here ever since. It had been a good decision. Now, seeing his friend Mallory again made his happiness complete.

"My daughter will be excited to see new people from outside. Especially when she hears one of you comes from the Island," he looked back at Astrid with a broad smile on his face.

"She's been dying to leave our town and see something of the world, but being an only child and her parents not getting any younger, it's been difficult. We expect her to lead the Family company when we are gone."

"Cheng and his family own one of the largest silk farms in Sinatown," Mallory explained.

"The best one," sticking his chest out, Cheng looked proud as a peacock. They all laughed.

During their walk to Cheng's place, they crossed many canals by wooden gangways leading to colourful houses, all with a pier attached. The houses had curved, sloping roofs built from some kind of pipes. Cheng explained the material was called bamboo.

"We use it for everything. It's a light but durable material and easy to use. We don't have many trees here, so it's better than using wood. This whole area used to be a swamp, which our people have partially drained over time. Our forefathers planted lots of Mulberry trees around the larger water holes. We use them to feed our silkworms. Ah, here we are, my friends" Cheng threw open a slightly smaller gate than the one in the main entrance and motioned for them to enter a brightly lit courtyard.

Though it was already dark by now, myriad lanterns showed them a yard full of beautiful flowers and small fruit trees set in multicoloured pots. The fragrance of the blooms reminded them of summer days at home. The welcoming, warm feeling did too.

"Anna, Anna, my love, look who I'm bringing you."

A delicate-looking woman, her jet-black hair done up in elaborate curls and plaits, came hurrying out into the yard. With the introductions done, Anna insisted they should all have a nice warm bath before joining her and her husband for supper. She ushered Mallory and Jonah to the men's bathhouse before leading the girls to a bedroom where she showed them a deep copper bath large enough to fit them both, where they could have a wonderful soak.

Astrid returned to the courtyard, all freshened up and feeling much better. A servant led them to a long porch looking out over the exotic garden. Cheng and his wife were waiting for them while kneeling on large flat pillows at a low table.

Mallory took one look and said: "My dear Cheng and dearest Anna, this old man has been hiking far too long with his worn-out body. If I have to fold myself up for any amount of time, I'll never be able to get up again. Could you please seat me at the horigotatsu? The young ones probably will be fine kneeling. Astrid, you can always join me if I'm wrong."

Their hosts both hid their laughter behind their hands and pointed him to a specific place at the table, where, as he showed the others, there was a hole dug out under the table, where guests could put their legs instead of having to kneel. His young companions took the pillows.

Servants brought out the most delicious Sinise dishes accompanied by a fiery liquid called Berry made from fermented mulberries. Their hosts warned them to mix the drink with water as the wine could make you very drunk, very fast if you were not used to it.

"Some of our people mix the ripe berries with unripe ones to give them good dreams. But don't worry, Anna does not allow that in this house."

Mallory filled the couple in on their adventures and why they had come all this way to find sanctuary. They listened attentively, now and then exclaiming in horror.

Astrid soon felt her head dropping on her chest after eating all the exotic food and drinking the diluted wine. Jonah and Mattie were nodding off too. Anna got up and led them to their quarters, wishing them a good night. Cheng and Mallory were so deep in conversation that they hardly noticed them leaving.

Harbour Cities Midland

Chapter Fifty-six

Mallory told his friend, whom he hadn't seen for such a long time, about the life he had after they had each gone their way. Cheng knew why his friend had to leave the Monastery and had been the one who helped him escape.

"How on earth did you end up with that devil Damien? I know you didn't have many options left but moving into the White Fort seems such a desperate move. You could have fled from Midland altogether and maybe gone further West?"

"I was on my way to do just that when his men caught me. Word had gotten around. I had medical knowledge, so they had been looking for me to take me to Damien. He was suffering from debilitating back pains but didn't want the Prior knowing about them as they would make him look weak. He ordered me to find out what was wrong with him and fix it in exchange for keeping my head. After examining him, I discovered he had kidney stones and was able to cure him. Then he didn't want to let me go, afraid the pains would come back, or he needed me again for something else. On top of that, he was probably worried that word would get out to Luton about his health. When he stopped keeping me under guard all the time, I found a way to get out of that terrible place and was ready to go."

"So why didn't you? You stayed for more than

five years?"

Thinking about how to explain about Mattie, Mallory filled his cup again:" I'm getting quite fond of this Berry stuff and telling a story is thirsty work. Shall I top you up too?"

Cheng declined: "No thanks, you guys can sleep late tomorrow, but our caravan will leave in one week. I have to get up early every day to ensure we have enough stock to fill our orders. Stay with us until the caravan is ready? Now tell me why it took you so long to leave the Fort."

"Well, one night, not long after I was ready to quit that place, one of the kitchen maids woke me up. She told me the men had found a small child who didn't speak and only made strange sounds. Damien wanted to know if she was a mute or just didn't want to talk. He was planning to sell her on, and it would affect her value. The maid took me to the kitchen where, sitting in front of the fire, I found this scruffy, emaciated little kid looking at me with terrified eyes. With her dark skin and white hair, I took her to be a Dinali, so I said something to her in that language. She jumped up and flew at me and held on to my knees for dear life, crying and saying: Dada, Mama. It nearly broke my heart. She must have gotten lost somehow. I asked Damien if I could keep her. In exchange, I promised I would stay put and not try to escape. He knew well I could if I set my mind to it. It is not easy to keep a monk, even a former one, locked up for long. He allowed me to take her under my wing. I sort of made my life there, trying to raise her and keep her out of trouble. The others in the Fort soon saw me as part of the furniture. After I patched some of them up, they grudgingly accepted me as one of them. The little one had to learn that it was a matter of eat or be eaten in that place at a very young age. I did my best to teach her some morals with more or less success. After we fled, we came through the Dark Towers, and I could have returned Mattie to her people. She refused. She has taken quite a shine to Astrid, and the feeling seems to be mutual. I want Mattie to go with her when she returns to her Island. The girl can have a proper education there and live amongst ordinary good people. I will miss the little demon but can't keep her with me forever. Too dangerous for both of us. I hope that Astrid can make them bend the rules a bit for her. As for me, I plan to finish my plan of going west, maybe even as far as Eire."

Mallory stared into the embers of the dying fire, thinking about how different their lives had turned out from the ones they had imagined as trainee science monks in Luton.

They were just about to turn in when the front gate clanged open, and a shadowy figure came walking in, slightly listing to one side. Like most drunk people, she, as it appeared to be a young woman, tried to walk in an exaggerated careful way not to show that she was inebriated, which made her look even worse for wear.

When the latecomer came closer, Cheng shouted: "Li."

It seemed to be Cheng's daughter,

"Oh hello, father, I didn't know you'd still be up. Don't you have an early morning tomorrow?" She was slurring her words slightly. Even though she was trying very hard to seem sober, they could both see and hear she was utterly wasted. The girl burped loudly and then started to giggle.

"Oops. Sorry, master stranger, I think I'm a bit tipsy."

Cheng looked furious but was trying to restrain himself.

"My apologies Mallory. Let me introduce you to my daughter Li, who was supposed to have come home early not to be too tired to help me with the loading and checking of the stock tomorrow. I apologise for her condition. You are lucky, my girl, that we have a guest, my old friend Mallory, or else you would've been in a lot of trouble. For now, just take yourself to bed and sleep it off. I expect you at the factory at first light sobered up one way or the other. If you aren't there on time, you'll not come with me to accompany my friend and his wards to Upavon on the next caravan."

The girl, her good looks not in any way marred by her state of dishevelment, was the spitting image of her mother. She gave a shrill cry and threw herself around her father's neck, not paying any attention to his stern face, which soon melted into a grudging smile.

"Thank you, thank you. I'll be there, I promise. I

always wanted to come with you to Upavon. Finally."

"Don't thank me yet. Make sure you help me this coming week, or you can stay with your mother. At least on the trip, I'll be able to keep an eye on you. There'll be no drinking or drugs if I can help it. You'll get a chance to get to know some young people who've had to learn the hard way that life is not a joke to be wasted away on foolishness. Hopefully, you'll learn something from them."

Li quickly left them with a look of 'parents are such a tedious nuisance' on her face.

"We might have transformed her into a girl, but she still behaves like some irresponsible young buck. Did you forget about our tradition, old friend?" Cheng asked when he saw the puzzled look on Mallory's face.

"No, I didn't forget but didn't think your people still adhere to the old Sinise customs. Is she yours?"

Cheng looked a bit uncomfortable at this direct question. He moved closer to Mallory and said softly: "No one is supposed to know, but she is. When we took her to London for her change, I secretly had her tested. My Anna doesn't know, and she can never know. She wouldn't understand. She prides herself on loving me for who I am and not for being Li's father. Luckily, we had various visitors that week, so in her eyes, the anonymity of the father is safe."

During their time at the academy, Mallory had been a bit surprised upon hearing about the custom of the Sinise, not wanting to know who fathered a child. For them, it was only relevant who its mother was. Later he understood that it all had to do with diversity and to keep the bloodlines healthy. The Sinise community of silk farmers had started with very few, so they had made it a custom that their women would welcome visitors to their bed. Their husbands would accept and love any issue as their very own without needing to know if the child was theirs.

"Did you stay long after I left Luton?" Mallory asked to change the subject.

"No, when you had to leave the Academy, I found the other monks mistrusted me as we were friends, so I decided to leave as well and go home."

Mallory felt guilty hearing his behaviour had ruined not only his career but also the stellar one of his best friend. When he mentioned it, Cheng refused to accept any kind of apology.

"You did me a favour. The way they treated you opened my eyes to what was going on in that place. I did some research and was shocked by what I found. No wonder you left. It is evil what they are doing. Now it is time for these two old fossils to catch some sleep." On this note, he got up and showed Mallory his room, bidding him goodnight.

Chapter Fifty-seven

For the next seven days, Astrid had a chance to recover from her harrowing journey. Once recovered, she joined in with some of the activities of the young Sinise friends of Li.

In the evening, she took part in the games the boisterous youngsters played. A lot of them indulged in copious amounts of Berry and a weird weed called Dama, which seemed to make everyone giggle uncontrollably. Sometimes a few of them would get their instruments out, and the night would end in dancing, singing and flirting.

It felt nice to be young and foolish for a bit though she held back from the drinking and smoking. She was still too afraid to lose control.

Despite her promise to her father, Li had no qualms about joining her friends smoking Dama and always tried to persuade Astrid to try it, telling her how much better it would make her feel.

The evening before their departure, Astrid finally let Li convince her to take a little puff when she saw Jonah showed no inhibition in accepting the pipe when it came around. She had tried to stay away from him as much as she could. He reminded her too much of all that had happened.

At first, she felt no different. She was a bit disappointed as the others seemed to be thoroughly enjoying themselves, rolling about at the most stupid jokes or even for no reason at all. Throwing all caution in the wind, Astrid let Li fill her glass to the brim with Berry and gulped it down. When the Dama pipe came around again, she took a deep draft, nearly choking to the others' great hilarity and felt herself floating away on a cloud of bliss. So this was what Li had been talking about.

Looking at Jonah, who was joking and laughing with some girls, his eyes sparkling, she felt an intense longing to be near him and hold him. Mother, he was gorgeous. Why hadn't she noticed before? He seemed to be a bit worse for wear but in an endearing way that made her smile. She had never seen him laugh so uncontrollably. It made his face light up like a bright fire, and she yearned to warm herself on it. He was sitting far too close to that giggling girl who kept touching his arm and leaning into him, the little hussy.

When she saw Jonah glancing at her over the girl's shoulder, she beckoned him to come over to where she was sitting. He raised his eyebrows but got up and came over without breaking eye contact, which made him nearly trip over a stool and her feel deliciously giddy.

The other boys and girls laughed and called out ribald encouragements, which under normal circumstances, would have made her cringe with embarrassment but now made her laugh out loud. The girl sitting beside her shuffled aside to make room for Jonah, calling Astrid a lucky girl.

He dropped right next to her, putting his arm around her waist and pulled her even closer. She felt a joy she had never experienced before and looked at him as if seeing him anew. He told her he had dreamt of her one day looking at him just like this. At the back of her mind, a small voice tried to warn her she was under the influence of the weed and Berry and had to be careful. She ignored it.

When Astrid gave Jonah a loud kiss on his cheek under the cheering of their new friends, he smiled that beautiful smile. He pulled her to him to return the favour, but she turned her head, so their lips touched. After that, she gave up resisting. How could something that felt so great, so right, be wrong? He pulled her on his lap and kissed her deeply. She answered with the same fervour, and it took some time before they came up for air. They stared at each other surprised at the hunger they felt. Jonah pushed her hair from her face and dug his hands deep into her hair. She put her hands on both sides of his face and kissed it everywhere, all the while murmuring how much she loved him. Everything around them seemed to disappear.

They were rudely interrupted by Cheng barging into the hall, commanding everyone to go to bed while frowning furiously at his daughter, who tried in vain to look sober.

It stopped Jonah and her from taking things further. He gently untangled himself and told her he would walk her to her room. When he pulled her up, she was so unsteady on her feet, he swept her up and carried her outside. She kept kissing him and telling him loudly how much she adored him. He smiled at her and told her he did too.

Jonah put her down in front of her door and, one last time gave her a long kiss before sending her, giggling and wobbling, into her room. Once she lay down, everything was spinning, but she felt better than she had for a long time.

Astrid woke up early the next day, her bladder bursting. Her head felt very strange. She tried to remember what had happened the night before. Her last memory was of drinking that lovely wine and trying to smoke a pipe. After that, everything was hazy. She could vaguely recall Jonah coming over to her and spending time with her. He had probably tried to convince her of his innocence again. She shook her head to try and clear it. A vague memory popped up about her kissing someone.

What did it matter anyway? Today was the day when they finally would be on their way again after a pleasant but slow week. She longed to be able to share her grief with the people who had known and loved her parents. She missed Nicholas, Marion and her little sister. She swallowed a big lump that had formed in her throat. Better not think of that now and just concentrate on getting there.

When she returned from the washroom, she heard a lot of commotion outside her bedroom window. Opening the shutters to peer down, a patchwork of colours greeted her. She listened to the crowd of brightly clad people laughing while working hard, piling huge rolls of silk on a long row of pack animals. The past week she had learned from Li these strange looking creatures were called Lamas.

Amongst them, she saw Cheng walking around ticking off items on a list. Now and then, he turned to his daughter, who was slouching after him. Even from this far, Astrid could see that Li was still a bit wasted from yesterday. The girl barely acknowledged her father's explanations.

Astrid couldn't see Mallory or Jonah down there. Mattie was still hiding under the covers behind her. As she was keen to have an early start, Astrid shook the girl's shoulder.

"Wake up, lazybones."

Mattie just mumbled something and tried to go back to sleep.

Astrid teased her: "Well, I guess you can always stay here. They seem to like girls, and Mallory wants you to be safe."

It got the expected reaction. Without a word, Mattie got up and quickly pulled on her clothes and shoes. She didn't bother to wash. Astrid thought that she would have to have a serious conversation with the girl about personal hygiene one of these days. It had been practically a religion on her Island. At least the girl's clothes were considerably cleaner. She smelt of lavender now instead of a small furry animal.

She stuffed her meagre belongings into her backpack and encouraged Mattie to do the same. Leaving their room, she heard Jonah and Mallory's voices coming from one of the rooms further down the corridor. She knocked a few times and pushed the door open, Mattie slipping around her like an eel, and started to hurry them along.

"When will we be leaving? Are you, guys, ready yet? We have packed our stuff already. Cheng said we would leave very early. Come on, let's go?"

"Yes, yes, we are ready to go too, " Mallory was smiling at the little girl's impatience. "Last night, Cheng told me, we will have breakfast on the road not to waste the early morning cool weather. They trooped downstairs feeling excited to join Cheng and his caravan and be on their way again.

Chapter Fifty-eight

Outside, everyone pretended to be too busy with their tasks to notice them. Staring at people was an insult in Sinatown. Astrid still felt very conspicuous. Except for Mattie, she and her friends looked like giants towering over these short, dark-haired men and women. The easily distractable girl gave a whoop when she saw the lamas and ran off to pet them.

"Ah, my friends, did you have a good sleep last night? Mallory, I see the caravan leader over there. Let's see if we can sort out our defence in the unlikely event we run into any trouble. You have a lot of experience with Damien's men and might be able to give him some tips. Li, you go and help finish the loading. Don't pull that face. It is the least you can do after yesterday's behaviour. Take your new friends with you."

Li, looking a bit embarrassed, bowed to Mallory letting her hair fall over her face. After her father left, she looked up at her travel companions, her eyes twinkling.

" And how are we all feeling today? I hope you made it to your rooms, all right? Or should I say room?"

Astrid tried not to look at Jonah, cringing at Li's assumption they had spent the night together. Other young people arriving in the square called out to Li, saving them from answering the question. They crowded around them, laughing and chattering, looking fresh as if they had never had been up all night partying.

Astrid saw Jonah staring open-mouthed at a delicate little figure, who looked ridiculously beautiful in her multicoloured silk dress, her hair tied up in a very intricate arrangement of loops and plaits, ending in a triumphant ponytail streaming down her back. It was her from last night who had been pawing him all the time.

The girl was twittering like a little bird, seemingly delighted with Jonah's undivided attention and begging him to come back soon. Astrid felt a slight pang of jalousie but reprimanded herself. Why would she care what he did or didn't do? It would be a nice change to have him run after another girl like a puppy dog. She could never return any feelings he had after what happened in Sevenoaks. She pushed the painful memory of her family's catastrophe quickly away. It would never stop hurting. The sooner she went home and put this miserable place behind her, the better. Only a few more days and she would never have to see or think about Jonah again. She would miss Mallory and Mattie.

Astrid looked around and heard the latter, never one to be shy, introducing herself to a few new admirers: "My name is Mattie. My Dinali tribe name is Jones from the Towers. I am nearly thirteen."

Seeing Astrid approaching, she went on:" That is Astrid, my best friend. We're taking her back home, at least as far as the harbour. She is from the Island, from the Gen people. She is a real Harrington. Do you know she was to be married, but that guy over there, Jonah, stole her from under her family's nose?"

She sounded as if she admired the bold deed and took a deep breath to continue.

Jonah, who had been listening too, stepped in and interrupted Mattie's account. He probably didn't want the girl who was still clinging to him like a barnacle to hear about his deeds. "Young lady, these people have a lot to do. Let's not stand in her way and bore them with our stories."

Undeterred by the fact that he might be a kidnapper, maybe even attracted by it, his hanger-on told Jonah she, Shao Mei, would be delighted to be bored by him.

Astrid saw Jonah's face taking on a hot red colour. He stuttered something unintelligible and busied himself with the straps of his pack.

Shao, who seemed to find his shy bumpkin act rather cute, fluttered her eyelashes at him and giggled at the effect she had on him.

"It would be wonderful if you came back after you've delivered your Astrid to her people. I'm already looking forward to it. Why don't we go and see which wagon you're on?"

With a naughty look at Astrid, who, to her surprise, felt annoyed by the exchange, Shao wrapped herself around Jonah's arm and led him in the direction of the caravan. There was not much else for Astrid and Mattie to do but look at their retreating backs.

Then Cheng tapped her shoulder and told her and Mattie to come with him. "You can either sit with Mallory and me or with my daughter and your friend Jonah."

Mattie insisted on riding with Jonah and Li and immediately fell in love with the two lama's that would pull her cart. "What are their names?" Upon hearing, they only had numbers, she, to everyone's amusement, christened them there and then 'Woolly and Puffy, as they look so soft'.

Astrid, ignoring Mattie's plea to sit with her, joined Mallory and Cheng on their wagon. She did not want to be the butt of more jokes about last night.

After everyone and everything was in their rightful place, the caravan leader blew a small horn and the procession of about ten carts, leading a long string of lamas, set on its way.

Soon the cart's swaying and her empty stomach made Astrid feel very queasy. When she told Mallory, he advised her to climb in the back of the wagon to have something to eat. The pungent smell of the sausage meat in the food basket made her nausea worse, so she stuck to the crispy dark brown bread spreading it with honey and accompanying it with fresh apple juice.

She made some sandwiches for the men and reached through the canvas to hand them their breakfast. They made short work of the sausage buns rinsing them away with some light cider. She decided to stay in the back for a while.

Looking out at the cart behind them, she could see Li having an animated conversation with Jonah. He was constantly laughing, his white teeth shining through his beard. Mattie, her head stuck between the two, was sharing in their enjoyment. Astrid could not imagine what they could be talking about that was so funny. Trying to put them out of her mind, she studied her surroundings.

  The caravan was ploughing through a steppe of tall grasses dotted with clumps of bright purple or yellow flowers. Now and then, a startled rabbit and once a fox ran away spooked by the noisy wagons. Though it was lovely to see all the colours of spring, the landscape got a bit monotonous after a while. She lay down amongst the bolts of silk and closed her eyes, nodding off to the gentle swaying of the cart and the soft voices of the men sitting in front.

  After what seemed like only a few minutes, a shout woke her up. Her heart hammering, she sat up and peered around Cheng to find they had arrived at a place with an abundance of green trees and bushes through which she saw the unmistakable crystal glitter of water. She realised they had come to Darkwater Oasis, which did not honour its name at all, lying there all blue and refracted sunlight.

Chapter Fifty-nine

"Darkwater Oasis." Cheng sounded relieved, "Remember, Mallory, when we were here last? When we were still in our prime and beautiful."

"Speak for yourself, old man. I can still attract the ladies." Mallory sounded more carefree than Astrid had ever heard him before.

Spending time with his old friend, sharing stories about their days as disciples at the Monastery, must make him feel young again. It was nice to see this grave, solemn man having such a good time with his friend Cheng like he had no care in the world. One day she hoped she could leave her bad memories behind her and feel that happy and careless again.

She looked back at the wagon stopping behind theirs, feeling a bit more inclined to be friendlier towards Jonah. That was until she saw him swing Li from their cart. The little minx was screaming with laughter and fell against his chest, pretending to have slipped. Jonah put her down, laughing uproariously too. Lady, was he going to start with Li now?

He made his way to where she was sitting. He stretched his hands out, smiling, indicating he wanted to help her down. With a sniff, turning her face away, she ignored his outstretched arms and jumped over the sideboard to stride off with her chin up in the air, nearly falling flat on her face in the process.

Looking back, she saw Mallory and Cheng looking at each other, shaking their heads and overheard them saying, "Young love. I so don't miss all that shit."

They slapped hands and went off to help unhitch the lama's, who were eager to get to the water. After completing the task, they sat down in the shade of a palm tree, smoking their pipes, being quiet as only good friends can be. They would spend the night at the oasis and, the next day, finish the last leg of their journey to Upavon.

Astrid, feeling a bit at a loss, wandered to the edge of the water. She could still enjoy the beautiful vista of the sparkling blue water surrounded by palm trees set against the arid yellow plains behind it. Her home looked very different, all lush green foliage and flowers in every colour, making you happy to be alive. The summers could be hot, but they never became as scorching as early spring was here. She felt sweat forming on her back, making her linen shirt stick to it. It must be impossible to travel here in the summer.

Turning around to see what the others were doing, she saw Jonah coming her way. He just didn't get it, did he? She wanted nothing to do with him. Let him go back to that ridiculous person in Sinatown or Li.

Ignoring her scowling face, he said: "Hey, Astrid. We were wondering if you wanted to join us. Li has brought her playing cards, but we need a fourth person for the game she wants to teach us."

His friendly blue-grey eyes looking directly into hers made her feel so strange. If it were not for the thing with the fire, she knew she could easily fall in love with him. It felt more real than her love for Nicholas had been. That had been a girlish infatuation, and she now understood why her parents had been so sure she would grow out of it. She was aware Jonah had feelings for her and would do everything for her if she asked. It would be so much easier if she could forget his part in the tragedy that had happened after they took her.

Astrid knew she should not blame him for the abduction and following assault by Solo. She still did, though there was that niggling thought telling her she was just as guilty. Maybe more than him. Suppose she hadn't gone to the beach and been so careless to leave the basement door open. Perhaps none of it would have happened. Jonah had just taken the opportunity she had handed to him. It was all he knew.

She sighed and relaxed her shoulders, realising how tense she had been the last few hours. Trying to hate someone you felt so attracted to was exhausting. Seeing her waver, Jonah tried another approach.

"I understand you don't want to be with me, but please don't punish Mattie. She had nothing to do with it all. She adores you."

Astrid's eyes strayed to the other two trying to pretend they were not eavesdropping. Mattie, with her sharp ears hearing her name mentioned, gave up all pretence and waved enthusiastically, shouting: "Come on, Astrid. We are waiting. You can play with me against them. Please?"

Astrid waved back and turned to Jonah. "Alright, then. Just to make Mattie happy, I will do one game." She swept past him to join Mattie and Li, with Jonah following her, careful not to show the smile on his face.

After Li explained the game of Sheng Ji, as she called it, Astrid soon started having fun trying to outwit the other pair, assisted by a boisterous Mattie who kept hugging her every time they won a hand. Life at the Fort had given the child cunning beyond her years. She used her impressive memory skills to help Astrid wipe the floor with Li and Jonah. There were many calls about 'that is cheating' and 'you can't be serious.'

When Cheng came to tell them their meal was ready, he found four young people simply having fun together. Astrid seemed to have rediscovered some of her joy of the last week. He ushered them to the campfire, where the others were already tearing into the roasted hares one of the guards had shot. Mallory looked up at his friend, who winked at him, pointing his chin at the kids, as they called them. Mallory answered with a hearty thumbs up.

By the time they finished the meal, it had gotten dark. The bumpy track through the steppes in the wooden carts, combined with the food and a cup, only one this time, of the fiery Berry, helped Astrid fall asleep the moment she lay down her head. Her last thoughts were of home. She felt much better tonight, getting ever closer to her goal. That was all that counted in the end. She would try to forget everything and make an effort to get her life back on the rails.

Chapter Sixty

Jonah looked at Astrid lying on the other side of the fire and, seeing her face relax into sleep, felt overwhelmed by such tenderness and hopelessness he had to swallow back his tears. He wished their trip would take another month instead of one more day. He was sure he could win her over if only he had more time. Being a born optimist, he tried to figure out how he could keep in contact with her, maybe even visit her one day, after she left. He felt that she was coming around. Holding that hopeful thought, he drifted off to sleep too. It was still dark when the caravan leader blew his horn to pack up and get back on their wagons. The last sounds had just died away when Jonah heard the man shout something unintelligible. He was pointing to where a cloud of dust was becoming ever larger.

Cheng had just sat down on the driver's seat. He swore loudly.

"We've got company. It could be Damien's men. They come from the Mining camp on the Red River. Damn, we have taken this desert route in the hope of steering clear from them. Let me do the talking. I have dealt with them before."

He ordered the rest of his crew to form a half-circle with the wagons behind him. The lake and its dense surrounding shrubs would protect their backs. All the drivers, men and women, checked their weapons and formed up behind him. It looked like they had done this before.

"Mallory, it might be a good idea if you and your charges make sure they can't see you. Damien has a long reach. Word about your escape might have reached even this far south. The sum of money he has put on your heads might be more than whatever deal I can come up with and encourage them to attack us anyway to search the wagons."

Mallory, who had taken out his sword and strapped on some knives for good measure, saw the sense of this. He ushered Astrid and Mattie to stay with Li out of sight behind the wagons loaded with the bales of silk. He told them he and Jonah were going to hide in the one nearest Cheng.

Astrid looked petrified and made no objections. She meekly let Li lead her to the furthest side of the caravan.

Mattie, however, her cheeks blazing, looked at Mallory as if he had lost his mind.

"I want to fight. I don't want to hide. I'm not scared. I've got my knives. We will look like cowards letting others do our fighting for us."

Mallory squatted down in front of her and explained what Cheng had said.

"You will be much more useful looking after Astrid. She is not used to this and will need you beside her for protection. Jonah has to stay with me, so it will be up to you to make sure she is safe. We will try not to get involved but might have to help Cheng if he can't reason with those guys. You won't be far away. Let's first see if Cheng can talk them down.

He has done this trip many times before and knows these men."

"Alright. But if those bastards come near us, I am allowed to use my knives, won't I?"

In the past, Mallory had made her promise never to stab anyone again unless her life depended on it. He had done this when, after a few mishaps at the fort, she was nearly hanged. She had, albeit grudgingly, agreed to this rule.

"You have my permission. However, the safest thing will be not to show yourselves at all. If everything fails and you see we cannot hold them off, you have to promise me to get Astrid out of here to Upavon. Take her to my sister. You do remember her name, don't you?"

She nodded. Mallory had told her stories about his sister when she couldn't sleep at night. She had loved to hear about the pranks the twins would get up to when they were children.

"Plaxedes will take care of Astrid and you. Take this bracelet. She will recognise it and help you get Astrid home. She made one for each of us when we were children. Now go and look after Astrid."

She must have realised the urgency of his request and shot off to do his bidding.

Mallory crawled into the wagon with Jonah following behind. They both hunkered down behind the canvas flap of the wagons, sweat rolling down their faces. The hot sun and acute tension made him feel like he was slowly being roasted in a small oven. They both laid their weapons within hand reach. With a sinking feeling Jonah saw the cloud of dust turning into a band of ferocious-looking men riding their horses as if possessed. Mallory cursed.

"Shit. That doesn't look to me like men come to barter. Let's hope Cheng's plan works, and they will settle for a bribe. We won't stand much of a chance against these wild animals if we have to fight."

"Do you know who these guys are then?"

"Not personally. But I do know the men slaving away in Damien's mines are some of the worst criminals in Midland, even the Archipelago. Their guards are only slightly better. Midlanders, who in any way threaten Damien's position, are sent to the mines to dig for iron ore. What is little known is that the monks send all who break their laws to Damien's penal camps too. This particular mine lies under a live volcano. No one working there lasts longer than a few years because of the atrocious conditions and appalling treatment."

"I knew about those mines. But I never thought the Church would send people from the other islands there as well."

Jonah didn't get the chance to give it much more thought. The raiders had arrived. He saw Cheng fearlessly stepping forward, looking every part of a leader. When he spoke, his voice was calm and firm.

"Greetings, what can I do for you, gentlemen?"

One of the men, a massive brute with so many

tattoos on his body there was barely any skin visible and enough metal pierced through his body to make him clang like a drawer of cutlery, snorted loudly. He smirked, looking at his men adorned in much the same way, circling his finger beside his head to show them what he thought of the little man facing them without fear.

"Ha. You can stop right there, little imp. The only thing you will do for us is hand over all that beautiful silk you've got there and your women. Don't bother to unload the silk from those fine animals. We'll take them as well. If you're lucky and don't make a fuss, we'll let the rest of you keep their lives."

His men started to move forward.

Cheng held up his hands, still trying to do his best to avert a fight.

"We, Sinise traders, have an agreement with Damien. We pay our taxes, and he leaves us to get on with our business. He won't be pleased when he hears one of his men breaking our deal" Cheng kept his voice low and steady.

The mountain of a man spit on the ground, barely missing Cheng, and laughed with his men joining in.

"Damien? He can go and fuck himself, the little fairy. It is time someone takes him and his girly girls down. Midland needs a real man as a leader."

He banged his chest as if to make sure they all understood who that leader should be.

Mallory sighed, and Jonah saw Cheng do the same. He knew why as he felt the same. Why did strong men always have to be so stupid? Everyone with a single brain cell knew Damien was where he was because he had the Monastery's full support, or at least the Prior's. The large number of raiders and the state they were in was starting to worry him.

Cheng must have decided to give it one last shot and try to educate these mongrels. Jonah didn't think it would change their minds.

"Why do you think Damien and his family have been in charge for so long? Have you ever heard of anyone challenging them and coming out as a winner or even alive? Hell, quite a few of your prisoners know what I'm talking about."

Cheng's speech didn't have the effect he hoped it would. The men in front of him started to laugh even harder as if he'd just told them a great joke. Their leader was grinning.

Jonah saw Cheng giving the secret hand signal for his men to cover him. The time for negotiations was over, and they all readied their weapons.

The big man spoke again.

"I do know what you're talking about. I am one of those prisoners, and so are all of my friends here." Seeing a look of horror appearing on Cheng's face, he continued: "I see you're starting to get it, little mouse. Better step aside and tell your crew to do the same. We're not unreasonable people. We'll take your caravan and have some fun with those little ladies I see over there and then let you go home with your head still on your shoulders."

Mallory whispered to Jonah:" Prison uprising. Not the first time. These sad cretins don't know that when Damien hears of it and he will, he will get help from the Prior and annihilate these fools. Get ready to fight, boy. These men are too stupid or too desperate to reason with."

Cheng seemed to have gotten to the same conclusion and let out a long shrill whistle using the volley of arrows his people rained on the raiders to jump behind the barricade.

Practically all the arrows met their targets, bodies dropping of their horses like sacks of dead meat. It stirred up the rest of the band like they had stuck their hand in a wasp's nest. The attackers were all on horseback, giving them a longer reach and adding the strength of the horses to theirs, but they were emaciated from a life in the mines. Harsh physical labour and abuse at the hands of their wardens had sucked all their strength and humanity from them. They knew that failing to get their price would mean certain death. They fought with the power of desperation.

Mallory and Jonah, jumping from the wagon after the first volley of the arrows, stood shoulder to shoulder with Cheng. They ceaselessly chopped and hacked their way through wave after wave of miners.

Jonah felt all his training flowing back into his muscles. He fought like a killing machine. Never losing his footing, he slaughtered so many of their attackers, he could barely see through the blood covering his face. His body, painted red, his mane of hair radiating from his face, made him look like a demon from ancient hell.

It was an uneven fight. The Sinise gave as good as they got, using skill and speed to overcome their far larger opponents. But the battle was weighed against them. They were starting to go down at an alarming rate.

Mallory made a decision.

"Cheng, leave this to Jonah and me. Go and get as many of your people out as you can. Your lamas are strong enough to take you through the bushes around the Oasis. Take Astrid and Mattie with you. We will hold them off as long as we can to give you enough time."

He looked at Jonah, who nodded as if to say, I hear you and will stay.

Cheng hesitated, but Mallory managed to give him a shove towards the animals at the same time taking down the next person unlucky enough to come within reach of his sword. With a last look of despair, Cheng ran to the back of the caravan, soon followed by the rest of his people.

"Boy, are you with me?" Mallory shouted.

For an answer, Jonah stuck his sword in the throat

of a tall, lumbering monster, who'd been one of the cronies of the big man. Mallory grinned, his teeth looking very white in his blood-covered face. Against all odds, they managed to keep their stand until the last brute was down. The older man's experience, coupled with his own stamina, made them overcome the onslaught. Surrounded by mangled bodies, using some of them to stand on higher ground, they had been able to hold their attackers back until the final sound of the departing lama's died away.

They looked at each other, and Jonah was just about to say they made it and they should follow Cheng when they heard a violent roar and the sound of galloping horses.

The large man, who had put himself forward as the leader, had been staying out of the fray. So had two of his lieutenants. Seeing the unexpected outcome of the attack, they were now galloping at Mallory and Jonah, swinging brutal-looking maces and howling like a pack of rabid dogs.

They were outnumbered and exhausted while these guys were still fresh as a daisy. Mallory shouted:" Jonah, go and follow Cheng. I've got this. I can keep them busy long enough for you to get out. No use us both risking our lives."

Jonah, clamping his jaw, shook his head.

Mallory bellowed, "Astrid needs you. Mattie needs you. Please go. I can handle them."

Their attackers were nearly upon them, and Jonah still was determined to stay and fight to the end, until Mallory added, despair seeping into his voice: "I will be fine. I will find you guys when I have finished here. Astrid needs you. She is pregnant."

It was as if he had hit the boy in his face with a sledgehammer. All fight went out of him. He stumbled backwards.

"Go. Do it for her."

With Mallory's words ringing in his ears, Jonah finally unfroze and fled, forsaking his friend to save another one. He saw Mallory had turned back to his assailants.

Jonah jumped over the wagons and ran in the direction he knew Cheng and the others had fled. Angry tears were flowing freely over his face. Not daring to look back, the last thing he heard was the clash of weapons and the bloodthirsty shouts of the attackers trying to kill the man he had come to love like a father.

Chapter Sixty-one

There was not much left from the cheerful caravan that had left Sinatown yesterday. Everyone was covered in white dust, making them look like cornmeal covered ghosts. Nobody was saying very much as they continued their journey to Upavon. They all had friends to mourn.

Mattie walked, staring ahead, clasping Astrid's hand as if she would never let it go. Leaving Mallory behind had taken all the joy out of the girl. Astrid was not feeling much better.

After a few hours of trudging along, she heard one of the lookouts let out a shout. At the top of a high scraggly hill behind them, a rust coloured figure had appeared. Looking like a spirit from the underworld, he staggered down the incline

Cheng waved to one of the scouts to ride towards the broken-looking figure. They all saw him pointing at their group and then himself. The scout helped him up on his lama and rode towards their small train. When he came closer, so they could see his passenger, Astrid was shocked. It was Jonah, alone, looking like death warmed up.

When Mattie saw him without Mallory and covered in dried blood, Astrid had to restrain her from running back into the desert. She was screaming to let her go. She needed to go back and help Mallory. She held the distraught girl and turned to Jonah, who had slid down from the lama.

"Where is Mallory?"

When Mattie heard Jonah say Mallory had still been fighting when he left him, she flew at him, cursing and swearing like a hell-cat.

"You're a coward." she ranted at him, pummelling him with her fists, "I would never, ever have left him. Why did you? I thought you liked him. Is he dead?"

Her voice broke, and she started to weep. Astrid pulled the child into her arms again. She held on to her as tightly as possible crooning little words like she did when her little sister had hurt herself. Over the sobbing child's head, she gave Jonah a cold, accusing stare. He started to say something but then, shrugging his shoulders, turned abruptly and went to speak to Cheng.

To think she had been ready to forgive him and accept his friendship. When he stayed behind with Mallory, she had thought him so noble. How wrong she was. Like all those dirty Midlanders, he was not to be relied on. Over the past few weeks, Mallory had always been there for them, keeping them safe even willing to give his life for them. How could he have left their friend behind? How could he let him die to save himself?

Li, looking stunned, came over and persuaded Mattie to go with her and sit with the other survivors. She told Astrid she could not believe Jonah would have left Mallory without a good reason. She urged Astrid to go and give him at least a chance to explain how he came to arrive here all by himself.

"We're all shattered by the news, Astrid. After losing half of our people, I didn't think it could get any worse. But now it has. Father was so sure they would both survive and rejoin us. He has taken it very hard, but he is willing to give Jonah the benefit of the doubt and talk to him to find out what exactly happened before judging him. There might still be something we can do for Mallory. Jonah didn't say he saw him die. Please go, and speak to my father. You might even offer him your condolences."

Berating herself for not giving Cheng's feelings any thought, Astrid swallowed the big lump in her throat and pushed a deep sense of hopelessness away. She was determined to find out what lies that craven deserter had come up with to explain himself. Cheng might not understand what Jonah and his people were capable of. Like the fires and taking her and…

With long strides, she stormed at the small group of Sinise surrounding Jonah. He was white as a sheet under all the blood and looked ready to drop down with exhaustion. He winced as she stepped close to him, moving his body back as if expecting Astrid to start hitting him as well.

She definitely felt like it. Never before did she have this compulsion to destroy another human being. Her voice trembled with pent up rage. She had enough. He and his people had stolen her from her home, abused her, and now this.

"So? What's your excuse this time? On my island, they teach us never to leave our friends behind, no matter what. You Midlanders may be a bunch of uncivilised barbarians, but you must have some sort of code of honour when it comes to protecting each other? Did they kill him? Is that why you left? Or did you run at the first opportunity you got?"

Jonah's face, if possible, became even paler than before. He tried to say something but couldn't speak.

Cheng, holding his hand up, spoke up his voice as if from steel. "I think that is enough, young lady. Come with me. Jonah is exhausted, and we still have half a day to go before we reach Upavon. I will explain to you what happened but think it better to do so in private. Dear boy, you go to Li to get something to drink and let them tend your wounds. Leave Mattie to her own device for a bit. I will talk to her later and tell her the truth."

In her anger and distress, Astrid had failed to notice a lot of the blood covering Jonah was his own. His body had cuts all over it, with a nasty head wound dripping blood into his eyes. He didn't look like someone who had run from a fight at the first opportunity. It looked more like someone who had gone through a meat grinder. He gave her one more numb look before turning to find Li.

Astrid let Cheng lead her to the lamas, who were waiting peacefully a little away from all those shouting humans.

The man seemed to have aged half a century in the last few minutes. The loss of nearly half his caravan and many of his tribesmen had carved deep lines in his face. The news that his friend, Mallory, had most likely succumbed to the criminals had been a hard blow.

His voice was strong, though, when he addressed her: "I know the young are quick to judge. You have not known that young man for a very long time, but from what I have heard from my dear friend Mallory, he is an honest lad and has always behaved with bravery and honour the time you were together. The least you could do is not jump to conclusions and give him the benefit of the doubt. Mattie is still a child. She was closer to Mallory than any of us. Her initial anger towards Jonah when he showed up without Mallory is understandable. But I would have thought better of you. You should be the last one to blame that boy for anything. He followed Mallory's order which was to leave him to take care of you. You are the reason he had to leave my best friend behind to die."

Astrid reared back as if he had smacked her in the face. She had not expected to be scolded by Cheng. "What do you mean? I wasn't even there. How can I be responsible for what has happened? Are we sure Mallory is dead? Did Jonah tell you? So why did he leave him?"

" Mallory insisted that Jonah leave him to finish the fight and go after Mattie and you. The boy tried to stay, but Mallory told him something so important, the lad had no other choice but to go and find you. And no, he did not see Mallory die before he left him. But he did see him about to start going up against the rebels' leader and his two lieutenants. Mallory is one of the greatest swordsmen I know, but even a born one like him might not have survived those odds. He would have caught up with Jonah by now. But I still have hope he survived. He might be wounded too severely to travel fast. I will send a search party to look for him as soon as we reach Upavon. My men here are too tired and too few. It might still not be safe. My agent can get a team together to track him down. If there is the slightest chance he is still alive, they will find him. I don't think he would let them take him alive. But that is not why I needed to speak to you alone."

Astrid, who had started to feel a glimmer of hope Mallory might still be alive, blinked her eyes and looked at him curiously.

Cheng looked dead on his feet, but his voice was steady when he told her what he knew, "Mallory told Jonah that you are pregnant and that it was Jonah's duty to look after you as it was his doing. Besides being an excellent fighter, my friend was, is, an even better doctor. He must have noticed. I know he would never make this up, only to get the boy to leave. Are you okay?"

A feeling of great despair came over Astrid. Seeing her with him and noticing their attraction to one another, Cheng must assume Jonah was the father. She understood now what had happened that night with Solo after she had blacked out. Her body had told her the truth, as had the bruises, but she had tried to ignore it, being too disgusted by the thought. That was why she had never contemplated that night could have consequences far beyond the physical damage. It was as if after she had blanked it out. She had accepted the partial loss of sight and tried to forget that man's filthy assault. Now she would have to live with the fact there was more. The bastard had put a child in her. She felt bile coming up in her throat. The pitying look in Cheng's eyes made it even worse. And Jonah knew too. She wanted to rip this thing growing in her out of her body like the abomination it was. Now, she could never go home. They would treat her like an outcast. She moaned.

Cheng gripped her by her arms and turned her to him.

"Child. Didn't you know? I am so sorry I told you in such an abrupt way, but I thought with you two getting along so well, you might not find it so terrible. I know your people will frown upon you having a child outside the tree, but there are more places than your Island to make a living if you two want to keep it. It is a lot to take in, but we will find a solution, I promise. We will soon continue to Upavon. I am sorry, there is nothing we can do about it now. Mallory told me you are to see his sister. She is a midwife and might be able to help."

Biting down on her bottom lip to stop screams of horror escaping, Astrid numbly pointed to the others as if to say she was going back to join them. Hugging herself tightly, she started to trudge in their direction—a pale shadow of the girl who was only yesterday laughing with her friends at a card game.

Jonah looked up when Astrid returned and seemed to realise Cheng must have told her what Mallory had shouted at him. He was holding Mattie's hand and had been speaking softly to her. The little girl seemed to have calmed down somewhat and seemed to accept his desertion hadn't been his idea but an order from Mallory.

Astrid wondered if Jonah had told her. Who else knew of her shame? Her life was ruined unless she could make it all go away.

She thought about what she had been willing to do that night with Nicholas to make him run away with her. It could have had the same result. At least that child would have been from someone she loved and not from a savage. How would he react if he ever found out? Would he still respect her? Probably not.

But she needed to get home. And the only way she could do that was to get rid of this thing and pretend it never happened. Her thoughts went to Mallory. That sweet man would have understood her despair and might have come up with a solution. But she should start looking after herself now. She had been far too dependent on others to keep her safe. She would have to grow up and fast. She would find a solution.

She straightened her back, swept her hair out of her face, and walked to the end of the line of pack animals. She was on her own now. She just needed more time to find a solution.

Chapter Sixty-two

A group of bedraggled people rode or stumbled silently into the harbour town of Upavon. It was still busy in the streets even at this late hour, and the inns and bars heaved with people. Errand boys were dashing between the crowd, and the market stalls were still open, their owners crying for customers to come and look at their goods.

Jonah tried not to look up at the painted boys and girls hanging from windows or over balconies, displaying their wares to all and sundry. He had heard Solo talking about them after one of his trips to this place. He had described these whores, as he called them, with great delight. Solo and Yaya had a big fight about it. Now he knew why.

He looked behind him to see if he could see where Astrid was at the back of their caravan. She still looked in a daze staring straight in front of her.

Jonah wondered what it would be like to grow up so innocent, surrounded by people who meant you no harm. When they were still on talking terms, she had told him how a chaperone had always accompanied her if she left the city. It must be nice to be always safe, though it didn't do much to prepare you for the pain and disappointments of the real world.

He still felt terrible about what Solo had done to her even though he knew he couldn't have stopped him even if he had tried. Solo would have killed him for interfering, maybe killed Yaya too if she had tried to stop him. He should never have trusted that mongrel. If only he hadn't been the one to tell him about the easy access to Harrington House or to suggest setting fires to distract the Sevenoaks people.

Jonah moaned softly. Astrid would never forgive him for indirectly being guilty of killing her parents and all that had befallen her since. Last four weeks, the girl had wormed her way further into his heart. Yes, she was beautiful, even with the scar on her face, but the way her spirit kept bouncing back, no matter what life threw at her, made him adore her. He had now lost any chance of Astrid returning his feelings. She was with Solo's child and would have one more thing to blame him. What was the point of even trying to change her mind? He should just move on and forget about her. Let Cheng put her on a boat home. He would go back to his mother in West Drayton and be a simple fisherman again. No more raids for him.

No, look at her. She was trying so hard to keep it all together. Astrid would need his help now more than ever. The Island people didn't look favourable on pregnancies outside their precious tree. Enough fugitives from their law arrived every year in Midland to prove that. He must stand by her and help her, even if it was to be from a distance. Not only because he had promised Mallory but because he, against all odds, still hoped she would one day return his feelings. He was a lovesick fool.

Looking around, Jonah saw Mattie not far away chatting with one of the drivers. She might be able to cheer Astrid up a bit.

"Mattie, why don't you walk with Astrid? She looks like she could use a friend. I have to go and ask Cheng where we're going to stay tonight."

Mattie didn't need much persuading and ran to the back of the caravan, where he saw her say something to Astrid. The latter bent over and hugged Mattie. Even from this distance, he could see Astrid's posture relax a bit.

As if he had read his mind, Cheng came over to inform where they would stay that night.

"By the Lady, I have never been so glad to see Upavon again. Normally I am not too keen on these harbour towns: too much noise and far too many uncouth individuals. I have sent Li to contact our agent and ask him to bring us some money. We can't all stay at his place, I'm afraid. I suggest we let Astrid and Mattie go with Li to stay at his house while we go to an inn. I have sent one of my men to book the rest of us into the Jade Dragon. I will bring the sad news to Mallory's sister. She deserves to hear it from me and not through the town's gossip. Will you tell Astrid?"

Seeing Jonah hesitate, he added, "You will have to speak to her sometime, you know. NowThis is your chance if you want one."

Cheng squeezed Jonah's shoulder. Taking a deep

breath, the young man pushed his way to the back to find himself face to face with Astrid. Mattie, wise beyond her years, made herself scarce, saying she wanted to see where Li was.

Jonah, seeing Astrid's uneasiness, felt sweat pearling on his forehead and said, stammering a bit: "Cheng has asked me to tell you he arranged for you, Li and Mattie, to stay with his agent tonight. The rest of us will stop at a place called the Jade Dragon. After freshening up, he wants us to meet again for a meal and discuss what to do next."

Astrid didn't say anything but looked at him as if she had never seen him before. Jonah felt his heart shrinking and didn't quite know what to do next. He searched her eyes, trying to see something of a response.

He pushed on: "I understand if you don't want to speak to me, but, please, is there anything I can do for you? I'm so sorry about everything. The last words Mallory spoke to me were to look after you. I would never have left him to his fate. I'm no coward. I would have fought with him to the end. But he told me I had to go because of you. I desperately want to do something, anything, to make all of this easier for you. Maybe today is too early for you to decide if you can let me help you. I'll stay in Upavon as long as you need me. You will only have to say the word, and I'll be there."

Looking over her shoulder, he saw Mattie tearing through the crowd towards them. He continued quickly, "I see Mattie is coming to collect you. Will I see you later in the inn?"

To his surprise, she nodded. He felt his heart leap. Maybe all was not lost. Walking away, Jonah looked back and caught Astrid looking down on Mattie's golden head, smiling a bit at the girl's irrepressible energy.

Mattie seemed to have bounced back from the terrible news about Mallory. The doctor had been, in anything but name, her father. She told him she couldn't believe he was dead and kept telling everyone who would listen he would come back and take her with him. Jonah hoped her faith in Mallory's survival would be rewarded. He doubted the outcome of that fight would have been anything but tragic. Mallory had been so tired, and those men had just waited their chance to hack them down. He would never forget the sound of the men galloping towards his friend and Mallory's last words to him.

Jonah let go of the breath he hadn't known he was holding. Why was everything Astrid did and said so incredibly important to him? They barely knew each other. She was an Islander. What could they possibly have in common? He'd better get himself to the inn to clean himself up before the meal. She would be there. That must count something.

Assembled at a large table set up for them on the broad veranda of the Dragon Inn, the Sinese fell upon the food as if they had not eaten for a year instead of one day. Astrid was just toying with hers. Hearing about their disastrous trip, the innkeeper had generously offered them unlimited bottles of his best wine on the house.

Jonah had installed himself opposite Astrid in the hope she would give him a chance to talk to her. Finally seeing her eyes resting on him, he took a deep breath and started, "Have you had a chance to think about what you're going to do?"

The word 'now' holding more meaning than that little word could ever contain.

Putting her fork down, Astrid gave a quivering sigh that pierced his heart.

"I want to find Mallory's sister and ask her if she can help me. Mallory told us to contact her if we were in trouble, and he was not there to help us," she took another breath, her eyes shining with tears. "Cheng said she knows what has happened to her brother, and I want to go and see her. Even if it was only to tell her how much he has done for me."

Jonah didn't understand how this sister could help get Astrid back to her people. She was a midwife, not a trader.

"Wouldn't it be better to let Cheng arrange transport to your Island and wait here at the Inn? I will leave Upavon after you have gone home. I need to find my mum and my sister. We will have to leave Midland and get as far away as we can from Damien."

Eyes blazing, she bent forward over the table, putting her face so close to his, he could feel her hot breath on his cheeks.

"Home, going home?. I thought you knew at least

a tiny bit about our people. You told me how you read so much. I can never return home carrying a child by that son of a whore. They would ban me from society, and for the child, they would make it disappear if I had any inclination to let it be born, which I don't. They would stuff me in some convent in a godforsaken place and erase my name from the Book of Life. I first need to get rid of it, and that is why I need Plaxedes, you moron."

Astrid spat out those last words out and sank back on her seat, all the while looking at him as if he were something she had found under her shoe in the farmyard.

He knew how deep her hate for Solo must be, which he understood, but he still felt her decision to callously want to kill an innocent child for not deriving from that precious tree as a direct judgement of himself and his family. He didn't think he deserved that and started to get annoyed.

"I understand you hate Solo's guts, but my people are not all monsters. These last four weeks, I've tried my best to help you get back home. I understand you detest anybody who had anything to do with your abduction and its consequences, but my mother is the kindest woman you'll ever hope to meet. You may think my sister Yaya is a hard woman, but she is capable of great love and loyalty. You Islanders don't have a monopoly on those qualities. I can't help it your people are such racists when it comes to children, not from anybody on that stupid Tree."

They were looking at each other with near hatred,

their faces white, red masks.

"Hey, you two. People are watching. Maybe you should go and have some sleep before tearing each other's throats out. We are all shattered by Mallory's fate, and you, Astrid, have had another shock to cope with. Tomorrow things might not be better, but a good night's rest might make them easier to deal with. I'll bring Mattie around to the agent's house a bit later. I don't have the heart to interrupt her while she is having a nice time despite her grief. The young have such a capacity to bounce back.

Jonah, you go and ask the innkeeper what I owe him and to put it on my tab. Then take yourself upstairs. You, more than others, need to rest after the day you've had. It must have been extremely grievous to leave my friend behind, not knowing if he would survive. It isn't easy to cope with something like that. Please don't be too hard on yourself. I have known Mallory for a long time and know that he would never have told you to leave if there had been any other solution. I have not yet given up on him. Neither should you. Now both go."

Before he would make a spectacle of himself bawling his eyes out at the kindness of this man, who had lost loved ones too, and hurting from his fight with Astrid, Jonah fled the room in the direction of the kitchen.

Chapter Sixty-three

Before leaving the Bunyip, Yaya and Wulf had stocked up on food and drink for their journey to Reading station. They hadn't been too worried about bumping into Damien's men, as the southern tip of Diggers Peninsula was under the supervision of a religious garrison, under the command of a warrior monk with a fierce reputation. The only people allowed entrance to Midland from that side of the Swamp had to undergo an exhaustive investigation.

There was a regular ferry service between the garrison of Boulder town and their post on the other side of the Sound. They planned to persuade a ferryman to smuggle them across

Freya embraced Wulf and kissed him goodbye, admonishing her son to be careful and wishing him luck in finding his friend.

Yaya tried to hug Solo, but he shrugged her off and walked away without looking back.

Eric sprinted after her, not letting her go until she had given him a big hug and told him 'that yes, Yaya loved him a lot and he would soon see her in London'.

Tish had gone to say goodbye to her family

They went on their way, guided by a pair of Bunyip, making sure they crossed the bogs safely. After the Bunyip had deposited them at the seam of a dark forest, they took their leave.

Yaya set off at a good pace. Wulf followed along, having no trouble keeping up with her, all the while trying to keep up a rather one-sided conversation. He told her he never would've thought his friend would choose his dad's name. He had hardly known his father. And when Jonah had left with Solo, Yaya and the girl, Wulf had wanted nothing more than to go with them. But his mother had begged him to stay, telling him Solo always meant trouble. At one point, she gave him such an annoyed look he must have realised he had been babbling and kept silent.

Wulf nearly walked into her back when she suddenly stopped and pointed. Huge, grey boulders lay directly ahead, forming a barrier between them and their destination. "Look. Behind those rocks lies Bouldertown. Everyone who lives there works for the Digger's garrison. There are mainly whore houses and bars. We will have to make a detour around it and go straight to the harbour. We can bribe a ferryman to take us across."

"But how are we going to get over those huge things?" Wulf asked her, pointing at the towering boulders.

"We'll take a goat-path at the right of it. A long time ago, the people living in Digger's peninsula cut stairways in and along those rocks to make it easier to travel over them. Time has worn many away, but quite a few still exist. Those are the easy bits. Most of the climb will be hell on your leg muscles. I hope yours will be up for it. It is all up to start with."

Seeing him looking doubtful, Yaya snorted, punching him playfully on his arm and set off, not looking back to see if he was following.

"You see what I meant?" Yaya pointed to the first part of their trail, which looked like the deeply worn stairs going up so high they could not see where they ended.

It wasn't too hard going at first. After every turn of the path, they looked near the top, only to find there were yet more stairs or gravelly uphill trails to follow. Wulf was complaining that his thighs were burning.

Sweat was covering her whole body, drenching her clothes and seeping into her boots. She tried not to think of the blisters this would cause. She was fit but felt it in her whole body.

After an hour and a half of torture, Yaya finally halted and turned to Wulf, who was trying not to breathe hard, failing miserably.

"How are you doing, little guy? We've reached the last set of steps before the top. We will have a little rest there. But we can't stay for long as our muscles will cool down, making going down worse. Believe me." With a groan, Wulf sank on a small boulder beside the path and told her he was just happy not to have to stand on his poor aching legs for a moment.

Yaya took a deep draught of her water bottle.

"Don't get too comfortable, my friend. You might think going down will be easier, but you just wait. Your knees will soon be crying for help. There'll be a lovely surprise on the way, though. Not afraid of heights, I hope?"

Wulf shook his head, looking up at her.

"How do you know about all these places? I never knew any of us ever came this way."

Happy to distract Wulf from his sore legs, Yaya explained: "Just after I joined Solo's scouting gang, we were fishing south of the Peninsula, just the two of us, when a storm dumped us on the coast here in the area of those woods we walked through before. We couldn't risk going back via the Bog, so we travelled this way and found this path. We were lucky. At that time, the garrison was not well established. There was no inspection to speak off. The townspeople helped us to get back home."

Yaya's prediction about their knees was correct. She was happy when they reached the surprise she had in mind. Though she would never admit it, she was finding the descend hard too. Halfway down the path was a narrow ridge from which the cliff took a steep plunge into the dark blue sea foaming white around the base of half-submerged rocks.

She usually had a good head for heights but still found herself shivering a bit when she looked down at the violent waves crashing loudly against the cliff.

The view further out, though, was breathtaking. In the distance, the low hills that bordered the marsh looked pale as smoke. The water was taking on all kinds of blue and green colours wherever you looked. All her aches and pains were forgotten by the sight of the sun, slowly turning the sea into molten gold.

"Beautiful, isn't it?" Yaya felt pleased, seeing Wulf looking at her with his eyes wide open in wonder. He nodded, speechless.

Realising it would get dark soon, Yaya started to descend even faster than before. Wulf had no choice but to follow her panting like a smith's bellow

When they arrived at the bottom, she told Wulf they should hole up for the night in one of the many deep crevices between the lower boulders.

Chapter Sixty-four

Spreading their blankets on the rocky ground in the dimly lit cave, Wulf and Yaya didn't bother eating before collapsing on their beds, exhausted from their forced march. They fell asleep like a log, only to be woken a few hours later by being poked with a stick.

A creaky voice sounded in the now pitch-dark cave:

"This is my cave. You better scram. I saw some soldiers coming this way. They're not nice people. I can tell you that for free. They know me and won't bother me, but they don't like strangers."

Her eyes adjusting to the dark, Yaya saw a small, crooked man, dressed in rags, standing over them, holding on to a long staff. A herd of pathetic looking goats was milling tightly around him. They smelt to high heaven, the man, as well as his goats. She saw Wulf unsheathing his knife, ready to defend them and put a restraining hand on his arm.

"Let's listen to him, Wulf. For all we know, Damien's alert has reached Bouldertown, and it would just mean a lot of trouble and a longer delay."

To the man: "Thank you for the warning, my good man. We'll be leaving now. Please, don't tell anyone you saw us. You would be doing us a great favour."

The man snorted and pinched his nose to deposit a

blotch of snot on the floor.

"I wouldn't help that idiot in the north whatever the reason he is looking for you. He has cost me my family and my home. Don't you, young ones, worry. If asked, I'll very helpfully point them the other way. May the Lady protect you both."

He grinned, showing four stumpy brown teeth.

Yaya bowed to him and urged Wulf to do the same. Now fully awake, they collected their things and wormed their way around the old goatherd and his flock. Diving in her bag, Yaya handed the old codger an Oro before she stepped outside. His lined face lit up, but before he could thank them, they had left him to his cave and hurried away, careful to make a detour around the town and a group of soldiers making enough noise to wake up the dead.

They needed all their breath to run as fast as their unfamiliarity with the terrain allowed. When she saw some dark shapes, Yaya stopped to get her bearings and gasped: "That's the garrison. We better hide somewhere out of sight until tomorrow. Let's see if we can find the ferry for Reading. We can ask if they will let us on board now.

The ferryman was willing to hide them for a sum of money that made Wulf grumble about fucking thieving sons of whores. Yaya shushed him. The bribe made quite a dent in their stash, but, as she told Wulf, the money would be no good to them either if they got caught and killed.

Sensing the bored ferryman was keen to have someone to talk to, Yaya took the opportunity to pump him for some information. She was careful not to mention any names or why they did not want the garrison to know where they were.

"Been very busy lately?"

"Just the usual. Could do with a few more customers like you two," the captain grinned at the sour face Wulf was pulling.

"Anything exciting happening? We've been travelling for quite a while. We don't get much news in the back of beyond in Digger's woods."

"Reading is Reading. Nothing much going on as per usual. We did hear Damien was having a bit of a bother. The monks got involved. Some guy snatched an Islander girl, someone important, and they want her back big time. Damien has put the word out he is looking for her and some guys who are with her. They pulled a fast one and snatched her right out from under his nose. Just bringing him some information about these them will earn you a pretty penny. I wish I weren't stuck on this boat. With that kind of money, I could go and buy myself a nice whore house and retire in style."

Trying to look suitably impressed by the captain's knowledge of the local news, Yaya snuggled up to Wulf and said:" Darling, once we've done our shopping, maybe we should join the search for those people. We sure could do with the money. We could finally get our own farm and move out."

Wulf pulled her against him with a little bit too much enthusiasm and planted a kiss on her head. She would make him pay for that later.

Holding her in his arms, he cooed: "But kitten, you know we have to go back. Your mother would never let us forget it if we upped and left without saying goodbye. Besides, what chance have we poor slobs when all of Midland is looking for them. ? Somebody probably has spotted or caught them already."

Yaya held her breath, waiting for the ferryman's answer. She finally might get some news about her brother.

"There have been more rumours about that lot than I can count on the fingers of my hand. That they went to the mountains, joined one of the caravans, or have fled to London City. I have not heard anything about anyone bringing them in. I think they're gone or dead already with Damien not telling anyone. He is probably afraid of what the Prior would do to him if he found out. The Monastery does not like to be taken for a ride. I don't know who is worse: Damien and his men or that pious lot."

He spat over the side of the boat.

"Glad to live far away from both of them. We have enough to do with them in the garrison."

They both mumbled their agreement and went down below to a tiny room stuffed with crates and ropes.

When Yaya woke up, she lay listening to the

harbour coming alive around them. The sounds of cargo dragged aboard and people shuffling into the passenger's cabin above them meant they would be leaving soon.

Feeling Wulf becoming restless, he was suffering being squashed in such cramped quarters with that large body. Yaya tried to distract him by laying out her plans in more detail.

"When we get to Reigate, we have to get off the ferry while they're unloading the crates and passengers. The guards in Reading Station harbour will be too busy checking the freight lists to pay much attention. Collecting tax comes first for them. We can continue pretending to be a couple going to the Reading market. It seems to work, and you seem to enjoy it."

Winking at Wulf and laughing when he blushed, she added: "A couple very much in love with each other apparently. People usually leave those alone."

Even in the semi-dark of their confined space, she saw his face got even redder. The bashful look he gave her nearly made her laugh out loud. She had always known he had a crush on her. Being her baby brother's friend, she had ignored it or made jokes about it with Jonah. Looking at this kind bear of a man, to her surprise, she felt strangely gratified by his infatuation. Still, she could not help herself teasing him a bit with it.

"Don't worry, Wulf. We can always pretend to be mother and son if you prefer."

Wulf quipped, "It's okay. I don't mind sacrificing

myself, having to smooch with such an old woman."

Yaya slapped his arm. She was relieved to feel the boat bumping against the quay and being able to leave their cramped quarters. As she had foreseen, they had no problems getting off the ship and walking to the outskirts of Reading undetected. She wanted to get to the rail tracks, connecting Reading with the next station, Penn.

"We can follow the tracks until we get to Penn. Damien has a countrywide call out for me and the others but not for you. Hopefully, travelling as a couple will keep us safe from his spies. Before we go on, let's see if we can get some more information."

"How?"

"You could go into Reading and see if there is some news about them. While you're there, buy some more food and something to drink for our trip to Penn Station. Be back here in about an hour. We still have plenty of daylight to cover one-third of the way. I'm going to have a rest in this orchard. I'm still tired from yesterday. I'm an old woman, after all."

After pinching Wulf's arm affectionately, Yaya strode into an apple orchard in full bloom and made herself comfortable under one of the trees.

Chapter Sixty-five

Yaya jumped up, her knife half out of its hidden place in her sleeve. Wulf was back panting like a dog. He told her about an attack on a caravan and that Jonah most likely had been involved. He could still be in a small harbour town called Upavon.

"They were talking about a monk and a Midlander. That must be Jonah and Mallory. They didn't say anything about the girl".

" You are right, Wulf. It must be them. We have to leave right away."

Yaya gathered her things. "Did you manage to find out how to get to this Upavon?"

"No, once the guy heard I was planning to get the ransom, he didn't want to talk to me anymore. Stupid of me. You told me they don't like Damien around here. I thought it better not to attract more attention and left straight away to tell you the good news."

Seeing him looking a bit sheepish at his mistake, Yaya decided not to waste any more words on it. They would have to take their chances finding their own way.

Walking ahead with long strides, she felt better than she had for days. Looking around, she noticed the trees had been showering them with pink, white blossoms like a pleasantly warm snowstorm. The sun had come out, warming her joints stiff from lying on the hard floor.

Heartened by the good news, and having no doubt it was Jonah, the Midlander, the man in the bar had mentioned, it took them only a few hours to reach the bend in the tracks, where they left the railway to follow their route due west.

They were lucky to meet some fellow travellers coming from one of the hamlets along the Silver River. It was a farmer travelling with his daughter and two cows in the opposite direction. He pointed at a nearly invisible track behind him and said in his strange accent: "Follow this here track until you get to a big river. That will be the Silver. You can cross it under the rail bridge or else pay the toll. There be a ford for the walking folk such as you and me. Follow the road some more until you smell the stink. That be the Ravines. Whatever you do, don't go near it but stay on the road keeping the mountains to your left. The path will then take you to the Darkwater Oasis. There be usually traders there to point you to that town you're after. Upavon, wasn't it?"

Thanking him for his help, Yaya and Wulf continued their journey. Everything panned out as the farmer had said. It was nearly dark when they started to smell a foul odour. Yaya decided they should stop before leaving the forest.

"We'll camp here within the tree line. Tonight, we'll finally have a warm meal if I can help it. How about you collect some wood while I catch us a juicy rabbit. I have seen plenty of them scooting around."

Yaya needed the exhilaration of the hunt to eliminate all the nervous energy generated by her impatience to see her brother again. The long march had done nothing to diminish it. Coming back a little later with not one but two rabbits, she found a neat campsite with a cheerful fire burning and heaps of wood piled next to it, promising a comfortable night.

Looking like the old married couple they had been portraying, they prepared the meal, each doing their bit without saying much. Without being told, Wulf had already filled their bottles for tomorrow from a small stream nearby. They devoured their meal talking about general stuff like hunting methods and scouting trips she had been part of.

Yaya, her face softening, looked at the big lad. "If I were fifteen years younger, I would ask you to marry me right away, Wulf. Never known you were such good husband material."

She laughed when she saw she had made him blush again. Wulf looked like he wanted to say something but then decided not to. He went to poke the fire and add some more branches to it, keeping his face away from her. The silly lad still had his juvenile crush on her. She thought that by now, he had given up.

Yaya nearly laughed again, imagining telling Solo she had chosen Wulf as her mate instead of him. That would not end well. She hated Solo's lack of empathy, but his lack of fun was his worse flaw. And the fact he thought he owned her. She had come to appreciate how Wulf treated her with respect. He had shown a surprising sense of humour too.

She got up to have a last pee in the bushes and wash her hands in the stream to give Wulf a chance to pull himself together. When she returned, he had rolled himself in his blanket on the other side of the fire. He kept his back to it pretending to be asleep.

Yaya decided to follow his example. She was dead on her feet. During the night, she didn't object when she felt a warm body slipping under her blanket, stroking her softly and starting to make love to her with a tenderness and enthusiasm that made her forget she shouldn't be doing this. He stayed with her after he finished holding her gently until she fell asleep again.

The next morning he was gone when she woke and only returned when she had packed everything up, looking shyly at her as if waiting for her to comment on last night.

She winked at him and handed him his pack. "Ready? We still have some way to go. Did you sleep well last night? I had such a nice dream."

Wulf's' shoulders slumped, and he looked disappointed only to start smiling again when she gave him a light kiss on his cheek and whispered there were a few days yet before they arrived in Upavon.

She shouldn't encourage him, but it had been

great, and she didn't see why she shouldn't enjoy it while it lasted. She would let him down gently when they had to go back to everyday life. Though at the moment, she had no idea when that would be.

Chapter Sixty-six

Astrid stretched, rubbing her aching back. It would not be long now before the time would come, and she would be free again. Sometimes, when she felt it kicking, she caught herself wondering if it was a boy or girl and what it would look like. But no, after the birth, she was leaving as soon as she could. Word had come to them through Cheng that Damien had been brought to heel by the Prior. That had been the good news. The bad news was that the Church now had sent some hunter after her to take her to Luton. She knew well what would happen if they found out about the child. She remembered when Jonah had come back from the market and told her about this Father Lucius.

"You will have to stay out of sight of the townspeople." Plaxedes had looked worried. "I know about him from my brother. Lucius was never good at his studies, so he decided to be the most devout Guardian of the Faith. The current Prior has given him the power to find fugitives by every means he thinks necessary. He is a ruthless man."

Plaxedes's house was on the outskirts of Upavon and lay hidden behind a high Hawthorne hedge.

Mattie had been told never to talk about Astrid. The girl had made new friends and started lessons at a school in the neighbouring village. She had vowed to become a warrior-monk despite them trying to convince her that the Church did not take on women.

"I will make them because that is stupid. I need to know how to fight better before I find Mallory again." She was always begging Jonah to teach her how to use a sword. He always gave in. They had become very close.

Jonah had found work as a fisherman and didn't see many other people besides Cheng or his daughter, who visited whenever they were in town. He was still trying to do his best to win her affection. It had been impossible for her to open her heart to him because she smelt the smoke and imagined her parents dying in that fire each time. He reminded her too of his people, not the least Solo.

She had been starting to feel safe until she overheard a conversation between Plaxedes and Jonah. It had been not long after he told them about the monk. She had gone to bed early but couldn't sleep and decided to do some sewing in the warm kitchen. She had passed the sitting room when she heard the soft murmur of Plaxedes having a conversation with Jonah. Just as she was about to join them, Astrid caught the word Yaya. She froze and stood behind the half-open door to listen.

"I can see you feel guilty not telling Astrid about their visit. Don't you think it might make her think a bit kinder of you when she hears what her people have done to your village? She is so bitter about what happened to her folks. I can see you suffering when she brings it up again when you try to get closer to her."

Before Jonah could say anything, Astrid had shoved the door open and demanded to know what they were talking about. Jonah had looked away, but she had seen his shoulders slump as if an enormous weight had been taken off them. Plaxedes had made her sit down and then let Jonah tell her about Yaya's visit. It had shaken her to the core.

" Not long after we decided to stay here until you had the child, I was at the fishmonger's in the market to sell him my catch. Wulf, the friend I told you about, surprised me by showing up there. I was so happy to see him. He was not there alone. My sister was waiting at the outskirts for him to find me and bring me to her. They had been looking for me for weeks travelling from Diggers."

Jona had swallowed and looked into the fire. When he looked up, his eyes were filled with tears.

"We got to Yaya, and it was so good to see her, but she seemed surprised to see me so happy. "You didn't tell him, did you," she said to Wulf. Then she told me about what happened to my mum and my village. Your people came the day after your abduction and killed nearly everyone. They burned everything. I will never see my mother again or go home even if I wanted to."

Astrid had felt shocked. Not only about the attack on Jonah's home and his terrible loss, but that he had kept this from her. She had lashed out at him so many times about his part in the attack. He could have thrown the grief done to him by the hands of her people into her face but hadn't. Still, she had to ask."How come they were there, the two of them? Does she know I am pregnant?" Astrid pulled her shawl tighter around herself by the idea Solo could have found out about her.

"They met when they were staying with a tribe in Diggers. She was on the run for Damien herself with Solo before they caught up with each other. Wulf's mother and Solo's brother were there too", seeing Astrid go white and knowing what she was thinking, Jonah had tried to put her mind at ease," He does not know about you and never will. I made them swear. I told them I was staying here and would look after the child. I had to promise them to follow them to London when it was safe to travel. They will remain there with Wulf's mother, Eric and Solo. Don't worry. I will make something up about the child when the time comes. He will never know it is yours." He hadn't added, "And his". She just had to believe him.

Plaxedes had taken her hand and told her it would be a good idea for all of them to go to bed and talk some more the next day.

Astrid still felt frightened but from that day on had gradually tried to be more forthcoming to Jonah, who even then had never blamed her for anything. She smiled when she thought of all the little presents he brought for her like a book, some soft, colourful silky wool, exotic fruit that was sometimes imported from Kent and made her think of home. The best thing was when he got her some news from home. Henry seemed to have taken on the Harrington Company. Astrid had been a bit shocked but not surprised when she heard he was now engaged to her younger sister. They were waiting until Lily came of age to get married. The story had been put about she, Astrid, had died in Midland. Jonah thought the Church must be behind that little tale.

    Astrid pushed the last loaves into the oven and started to walk to the pantry when a crippling pain shot through her. She could hardly breathe. It was too soon. She still had at least a month to go. Before she could finish that thought, another jolt shot through her body, making her cry out, and Plaxedes running into the kitchen.

    The midwife took one look at her and nodded. " It's time. I will send for Jonah. He asked me if I would when the time came, and I will need an extra pair of hands."

    After that, all Astrid knew were the pains and the blissful pauses in between. At some point, she felt Jonah's hand on her arm, his warm voice telling her it would be alright, making it all more bearable. The pain came in ever-faster waves rolling over her with breathtaking power. When she thought she could not stand it any longer, Plaxedes told her to push. Screaming, she obeyed her again and again until she heard the thin wailing of a baby. Jonah, his face shining like the morning sun, told her that she had a beautiful daughter. It didn't mean much to her. All she wanted to do was sleep for a very long time.

Chapter Sixty-seven

When Astrid woke, the first thing she saw was Jonah fast asleep in a chair next to her bed with his hand laid gently on the crib he had made.

For some reason, this made her weep as if her heart was breaking. All the memories of those first weeks in Midland came flooding back. She had managed to ignore them the more distant they had become. Everyday life and her growing feelings for Jonah had pushed the nightmares away. She wanted her mother.

Sitting up, he asked her if she was in pain. She shook her head and assured him she wasn't. As if feeling her mother's distress, the child started to cry as well.

Plaxedes came in and picked up the little bundle from the crib, holding her out to Astrid."She is gorgeous. Don't you want to hold her just for a moment?"

She felt herself go all cold and shook her head. She couldn't, even though her whole body was aching to hold this being that has shared her body for all those months, whose movements have kept her awake at night, and her heart told her to love.

During her pregnancy, she kept telling Plaxedes how she would leave after the child was weaned and wasn't interested in learning how to look after it. She didn't want it.

The old midwife had said to her that the force of nature was strong, and the bond of a mother with her child was nigh impossible to ignore. She might feel very different when she held it in her arms for the first time. She started to understand it now.

Jonah turned to Plaxedes and asked her to give the child to him. She placed it gently in his arms, and he gazed down at it with a face filled with so much love, Astrid was moved to take a look at her newborn baby herself.

Dark golden tufts of hair crowned the tiny little face of the sleeping infant. Her fists were balled as if she was ready to take on the world. She was so small. She reminded Astrid of her little sister Lily, who, when born, had the same colouring. She felt drawn to it despite all it represented. She stretched out her arms and accepted the child from Jonah, who looked relieved.

Plaxedes came over to help her put the child to her breast for the first time. They had discussed this over the last few months when Astrid told them she didn't want to bond with the child in any way.

"You will have to feed it for the first three months, my child. It won't survive otherwise. Islander babies don't thrive on outlander milk. Something else we have those monks to thank for."

Her eyes scrunched shut, the baby eagerly found the breast, and it all seemed to click in place. Astrid looked down at the tiny hand resting on her breast and was overwhelmed by an intense protective feeling. She settled back in her pillows and felt something she hadn't for a long time, peace.

"What will you call her ?" Jonah asks softly.

"You choose. It is the least I can do for you."

" Are you sure? Maybe you will want to later."

She assured him she didn't, and he told her he would like to call her Nessa, short for Vanessa.

"It means butterfly in one of the ancient languages. Mattie will be pleased."

When the child had finished, Astrid looked down on the contented little face with wonder. Would it be possible to love her just for herself? She was part Harrington too. Maybe she could stay a bit longer here with Jonah and Plaxedes to get to know her. She looked at Jonah about to say something to this effect when the child opened its eyes and looked straight at her. Astrid let out a gasp, remembering seeing that same look all those months ago. She pushed it abruptly to a bewildered Jonah.

"Here, take her. I can't bear it. Look at her. It' him. " She started to cry with the baby joining her.

Jonah handed the distraught child to Plaxedes, who rocked it in her arms until it stopped crying. They both looked down on its fuzzy head, and Jonah understood. The girl looked at them with the same obsidian eyes he remembered seeing in the face of the man who was undoubtedly her father. "Solo, " he whispered.

Plaxedes must have understood. She silently put the child back in its crib in front of the fire and tucked it in with only her shaking hands showing how the scene had affected her. She told Jonah to go and brew a calming potion for Astrid. She would be with him shortly. Mattie would be home shortly, and someone should stop her rushing in, waking Astrid to see the baby. After a last look at his beloved and the crib, he left.

Plaxedes helped Astrid out of her bed and told her to strip and wash at the basin while she would put clean sheets on the bed.

"You and I need to have a word about this, dear. I understand all of this has been challenging. I admit it must be hard under the circumstances for you to accept the child, but we are talking about a brand new life here that deserves to be cherished. That little girl should not have to suffer for the awful way she was begotten. You and she are very lucky to have that honest, hardworking young man who loves you both so much he has given up his family, his whole life, to look after you two. By all means, throw it away and leave them behind, but not before you have given the little one a decent chance to survive. I thought we had agreed on this. Maybe you can find it in your heart to show some kindness to your daughter and the lad as well. You don't have to answer me now. Just think about it in the coming weeks. Now have that tea, and I'll bring you something to eat." She tucked in Astrid, who had crawled back into her lovely clean bed, with a bit more force than was necessary, her face trembling a bit.

    Astrid felt dreadful that this woman, who had treated her with nothing but respect and kindness, felt so upset. Despite her grief about her brother, Mallory's sister had taken them in, ensured Jonah got a job and kept them safe. She had concocted a story about how Astrid and Jonah were her cousins expecting their first baby.

    Astrid decided she would do her best to keep her promise of making sure the child got a good start in life. As for going home, that would have to wait until the child was weaned. She felt her eyes close. The birth and the emotions following it had made her bone tired. She didn't need Plaxedes' potion after all.

Chapter Sixty-eight

"The Island ahead." a loud voice was shouting.

The captain looked at the austere, beautiful young woman who had come out on deck. Locks of her auburn hair had been swept from her hood and softened the sharp features of a lovely face with bright green eyes looking happy despite tears wetting her cheeks. Even after more than a week at sea, sharing their meals, and not much space to avoid each other, she was still an enigma to him.

Since they left Upavon, his passenger had kept to herself during most of the trip, spending a lot of time standing on the deck staring out at sea or when the weather was rough, reading in her cabin.

The captain had gotten paid handsomely by the young man who had booked her passage. The fellow had been carrying a small baby in a sling. On the clerk's question, if the little one was coming too, the young man had shaken his head, not giving an explanation.

Taking the young woman to the Island had meant they had to sail a bit off their usual route, but the generous compensation the young man had offered had quickly made his mind up. To the captain's surprise, no one had been at the dock to help her onboard or wave her goodbye. She had gone straight to the back of the ship, her eyes searching the quay as if looking for someone. It was all a bit of a mystery.

Upon sailing away from the harbour, he had caught a glimpse of the young woman's face before she went downstairs. It was so full of sorrow that it had affected him deeply at the time.

The captain turned to her.

"You must be glad to be rid of us after a whole week at sea with only us sailors for company?"

She looked at him, smiling.

"On the contrary, you've all made such an effort to make me comfortable. It is lovely to see my home country again. A lot of things have changed while I was away."

Her mouth trembled, and her hands shook. Only her proud bearing and knowing the Islanders' dislike of being touched by outsiders kept the captain from putting an arm around her.

"It won't have changed that much, surely? How long have you been away? We all heard the stories about the fire and the abduction of Harrington's daughter one year ago. Since then, there has been a change in management. A man called Redwood, I believe, is now in charge."

Seeing the young woman wince at this, he now realised his hunch that she was the girl everyone had been talking about was correct.

She must have felt his questioning look and gave a big sigh.

"Yes, you have guessed right. I am Astrid

Harrington, that daughter. It has been a bit over a year since they took me from my home. It seems more like a decade to me. "

She sighed and put her hand above her eyes, looking up at the large edifice proudly standing on top of the cliff towering above Sevenoaks harbour, not offering anything else.

The captain went back to oversee the mooring of his ship. He could not see any sign of a welcoming party on the quay. When the gangway had been let down, he solemnly wished the young woman all the best and stood for a long while watching her walk up Harbour road.

Epilogue

The weather was glorious as if welcoming her home. It was sweltering, but Astrid kept her hood up, hiding her face as she was slowly walking up the hill. The smells and sounds of Sevenoaks were so familiar as if she had never been away. But it was a different life she was going to have to face up to. Her parents were gone, and Henry was in charge of the company. She felt she had changed immensely beyond that silly, innocent young girl, dreaming about her childhood love and moaning about her arranged marriage. The last year had taught her that there were so many things that much worse could happen to her. It had shown her, too, that most things could be borne when you set your mind to it. She knew how to look after herself now. She felt stronger than ever.

Living with Jonah had gradually become a pleasure these last few months instead of something she had to endure. Oh, Jonah. But no, she should not think about him nor Nessa. It was too painful.

She straightened her back, pushing all that raw emotion to the back of her mind. Soon, she would be home. That was what was important now. It had felt like she would never see Harrington House, her family and friends again.

Now here she was. The main gates were open, and there was the usual bustle of people going about their business.

They would be so surprised to see her. For reasons she didn't even understand herself, she had not let anyone know she was coming back. Memories started crowding in about what had brought her to this moment.

That other spring day, one year ago, had started just as lovely. Who could have imagined a trip to the beach would have resulted in her coming home like this, damaged and alone, pining for someone she hadn't even known then.

Like that day on which her story began, today was one of those early April days that seemed more like summer than spring. Stepping into the shadow of the great towers, she threw back her hood and walked up to the house.